BLIND
PERSUASION

By

Linda Riesenberg Fisler

Published by Linda Riesenberg Fisler
DBA Kit-Cat Press
Middletown, OH

ISBN: 978-0-9967479-5-0

Author's Note:
This is a work of fiction. Names, characters, places, and incidents either are the product of the author's imagination or are used fictitiously, and any resemblance to actual persons, living or dead, events, or locales is entirely coincidental.

Many thanks to Sonja Sweeney, Editor
Cover design by Linda Riesenberg Fisler

Other Books by the Author

The Blind Series:

Blind Intention
(Available as a free download at www.LindaFisler.com)

"This is a great primer to get readers to fall in love with the characters and want more. I'm so glad that I read it. I purchased Blind Influence right away after reading this." – M.E.

"This is a real page-turner! A great way to introduce the main character and her background." –A.

Blind Influence- Three-Time Award Winning novel!
"Interwoven plots of international intrigue propel the storyline. Through all the twists and turns, the author uses solid dialogue and three-dimensional characters to keep the pages turning! There is a visual experience in the words that demonstrate her other talents. Linda is equal parts writer and artist –a rare combination that brings her story to life!" -A.M.

"I just read this book while on vacation. My only complaint is I couldn't put it down to do anything else! The author has written a gem. The characters are compelling and the plot engrossing and fully fleshed out. "It and they" pull the reader in and don't let you out! Looking forward to reading the prequel now...and EVERY book in the series as they appear. Please don't make us wait too long!" –M.D.

Other books by the Author:
Best Selling Art Instruction Book
(#1 Hot New Release and as high as #3 on the Best Selling List on Amazon)
How to Paint from Brush to Palette Knives
Creating and Painting Forms with Value and Color
In the Artist's Words: Interview with Quang Ho
In the Artist's Words: Interview with C.W. Mundy

Time Management
Take Back Your Time

Acknowledgments

To my readers, who inspire me to keep telling stories, thank you for shouting from the mountaintops, always asking when the next book is due out, and your unending support. I love you guys!

To my editor, Sonja Sweeney, thank you for your help, thoroughness, and guidance.

To Tom, who has endured many late suppers because of my dream, thank you for all you do.

"Remember, democracy never lasts long. It soon wastes, exhausts, and murders itself. There never was a democracy yet that did not commit suicide."

—John Adams

Chapter One

January 1980

Darkness! Winter was always dark and gray even on the sunniest of days. In the darkness, foreboding thoughts crept into the recesses of a person's mind and soul. Maybe it was because the trees were barren; their charcoal black branches a shade darker than the gray puffs of clouds that billowed upward, away from yet another gray shape that formed the foothills of the mountains beyond. The darkness became the playground for the demons that feared the light. The only saving graces were the festive complementary colors of red and green. These warm colors brightened the mood, decorated the buildings, and adorned most people for the month of December. It was a stark contrast to the bleakest month of the year: January. The joyous refrains became an echo among the inhabitants of this quaint town nestled in the foothills of the Smokey Mountains. The bitter darkness made the labors of the town's inhabitants seem harder than usual. This especially harsh winter weighed heavily on a few souls in particular. The cold, blustery winds whistled outside their windows giving their demons a voice. Oh, the darkness: Only those who suffer in its demoralizing anxiety can understand the toll it takes on them.

A man walked the lonely streets of this small North Carolina town. His new parka was zipped up all the way, and its hood shielded the man's face from the cold. While he had been seen about town to buy the basic necessities such as food, personal care items, and libations to ease the pain of what some folks assumed was a broken marriage or refuted lover, he never spoke of his problems. In fact, he never spoke at all. He showed up in their town a month ago and quietly rented one of the vacant houses out by the nearby lake.

He didn't bother anyone, and he made it clear he didn't want to be bothered. His beard was wild and unkempt. His emerald-green eyes pierced through all the black hair that was getting long and in need of attention. He appeared older than he truly was.

Speculating on the man's misfortunes became the favorite pastime of the locals. Whole dinner conversations revolved around the latest theory or rumor invented earlier in the day. The only fact that everyone knew about this man was that he was not from "these parts."

At one point, some people thought that the man had left as mysteriously as he had arrived. They had not seen him for a few days. They even admitted that not having him around made their lives boring. But they were wrong! Eventually, the man emerged from the lake cabin once again. He walked through town as if he had the weight of the world on his shoulders. Walking to the local store, he was aware of the finger-pointing, gasping, and whispering that his appearance generated.

The mailman reported that the stranger had received some mail a few days ago. It was a very nondescript envelope addressed to "Smith." The mailman declared that he would call him "Smitty," which seemed appropriate. Others only laughed at the mailman's attempt to humanize the odd, lonely man.

The man reached the local store in the curious little town. He wasn't going to buy much. After all, he had to walk the seven miles back to the cabin he was renting. Grabbing a small basket he made his way through the store. He picked up some skim milk, pasta, and sauce, and then at the end of the aisle, he eyed some small backpacks. Realizing he could purchase more food and make fewer trips into town, he tried a black one on over his coat. While it was not as comfortable as he would have liked, he decided he could make it work. He tossed the pack into his basket and moved on to the soup aisle, opting for the dry mixes. Out of the corner of his eye, he noticed that he was being watched. Inquisitive eyes were observing his every move. This made him uncomfortable, so he hurriedly selected some beef and frozen vegetables. He also wanted to stop at the liquor store on his way back. He made his way to the cashier to pay for the items.

"Hello," the cashier greeted him in her cheerful southern accent. The man gave her a quick smile, barely noticeable beneath his beard and moustache, as he set everything on the black conveyor belt. The young, pretty, dark-haired clerk looked at the man, trying to make eye contact. She thought she felt sorry for him. Maybe it wasn't her sorrow she was feeling, instead feeling sorrow emanating from him. She decided to be brave and ask, "Sir, are you all right? Is there anything I can do to help you?"

At first, the man was taken aback by her forwardness. He looked at her, their eyes meeting, and he could tell she was genuine in her concern. The clerk took notice of his bloodshot eyes. The man forced himself to say the first words he had spoken to anyone in six weeks. He tried to smile and disguise his voice. "I'm fine. Thank ya. Y'all don't need to worry." He cringed. His attempt to mimic the southern accent was horrible. Inside he was actually laughing at his pathetic attempt. The clerk wasn't sure if he was mocking her. The fake accent left her confused and speechless. She returned scanning the items only speaking to finish the transaction. He opened the backpack and placed the items inside, adjusted the straps, and slung the pack over his shoulders. Giving a nod to those standing in shock after hearing him speak, he started for the doors and walked out of the grocery store.

His next stop was the liquor store for the libations that would provide temporary relief from his pain. He grabbed a bottle of gin and a bottle of scotch from the shelf. After paying cash, he placed the bottles in the small pack and readied himself for the long hike back to his cabin.

It would be dark by the time he returned home. He didn't mind walking, and he wasn't in a hurry to get back. He knew what waited for him in the darkness. It was surprising to him that nightmares still haunted him. They were not the same nightmares from his past though. These nightmares were a mix of future and past events. In them, a woman he had pulled into his world was killed. Each night when she was shot, he awoke in a cold sweat. He couldn't understand why he was dreaming of her death. Nicole Charbonneau was safe, and the Serpent was dead.

As he walked up to the house in the dark, he took the key out of his coat pocket to unlock the door. After going to the kitchen to unpack the groceries and start his dinner, he smiled as his mind took him back to the beach house. He closed his eyes envisioning Nicole unpacking the groceries. Seeing her made him happy if only for a few minutes. He cherished those images. His smile faded as he recalled his current nightmares and wondered if he had failed her in some way. Why was he having these nightmares? He knew she was safe; he had saved her. So why did the torment continue?

Sean shook his head wondering if his mind would ever accept the truth and whether he would ever be able to sleep well again. Taking off his coat, he threw it on a nearby chair. He then removed his gun and holster. He set them on the counter and decided on soup for dinner. He retrieved a small pot from the cupboard and began to read the instructions on the dry soup bag. As he was preparing the soup, the phone rang. He turned the burner on the stove down and walked across the kitchen to answer the phone which hung on the wall.

"Hello."

"Sean, it's Charlie." Charlie Dawson was calling from London to check on his agent. "How are you doing?"

"I'm fine, Charlie. Did my dad put you up to this?" Sean asked.

"No, Sean. As per your wishes, I've not told anyone where you are. I'm calling from my home," Charlie told him. "I thought you'd be back home by now. If there are any problems, we'll be happy to help you. You do know that, don't you?"

Sean smiled. "I know, Charlie. I can't put my finger on it, but I'm just not ready to come home yet. I'm working through some things here, and it is just taking longer than I thought it would."

"What things are you working through?" Charlie asked with a hint of concern in his voice.

"For one thing, I'm not sure I want to continue to be with SIS," Sean replied. He was somewhat surprised that came out of his mouth. He had never thought about leaving the Secret Intelligence Service before.

Charlie sat quietly for a moment, wondering if Sean was going to elaborate. When he didn't, Charlie gave a bit of a sigh and responded, "Well, there are other jobs available that I think you would excel in, so don't be too quick in that decision."

"I understand. I know that I don't want to be in the field again. I think I've paid my dues if you know what I mean."

"I do indeed." With his next question, Charlie's voice took on a hesitation that revealed his concern for Sean. "Are you still having nightmares, Sean?"

There was a long pause. He sat down. He wasn't sure he wanted to tell Charlie, but his solitude wasn't helping either. "Yes," Sean said quietly, embarrassed to admit it. "It isn't the same nightmare though. Now I dream that it is Nicole that has died. I dream I failed in keeping her safe."

Charlie smiled. "You didn't fail. Nicole is quite safe. In fact, if you have access to television there, you might want to turn on the news."

"Why?" Sean asked.

"You'll be able to see that she is on the arm of our friend, Senator Bobby Jenkins," Charlie said with the sound of a smirk on his face.

Sean sat back in his chair, not sure how he felt about this turn of events. "Charlie, I've got to go. I've got something on the stove and, well, I'm not that great of a cook to begin with," he said standing up.

"Please consider coming home, Sean. We're all here to help you."

"Thank you, Charlie. It's good to hear your voice," Sean did have to admit that hearing from Charlie seemed to help. "Goodbye." He hung up the phone and said out loud to no one, "So, Nicole, that does make a lot of sense. Senator Jenkins is one lucky fella."

He walked back to the stove to stir the soup that was about ready to eat. "Maybe it is time to catch up on the news," he said to himself.

He walked over to the living room and, for the first time in over a month, turned on the television. He made trips between the kitchen and the living room. After pouring a bowl of soup, he sat down at a small table and tuned in for the six-thirty news. There was a small part of him that hoped the senator would be on the news with Nicole on his arm so that he could see her with his own eyes. What he didn't understand was the pang of jealousy he felt toward his old friend Bobby Jenkins.

As he watched the news, it seemed in his absence from the world that very little had changed. There was a follow-up report on the beheading in Mecca and a lot of talk about whether or not the US would attend the Summer Olympics in Moscow. One report though, Sean watched with more interest. The IRA had prematurely detonated a bomb on the Dunmurry train outside of Belfast. The bombing killed three people and injured five. With that report, the news was over. Sean drank the last bit of soup from the bowl and walked over to turn off the television. While he had been hopeful he would see Nicole on the screen, he was not sad that he didn't see her. Maybe Charlie misinterpreted what he had seen. Maybe Nicole and Jenkins were just friends. Sean put his hands to his head trying to squash his thoughts. "Why in the world would she ever be interested in you?" Sean shook his head.

He knew it was time to get on with his life. He needed to understand his feelings and gain control of the demons that still haunted him. He walked back to the kitchen where he cleaned up and put the remainder of the soup in the refrigerator. He caught his reflection in a mirror that hung in the entry of the cabin. He almost didn't recognize himself. He had lost a considerable amount of weight, and his face was gaunt. The facial hair did him no favors. He was startled at how he looked and how he had let his demons control him. He needed to get tough with himself again. He couldn't return home looking like this. The sight of him in the mirror made him realize that if he wanted any chance with Nicole, he had to pull himself together. It was time to kick his demons to the wall and out of his life forever. He began to search the house for some paper and a pen. He wanted to write down his thoughts. After he was satisfied that he had captured his fears and any demons that were lurking around him, he burned the paper in the fireplace using matches he had found in a drawer in the kitchen. He watched the paper turn to ashes. The orange flames turned to smoke that rose into the chimney. Sean envisioned his demons leaving him with the smoke.

Then he searched the cabin for a pair of scissors, deciding it was time to get rid of the long hair and beard. As he cut each snip of hair, he knew he was beginning the long journey back from his personal hell.

{II}

"Happy New Year, Bobby and Nikki," Mrs. Louise Barker said as she opened the door to their lovely home. Senator and Louise Barker were famous for their New Year's Day parties in Washington. It was an affair that everyone wanted to attend. A select number of prestigious insiders counted their blessings to be among the chosen. The party was a bright beacon keeping the gray doldrums of January at bay, if only for a few more days. Louise always had a theme for her parties, and this year she decided that she would usher in Mardi Gras a full seven weeks early. She had the house decorated appropriately with beads and masks, a band playing New Orleans jazz and a fortune-teller. She had even hired magicians and drama students to wander around and engage her guests. It certainly felt like you had walked into a house party on Bourbon Street the night before Ash Wednesday.

"Happy New Year to you, too," Jenkins returned as he kissed Louise on the cheek. "You have outdone yourself this time," he added, smiling at all the noise and commotion emanating from the other rooms.

"Happy New Year, Louise," Nicole greeted her with a hug and kiss on the cheek.

"Larry is in the great room down the hall, Bobby. I'll take your coats." Louise was an elegant lady, a quality that Nicole envied. "Nikki, you simply must visit the fortune-teller I've hired."

Nicole was unbuttoning her coat and stopped to look at Louise. "Why?" She blurted out. The tone in her voice caused Louise's smile to fade. Nicole noticed the tone, a tone that showed her aversion to the thought that someone could predict what was going to happen in the future. She quickly followed her contemptuous question by firmly stating her belief—or disbelief. "I mean, I really don't believe in that sort of thing." She removed her coat and handed it to Louise.

"I have my reasons, my dear, but mainly because of your circumstances in the past year," Louise replied. She paused a moment to rephrase what she was about to say next. "Well, let's just say things are looking up and you have so much to look forward to this year compared to last year." She smiled. "I would think you would love to know just what is in store for you."

Nicole tilted her head in confusion. What happened to her last year could not have possibly been foretold by a fortune-teller. She flipped a lock of curls from her face while forming her next response. She smiled uncomfortably. "Well, I don't believe that someone can tell me what my future holds. Had someone told me that I would have lost Carol at the end of the year, I would have taken her up on that vacation she showed me just before her death." Nicole paused. *But then, I would have never met Sean.* She shook her head, mainly to get the thought of Sean out of it. She smiled, turning her doubtful gaze to Louise. "In any case, I do believe that I control what happens to me and I don't think I'm that predictable."

"You are more predictable than you like to think, my dear," Jenkins chimed in. He put his arm around her and kissed her on the cheek.

Nicole returned his look with surprise. "I would love to see if this fortune-teller could guess what did happen to you."

Nicole felt a need to defend herself. "I consider what happened to me to be abnormal. What are the odds of having another assassin threaten my life or anyone else for that matter? Other than trying to determine if I'll return to law, I don't have any earth-shattering decisions coming up in my life. Really, Bobby, I'm not that predictable." Nicole gave Jenkins a look that let Jenkins know when he was treading on thin ice.

Jenkins smiled at the look he did not fear. He then chuckled as Nicole tried to make her look more menacing. "See, even receiving 'the Look' from you is predictable!" Nicole's mouth curled into a smile as she couldn't stay mad at Jenkins for very long.

Louise smiled at them both. "Oh, I think there might be one or two earth-shattering decisions in your near future." She winked at Jenkins, who suddenly became embarrassed and started to blush. "See what I mean?" She and Jenkins laughed as Nicole smiled. Nicole suddenly felt uncomfortable with the thought that she and Jenkins would marry in the coming year. Jenkins's embarrassment made her believe that Louise wasn't far from the truth. "Now I really want you to see that fortune-teller," Louise said as she handed the coats to a butler who appeared from the adjoining room.

"I'm not making any promises," Nicole countered. "I'll see you later." She turned away from Louise taking Jenkins's offered hand. Neither of them spoke as they walked down that hallway to the great room. Jenkins was too embarrassed, and Nicole didn't want to start the conversation. She didn't want to get married; it was far too soon. She still had a lot to process with all that had happened before Christmas. Nicole still didn't know what she wanted to do with her life now that it had changed so drastically. She smiled as her eyes caught Jenkins gazing at her just before entering a room full of notable guests.

Larry Barker, the tall, distinguished, senior senator from the state of Texas, stood out like a sore thumb. Barker was in his late sixties and had the respect of both sides of the aisle. He was known for his negotiating skills, even if some of those negotiations required heavy persuasion. These persuasions were typically accompanied with some kind of dirt acquired from snooping into his opponent's background. Jenkins was sure Barker had a secret room somewhere in the house that contained information on just about everyone. At times, Jenkins wondered just what information Barker had on him. It didn't matter though, as Jenkins didn't plan on crossing his mentor anytime soon. They worked as a team, which brought both men credence from others in Congress.

When Barker saw Jenkins and Nicole enter the great room, he broke away from his conversation to greet them.

"Hello, Bobby," he said, extending his hand, which Jenkins accepted and leaned in to give Barker a quick hug as well.

"Happy New Year," Jenkins greeted Barker.

"You too," Barker responded. He turned to Nicole and opened both arms to hug her. "Happy New Year, Nikki," he said as he took her in his arms.

"Happy New Year," Nicole said breathlessly as Barker's hug squeezed all the air out of her. As he let go, she cleared her throat and gave a bit of a chuckle. "I don't think I'll ever get used to those bear hugs."

"Well, seems I'll have to give Bobby some lessons. He should be holding you tight every chance he gets," Barker responded with a sly grin.

Nicole didn't like Barker's hugs. She found them quite annoying. At the risk of embarrassing Jenkins, she said, "I like the way that Bobby holds me. It doesn't ruffle the feathers."

A quick shake of his head accompanied Jenkins's smile. Barker was taken aback for a second, but then he gave a smile and a quick punch to Jenkins's upper arm. "Good for you!" Barker said following it with a hearty laugh. "You do have your hands full with this one, Bobby."

"I wouldn't have it any other way," Jenkins replied.

"That's hard to believe coming from a southern gentleman."

"I consider myself a modern southern gentleman," Jenkins corrected Barker. "I'm very secure in the fact that women are equals. Nikki provides valid counterpoints to any number of topics we discuss." Jenkins looked at Nicole and smiled. "I find her insights enlightening."

Barker smiled at Jenkins. "I suppose that is the new way of handling things." Nicole furrowed her brow.

"I suppose it is," Jenkins confirmed while he had the chance.

Barker thought that women should be seen and not heard. While his wife provided her opinions, typically it was with other women and not in the presence of her husband. Nicole began to wonder if Louise ever had any input to Barker's decisions. She recalled a time at a dinner party when she voiced her opinion to Jenkins on legislation that was being discussed. Louise gently took her arm and steered her away from the conversation. It was clear now why she was taken away from the discussion, and it saddened Nicole to realize that her opinion was not welcomed.

"Nikki is very astute in the field of politics, and I do appreciate her point of view," Jenkins continued, smiling at Barker. "I have had some private conversations with your wife and find the same is true. I know behind closed doors; you listen intently to what Louise has to say. Times are changing, and we need to embrace that change if we are to be the party that represents all people."

Barker laughed. "You got me there." He raised his glass in a salute. "Now, if you'll excuse me, I see more people have arrived. You know where the bar is."

When Barker was out of earshot, Nicole gave Jenkins an appreciative glance, acknowledging him defending her.

"Thank you," she said.

"Are you feeling alright?" Jenkins inquired.

"Yes. Why?"

"I was expecting you to answer first." Jenkins smiled at her. "It's not like you to back down from a fight."

"I guess I'm not up for it this evening. My mind went back to a party a few weeks ago and how Louise led me away from a conversation when I started to voice my opinion." Nicole gave a crooked frown with her lips. "I should choose my battles more carefully I suppose."

"Just remember, your feistiness is what attracted me to you," Jenkins said. Nicole smiled at him just as two senators' wives walked up to her. Jenkins smiled back and excused himself, leaving Nicole as he was called over to join Barker and Senator Daniel Mercer, who were deep in conversation. "What happens to be on the minds of you two gentlemen?" Jenkins inquired as he joined them.

Senator Mercer was the first to speak. "Larry and I were wondering how the investigation into the assassination is going. Is there any chance that you'll be able to make some kind of announcement in the coming weeks?"

"We are still investigating some leads. I'm not very comfortable with announcing anything until I have a few more facts confirmed." Jenkins was stalling.

"The sooner we can put this behind us the better, Bobby," Barker replied. "This is an election year, and we need to focus on the congressional races and, of course, the White House. If there is some evidence that can help our chances, then we need to use that to our advantage. The party has to decide and put its collective weight behind a front-runner."

"I understand your concerns. I want to have another look at where we stand before I commit one way or the other." Jenkins's mind was churning. The internal battle of whether to show Barker and Mercer the Sipes confession tape began again. He needed to sit down and determine the pros and cons of any action he would take. He needed to make this decision, but not without some careful thought and confirmation.

"Have you given any more thought to our suggestion about declaring your candidacy?" Barker asked. "If there is an indication that some committee hearings on the assassination are needed, that would be a perfect avenue to show your leadership."

"I have been considering it," Jenkins replied. "I was thinking of throwing my hat in the ring if only for the experience of running a presidential campaign."

"Good," Barker said, turning to smile at Mercer. "I think we need to confirm your candidacy and quickly. The Iowa caucus is crucial and only twenty days away. I took the liberty of drawing up the necessary documents after our last discussion."

"I think you need to call a press conference tomorrow, Bobby, to make it official," Mercer added. "We'll be happy to stand by your side."

Jenkins swallowed. He understood the importance of the Iowa caucus, and he had led the press to believe he would officially declare after the holidays. He wasn't sure he liked the fact that Barker had taken liberties. He had not discussed a presidential run with Nicole, and he wasn't sure what her reaction would be.

"I suppose the sooner, the better," he said.

"Yes," Mercer responded. "Have Chris call the press together at one o'clock tomorrow. We'll announce on Capitol Hill." Jenkins smiled and nodded his agreement, making a mental note to call his aide, Chris, in the morning. Jenkins snatched a quick glance to see Nicole sitting at the fortune-teller's table. "...And you know that Nikki would make a wonderful first lady," Mercer finished.

Jenkins realized he hadn't heard a word Mercer had said. There was an awkward silence in the air when Jenkins turned his head to see both Barker and Mercer staring at him and on the verge of laughing. "I'm sorry gentlemen. I didn't hear what you said."

Barker took the initiative this time. "Daniel was commenting how Nikki would make a wonderful first lady."

Jenkins began to blush slightly as he again looked over in Nicole's direction. "I believe we are a bit far away from that happening. Excuse me; I'd like to get something to drink," Jenkins walked past Nicole on his way to the bar.

"This is Nikki," one woman said. "She says she doesn't believe in this stuff."

"I have many who don't believe at first," the fortune-teller attested, smiling at Nicole. She looked at the two women escorts and said, "If you will excuse us, I will do Nikki's reading now." The two women walked a short distance away. The fortune-teller looked at Nicole, smiled again and said, "You have a number of people here who want to talk to you."

Nicole gave a brief chuckle. "I kind of doubt that."

"You have a lot of doubt, but you never used to be that way." The fortune-teller, who was more of a medium than a predictor of the future, picked up one of her tarot decks. She began to shuffle the cards. She set the deck down and picked up a pen and piece of paper. Reaching over she grabbed a business card and handed it to Nicole. "This has some information about me in case you ever want to get in touch with me again. What was your full name at birth?"

"Nicole Rae Charbonneau. Rae is spelled R-A-E." The fortune-teller asked her to spell her last name. She asked for Nicole's birthday. Nicole watched as the fortune-teller wrote down numbers and added them together. Nicole decided she was doing some kind of numerology.

"You are Hierophant, which is a counselor," The fortune-teller declared. "What do you do for a living?"

"Guess," Nicole said snidely.

"I read cards and listen to my guides. I do not read minds," The fortune-teller replied. Her tone was becoming a bit more serious.

"I'm a lawyer but not sure I want to go back to that profession," Nicole declared, resigned to the fact that answering sarcastically would only prolong the experience.

The fortune-teller smiled. She picked up another deck and shuffled it. Returning to the first deck, she commented, "You have quite a few people watching over you. Your parents are on the other side." The fortune-teller was still shuffling the cards. "They are proud of what you have achieved and especially with something that has just occurred or ended?"

Nicole's brow furrowed as she listened to the fortune-teller. "Did someone tell you what happened?"

"No. I'm just passing a message on to you. But your parents passed some time ago. This was in some kind of accident."

Nicole sat back. She scanned the room. No one in the room knew how Nicole's parents had passed. "OK, I'll give you that one."

"Give me that one? I'm not sure I understand."

"No one here knows how my parents died, or when for that matter."

The fortune-teller smiled. She didn't feel a need to convince Nicole that she was a true medium. She had her share of nonbelievers in the room this evening. She decided to move on with the reading. She removed the Hierophant card and laid it on the table that was between them. She covered the card with two cards. The Eight of Swords and the Two of Pentacles were now facing Nicole. "There is something to which you are blind. There is something of importance that is being kept from you."

Nicole looked at the cards and then at the fortune-teller. "By who?"

The fortune-teller pulled the Two of Cups. "It's someone close to you. It is someone who you have been with as a friend or a lover."

"Considering I'm dating a senator, there are probably a lot of things he is keeping from me. As for my friends, my closest friend was killed. I don't have many friends."

The fortune-teller paused for a minute. "Carol wants to say hello."

Nicole was shocked. She turned pale at the mention of her best friend's name. "That's not funny."

"I didn't intend it to be funny. She wanted to make sure that you knew she was here. She just spoke to me when you said you don't have many friends."

"Who told you about Carol?" Nicole demanded.

"No one told me." The fortune-teller looked at Nicole. "Carol wants you to know that she appreciated that you were by her side when she passed." Nicole was still pale and in shock. "And she is laughing now because of the look on your face. I take it Carol was a bit of a prankster in life?"

"Yes, you might say that," Nicole confirmed. "Is she okay?"

"She's fine. You being there when she passed helped her. She felt your love for her. She is watching over you." The fortune-teller placed the Four of Cups on the table. "You are to be given a gift."

She pulled two more cards and laid them next to the Four of Cups. The first card was the Seven of Swords, and the other was the Devil card. She watched Nicole as she started to retreat from the cards, both of which seemed ominous to Nicole. The fortune-teller put her fingers on the Seven of Swords.

"This card is indicating that there may be some kind of betrayal associated with the gift. The Devil card represents hopes and fears in either direction."

"I don't understand," Nicole said leaning forward now. "Can you tell me what the gift is? Is it something bad?"

The fortune-teller shuffled the deck a few more times. She pulled the Hermit card and laid it on top of the other three cards. She took the Four of Cups and placed it directly below the Hermit card. "There will be a need for an investigation. During this investigation, you will see someone close to you in a different light. A side of him or her will be exposed." The fortune-teller then drew two more cards from the deck. It was the Queen of Wands and followed by the Temperance card; she laid them on top of the spread.

"A lot depends on the decision that someone close to you needs to make. If this person decides in a way that you can't abide by, you will need to escape. You'll feel trapped and feel a need to get away."

"You can't tell me who this person is?" Nicole almost sounded desperate.

The fortune-teller sat for a minute concentrating and asking her guides for assistance. She shuffled the cards once more until she came upon the card she was directed to pull from the deck. She laid the card on the table. Nicole looked at the card and needed no explanation. She immediately stood and walked away from the table. The fortune-teller had placed the Lovers card on the table.

Nicole briskly walked out of the room and headed for the bathroom. She needed a few minutes to compose herself, alone. She locked the door behind her and stood with the palms of her hands bracing each side of the sink. She realized that she was breathing hard, extremely hard. She began to feel light-headed. She was about to hyperventilate. She sat down on the toilet. "Why am I feeling this way?" she whispered. "You don't believe in this stuff. Why do I feel like I've just been stabbed? I can't breathe." She rested her elbows on her thighs as the adrenaline continued to surge. "Just breathe." She started to slow her breathing, resisting the urge to take short breaths. She held her breath, counting to five then letting it go. With each breath she counted a little longer: first to seven, then ten. She started to breathe normally. She sat up and then stood, regaining her composure. She ran cold water over her hands taking her right hand and putting it on the back of her neck.

There was a knock on the door. It was a gentle little knock showing no urgency. "Nikki," a southern voice said softly with a hint of concern. "Are you alright? Is something wrong?"

It was Jenkins. He had witnessed her rapidly paced exit from the room and excused himself from his conversation with another guest to check on her.

Nicole looked in the mirror. Her eyes were wide open with fear. She shook her head and whispered, "Quit this; quit being stupid!"

"What? I didn't hear you," Jenkins said, straining on the other side of the door and answering quietly, trying not to draw attention. "Nikki?" The door to the bathroom opened. Jenkins saw a pale Nicole standing before him. "You are as white as a ghost," he said. He took her gently by the arm and led her to Senator Barker's study shutting the door behind them. "What happened? I saw you quickly leaving the room. Are you feeling alright?"

Nicole sat down in the chair closest to her. "Yes, I'm fine. Something that fortune-teller said upset me, but I'm okay now." She tried to smile.

"What did she say?"

"It makes perfect sense now that I think about it. I just had a moment of fear or something. Maybe I haven't recovered fully from everything that has happened." Nicole stood but lost her balance a little.

Jenkins moved quickly to her side and helped her sit back down. "I think we better head home. You stay here. I'll give our regrets to the Barkers and retrieve our coats."

"No, don't do that. I'll be fine."

"No. You need to rest. I'll be right back." Jenkins left the room, closing the door quickly behind him. He found Louise, and she went to retrieve their coats. He apologized to Senator Barker as well. He met Louise outside the study where she handed Jenkins their coats as he entered the study.

Peering over Jenkins's shoulder, Louise asked, "Nikki, what happened?"

"Just some kind of bug I guess," Nicole offered. Jenkins set the coats down to help Nicole to her feet. He turned to get Nicole's coat and held it while she put it on. He quickly put his coat on and offered his arm to Nicole.

"Please tell Senator Barker that I'm sorry to take Bobby away from the party," Nicole said.

"I will tell the senator you weren't feeling well. He'll understand. Don't give this another thought." Louise watched Jenkins. She admired the way he cared for Nicole. She remembered the days fondly when her husband acted in the same manner. She longed for those days again. The years of disagreements had taken their toll. She wondered if Jenkins and Nicole would survive all that lay ahead of them: the good and the bad. "I hope you feel better soon, Nikki. If there is anything I can do, call me," she added.

"That's very kind of you. I'll be fine. I just need to lie down I think." She placed one arm under Jenkins's offered arm, moving her hand to rest in his hand. She looked at Jenkins and smiled. "Thank you both for your concern. It must just be the flu or something."

"Thank you again," Jenkins said as they started down the hall. "Happy New Year to you and Senator Barker," he said when they reached the front door.

"The same to both of you," Louise said as she opened the door. She watched them get into Jenkins's car before returning to the party.

As Jenkins drove away from the Barker's home, he waited patiently for Nicole to speak. Nicole, however, was in no hurry to talk about the reading. She calmly looked out the window, silently wondering just what the reading meant. Jenkins ran out of patience and finally asked, "Will you please tell me exactly what happened?"

Nicole turned her head and looked at Jenkins. "It's nothing, Bobby." Jenkins gave her a quick glance-a glance with which Nicole was becoming very familiar with and received when Jenkins wasn't very happy with her. "It was something the fortune-teller said. I didn't want the fortune-teller's reading. I don't know how she knew some things."

"What things?"

"She knew my parents died in an accident. She knew about Carol. She guessed that I had been through some ordeal and that my parents were proud of how I handled it. She said that Carol was glad I was with her when she passed, that my love for her helped her pass." Nicole looked at Bobby. "How did she know all this? Have you told anyone about...?"

"How could I have told someone about your parents? I don't know anything about that. In fact, you've never mentioned your parents. As for Carol, her death was in the newspaper."

"It was all so strange," Nicole murmured.

"I still don't understand why this upsets you so much."

"That wasn't what upset me. The most upsetting thing was her telling me that someone close to me may betray me. That they are withholding information from me."

"And that person is me?" Jenkins asked. The hurt was evident in his voice.

"It could be," Nicole answered. "I know you can't tell me everything, Bobby."

"No, I can't," he confirmed. "I'm on the Intelligence Committee, for one thing. I can't share everything with you. There will always be a portion of my service I can't share. I thought you understood that."

"I do. I know I'm being silly." Nicole paused. A part of her didn't want to continue. "But, she indicated whatever you are withholding will hurt me in some way."

"What?!" Jenkins yelled back. "I would never intentionally hurt you."

"I know. But I can't get this out of my mind."

"Well, unless you can tell me what it is that I'm supposed to be keeping from you, I can't help you," Jenkins said, clearly frustrated.

"It has to do with a gift of some kind."

"Now that makes no sense to me at all. Any gift I give you would not hurt you." Jenkins was getting more and more agitated.

"I know. I'm sorry. Can we just forget about it? It all seems so silly now."

Jenkins sat quietly and then decided that it was probably better to tell Nicole about the conversation he had discussed with Barker and Mercer. "Nikki, there is one thing I do need to tell you."

Nicole's heart started to beat faster. She couldn't imagine what Jenkins was going to tell her and there was a part of her that didn't want to know. With reserve evident in her voice, she asked, "Yes?"

Jenkins hesitated a moment when he heard her tone. "Barker and Mercer approached me a few weeks ago. They want me to consider running for president. Of course, I would be one of many candidates, but with Barker and Mercer behind me, it is something I have to consider."

Nicole was relieved that it wasn't a proposal of marriage. "I think that's great, Bobby. You should run."

"You think so?" Jenkins responded. "They seem to think the time is right. I think it provides experience in running a presidential campaign. I doubt I'd get the nomination."

"I think you are underestimating yourself," Nicole said. "I think this might just work out for you."

Jenkins smiled. "We make the announcement tomorrow at one. Can you be there with me?"

"Absolutely," Nicole confirmed. "I wouldn't miss it."

{III}

Meanwhile, at the White House, President Stevens was having a small gathering of close friends to celebrate New Year's Day watching football games as the wives chatted about upcoming events. It was one day that Stevens didn't want to be the president. Being president and trying to honor his predecessor's plan was excoriatingly painful. Many of Andrew's policies were counter to his own. He couldn't wait to be his own man again and end the charade he was playing. Stevens was waiting for one more of his friends to arrive. He was hoping that Tony would show up with Nicole on his arm.

Stevens had seen the tabloid photos that proclaimed the most eligible bachelor on Capitol Hill was off the market. He had witnessed the state dinners with Nicole on Senator Jenkins's arm. Stevens never like Jenkins and was not happy about their relationship. He wanted to talk to his old friend and confidant, Tony, to see if there was some way to get Nicole away from that southern snake.

Since the death of Norman Sipes, Stevens had seen very little of Tony. Having called Tony a few hours earlier and finding himself still waiting, he was beginning to wonder if he would have to call Tony again. Just as he was getting up to do so, the butler opened the door to the room and in walked the sun-bleached white-haired, debonair Tony. "Where have you been?" Stevens asked as he walked over to shake his friend's hand.

"On my yacht," Tony answered, grasping Stevens's hand.

"Grab yourself a drink and join us. We're watching the Rose Bowl." Stevens walked back over to his seat while Tony poured himself a drink at the wet bar.

"Now that I have you all here, I want to talk to you. Joe?" Stevens said as he sat down across from Wall Street financier Joseph Engle. Stevens and Engle had been friends for decades. Engle, who was now handling Stevens's investments while he was vice president and president, was treasurer of every political office for which Stevens campaigned. "I think you should take over Sipes's company and prepare to drill for oil in ANWR. The bill is due…"

"Mr. President," Tony interjected. "I don't think it is proper for you to discuss…"

"That's bullshit!" Stevens interrupted. "It's just us, talking during a football game."

"I beg your pardon, Mr. President," Tony said, setting his drink down on the table in front of him. He stood up. "But quite frankly, I'm tired of covering all your asses."

"Tony, we'll need your help on this," Engle said.

"Count me out," Tony replied.

"Then assign Nikki to this," Stevens said. He was hoping it would provide an opportunity to see her.

"No," Tony responded. "Why do you need help?"

"Sipes's estate has not been settled yet. A reading of his will is in order," Engle stated.

"So?" Tony questioned. He was not sure why the reading was necessary.

"We don't know what is to become of Sipes Oil Company. As an investor, I want to know what happens to the company," Engle stated.

Tony looked at Engle astonished. He then started to chuckle which turned into a loud, hearty laugh. "Are you serious?" He managed to get out. "The man was flat broke! He owed money on his house, car—you name it! Any assets that company had will be used to pay off his debts. For Christ's sake, Engle, I thought you out of everyone here would be able to figure that one out."

"I still want to have his will read. I think as investors we have a right to petition for that."

Tony scanned the room. FBI Director Jefferies, Stevens, and their wives became silent during Tony's rant. Every eye was now on him waiting for an answer. "Sipes didn't have any surviving family members. It's in probate. I'll check on the status when I get back to the office in a few days." He started for the door.

"Tony, where are you going? Stay here and watch the game with us," Stevens called.

"I'd rather not be present when you talk about things that you shouldn't be talking about, Mr. President. I just don't care enough to be interested." Tony forced a smile and added, "Happy New Year, sir." With that, he turned and walked out of the room.

"What's up with him?" Engle asked.

"I have no idea," Stevens replied.

{IV}

Jenkins called Chris at home, waking him up early and giving instructions to organize a press conference on Capitol Hill. Jenkins knew this was just a formality, but it still felt rushed. He jumped in the shower and then quickly got dressed.

He walked down the stairs to the kitchen where Nicole was standing drinking a cup of tea and staring out the window. She had on a stunning forest green dress, conservative in style yet daring enough to reveal her voluptuous figure. Jenkins stood a moment, taking in her ravishing beauty and mentally slipping the dress off her shoulders, exposing her sensuous body underneath.

"Good morning," Nicole greeted him, knowing exactly what he was doing.

Jenkins smiled but did not blush at being caught in the act of undressing her in his mind. "Good morning." He walked up to her, took her in his arms and kissed her.

"Chris called when you were in the shower. He said everything is ready. Do you have your speech?" Nicole asked.

Jenkins poured himself a cup of coffee. "Yes, I do." He patted his coat where his breast pocket was located.

"President Robert Jenkins. President Jenkins." Nicole was speaking his name out loud as if testing it to see how it sounded. "President Bobby Jenkins."

"Enough!" Jenkins exclaimed with a hint of laughter in his voice. "I'm nervous enough as it is!" He enjoyed when she teased him. "You look marvelous in that dress."

"I thought you might like a bit of a distraction."

"We better get going," Jenkins said. "Barker has some people dropping by that he wants me to meet."

"People?" Nicole questioned. She took the last sip of her tea and followed him out of the room to the foyer.

"Yes, my campaign manager and treasurer."

"Oh, Bobby," Nicole started. "He's not letting you choose your campaign manager?"

"We talked about this a few weeks ago. He gave me a choice. After reviewing their credentials, I selected the ones I'd like to work with." Nicole frowned as Jenkins helped her into her coat. "Nikki, it's the way Barker is. There is no sense arguing with him. Besides, we both know I don't stand a chance of getting the numbers I need in Iowa."

Nicole became irritated. "That's enough of that talk. You will get the numbers you need, and you know it."

The drive over to Capitol Hill was a pleasant one. Congress was still on break, so there was less traffic and plenty of parking. Upon arriving, Jenkins retreated to his office where he began to study and then practice his speech. Chris was busy fielding calls from the press and from Senator Barker's office to coordinate meetings with Jenkins. Nicole volunteered to head down to the area where the press would be gathering to make sure everything was ready. She returned shortly before noon and reported that all was indeed ready, and she had even tested the microphones with the staff that were setting up the room.

A few minutes later, Barker walked into Jenkins's outer office with two gentlemen. He greeted everyone in the room and told Chris he was ready to meet with Jenkins. Chris excused himself and walked into Jenkins's inner sanctuary to announce their arrival. Nicole admired Chris's loyalty. He never let the stature of the person wanting to meet with Jenkins intimidate him.

"Hello, Nikki," Barker started. "I'd like you to meet Nelson Keaton and James Carson." The two men walked over, meeting Nicole halfway. She extended her hand to shake theirs.

"It's nice to meet you," Nicole greeted each one who respectively returned the sentiment.

Barker finished the introduction. "Nelson will be Bobby's campaign treasurer and Jimmy will be his campaign manager."

"Of course, Mr. Carson, now I recognize your name," Nicole said. "We're honored to have you on board."

Carson gave Nicole an odd look. He turned and looked at Barker with confusion. Barker smiled. "Nikki is Bobby's fiancée."

"No, I'm just a very good friend," Nicole corrected him.

"Well, that won't do," Carson retorted. "The most eligible bachelor on Capitol Hill needs to show the American people that he is in a serious relationship now. So, either you are his fiancée, or you are a friend who isn't part of his inner circle."

The door to Jenkins's office opened. Chris noticed the stare down between Carson and Nicole. "You can go in now."

"If that is the choice you are giving me, Mr. Carson, then allow me to reintroduce myself. I'm Nicole Charbonneau, counsel to Senator Robert Jenkins. I'm sure you are aware of my firm, Rosen, Shafer and Pruett?" With that, Nicole walked past Chris giving him a smile and wink. Chris wasn't sure what exactly happened but he knew Nicole just upped the stakes in the conversation.

Carson looked at Barker and then at Keaton. The three men walked into Jenkins's office. Barker made the introductions and Jenkins shook everyone's hand. "Good afternoon, gentlemen. It's an honor to have you on my campaign, Mr. Carson."

"Call me Jim or Jimmy," Carson said. "I'd like you to understand you are six weeks behind everyone else and the Iowa caucus is a short three weeks away. You need to give the appearance from the start that you are serious and that you are ready. I've taken the liberty of starting up your campaign staff in Iowa, New Hampshire, Minnesota, and in Maine."

Jenkins was shocked that this was moving so quickly. "I see," he said. He didn't like that Barker was so entrenched in his campaign, and he was beginning to feel a bit smothered. He looked at Nicole. She smiled and then sat down in a chair off to the side. The others took her cue and sat down. Chris started to exit and close the door. "Just a minute, Chris, I need you to take some notes. Chris will need the phone numbers for each of you and the campaign offices."

"I'll have an aide from my office dispatched immediately to get all the information Chris needs." Carson countered, dismissing Chris with a wave of his hand.

Chris didn't move and Jenkins didn't like Carson ordering his aide around. Jenkins motioned him into the office and handed him a legal pad and pen. "Have a seat, Chris, and if you would be so kind as to take some notes for me."

"It would be my pleasure, sir." Chris replied as he took the items from Jenkins. He looked at Nicole and smiled, beginning to understand what he had witnessed between Carson and Nicole. He sat down, off to the senator's other side. Nicole noticed how the people Jenkins could trust the most now flanked him.

There was an awkward silence in the room. No one was sure who was going to talk or what they wanted to say. Nicole was trying her hardest to mentally nudge Jenkins to take control. She wondered if anyone heard her expel the breath she was holding when Jenkins finally did speak.

"Mr. Carson, I appreciate all you have done to get this campaign off to a rousing start, being, as you say, six weeks or more behind. However, I will not allow mistakes to occur in our haste that may be determined as taking a different stand on an issue, for example, in the near future. I trust you haven't made any policy statements for me that I don't know about or that I couldn't possibly endorse."

"I've made no public statements. I wouldn't do that until we have a chance to meet and discuss what your stances are and what our campaign is about. We'll need to do that this afternoon, Senator." Carson paused then added, "Alone, without your counsel present."

"My counsel?" Jenkins questioned.

"Ms. Charbonneau," Carson replied.

Jenkins looked at Nicole, his eyebrows furrowed in confusion. Nicole smiled at his confusion.

"Allow me to explain," Carson started.

"I think I'd rather hear from Nikki if you don't mind," Jenkins stated without taking his eyes off of Nicole.

Nicole was grateful for Jenkins's authoritative response. She smiled and said, "It was necessary action, Senator. You see, Mr. Carson wants me to be your fiancée or I will not be included in your campaign or discussions. In light of that decision, I took the liberty of becoming your counselor on behalf of Rosen, Shafer, and Pruett."

Jenkins held his gaze at Nicole for a few seconds. Nicole could tell that Jenkins was angry. He slowly turned his head, first looking at Barker and then at Carson. "Nikki is not my fiancée, and we will not put on a show for the public. When and if I ask Nikki to marry me, she will be the first to be asked. Our relationship is very strong, but it is also very young. Senator Barker and Mr. Carson, I will not allow either of you to manipulate our relationship in any fashion. Is that understood?"

"Are you sleeping together?" Carson asked.

"That is none of your business, Mr. Carson," Jenkins shot back.

"Oh, believe me, Senator, if the people of this country find out that you two are shacking up, it will become my business."

Jenkins was fuming. His brown eyes flashed the anger, and his facial expression also revealed it. He gritted his teeth as he formulated his response. When he spoke, he enunciated every word taking great energy to show the anger and assertion behind each one. "My personal life is not and will not be a pivotal part of this campaign. If you cannot convince yourself upon receiving any questions, that you answer that it is none of anyone's business, then I'm afraid we will have to part ways now."

"Bobby," Barker jumped in quickly. "I think there is a bit of an over-reaction here. If Nikki wants to be your lawyer, then let her be your lawyer. It answers a lot of questions conveniently."

Nicole chuckled. "So, you don't see it as a problem when the press finds out that Senator Jenkins, a candidate for president, is discovered shacking up with his lawyer?" Jenkins lowered his head trying to keep himself from laughing. "Because frankly, gentlemen, I think the bar would find that bit disturbing."

"So, to be clear and to determine if you are to stay my campaign manager, Mr. Carson, Nikki is not my lawyer. Nikki and I are in a relationship. She currently is not my fiancée and will not be my fiancée until the time upon which I ask her to marry me." Jenkins looked at Carson.

"You realize this could sink us?"

"If you think that my relationship with Nikki is the biggest problem this campaign will have, then I believe it is better that you leave now." Jenkins's voice was very calm, but he was furious. "Do I need to remind you that Iran and Iraq are about to go to war. The Soviet Union just invaded Afghanistan. Americans are being held hostage in Iran, and that's just the tip of the iceberg. Our economy is in a deep recession, and I don't think my Republican counterparts have the correct answers to stop this plunge. Our first campaign stop is Iowa, an agricultural state, whose farmers have been hit hard because of declining exports, crop prices declining and interest rates rising. The sharp rise in oil prices and fears that we may be going into another oil crisis has Americans in a panic." Jenkins looked at Carson. "And you are worried about our relationship being the biggest issue of my campaign?"

Carson looked at Jenkins. "If you can answer every question about your relationship with the same conviction you just showed me, then I am not concerned about your relationship."

Jenkins smiled. "Let's get to work then. We only have twenty-five minutes until the press conference." Jenkins looked down at the papers that contained his announcement speech. He picked up a pen and began writing some notes in the margin. He looked up and announced, "I wasn't planning on saying much at the conference or taking any questions. I think we should keep it short and sweet with an invitation to join us in Iowa. What's our first stop?"

"That depends on our strategy. Are we going to focus just on the urban areas? Should we focus on college towns? You are young, and that will appeal to college students. Do we ignore the small farm towns, which typically caucus for the Republicans?"

"Why would you ignore anyone?" Nicole asked.

"Because we only have three weeks to ensure that Bobby becomes a viable candidate," Carson informed her. "The caucus process is different. It's not a vote. For Jenkins to be a viable candidate and receive the media endorsement on January twenty-first, he will need to have at least fifteen percent of the attendees backing him—as in literally standing under his banner when the evening is through. If he has the highest percentage, the press will then officially dub him the front-runner."

"So you need a strategy that will ensure that Bobby gets that fifteen percent consistently," Nicole stated.

"My preference is to hit the urban areas and the college towns. I can stop at some of the agricultural towns in between," Jenkins said.

"That would be my best counsel," Carson replied. He looked at Keaton. "Nelson, we need to generate some money fast and some endorsements." He looked at Barker when he mentioned the endorsements.

"I'll start lobbying some PACs now." Nelson stood up and started for the door.

Barker was thinking. "I have a few friends that I can call tonight. I'm sure we could wrestle up some endorsements by this weekend." Barker stood up. "I'll let you alone to work out the details of the campaign. I'll see you in the conference room in about fifteen minutes."

Carson, Jenkins, Nicole, and Chris started to discuss the campaign strategy. Nicole listened without contributing much. This position was her preference. This race to the White House was Jenkins's to win or lose. Jenkins was writing notes, scratching out sentences in his speech. With five minutes until the announcement, Jenkins stood up gathering his notes, and everyone started out the door to the conference room.

Jenkins held Nicole's hand as they walked to the room. His notes were in his leather folder that he carried in his other hand. Jenkins was quiet, and Nicole took notice of him caressing her hand with his thumb. She could tell he was nervous.

"Want some advice?" Nicole spoke quietly.

"I'm not sure." Jenkins wondered what Nicole might have to say.

"Just be yourself. Say what Bobby Jenkins would say, not what Barker or Carson or Mercer would say. When you stray from your truth that is when it will trip you up." Jenkins smiled at her. "You didn't get to the Senate on Barker's or Mercer's coattails. The people of North Carolina saw your vision. The country needs to see your vision now, so make sure it is always your voice they hear—your decisions and your thoughts. Do that, and you'll be a lot happier in the long run."

They reached the conference room. Mercer and Barker were waiting. Mercer shook Jenkins's hand. "It's an exciting day, Bobby." He turned to look at Nicole and gave her a quick hug. He smiled and said to Jenkins, "I can't tell you how pleased I am that I'm going to introduce you today. Shall we?" Mercer walked through the door to the stage, followed by Jenkins, who was still holding Nicole's hand. Carson, Chris, and Barker followed behind.

"Good afternoon," Mercer started standing at the podium. "I have witnessed many senators and representatives come and go in my long career. But I have never witnessed a senator with the intelligence and quickness that I have seen in Senator Robert Jenkins. His career in the military, albeit brief, was honorable. His experience stirred his desire to continue to serve his country and led him here, to Washington, DC. He has written many bills, and I have witnessed his negotiating skills and his ability to reach across the aisle to find common ground over and over again. Quite frankly, this young lad impressed me from our first meeting. I'm proud to introduce Senator Jenkins today and to say to you that the Democratic Party is proud to have him run for president." Mercer turned to shake hands with Jenkins. The flashbulbs from the press were blinding. Nicole wanted to shield her eyes, as did everyone else on the stage, but all resisted.

Mercer motioned to the podium, and Jenkins walked up to it, opening his leather folder. He paged through his speech. "Thank you all for coming this afternoon. You are probably wondering why I'm throwing my hat in the ring now. It is not entirely a new concept, my running for president. I think every talk show has hinted that I had an interest. Well, today I am officially announcing my campaign for president of the United States. I'd like to thank Senator Mercer and Senator Barker for their great counsel and support while I thought through what this means and why I feel I'm the best candidate for the job. Our country faces many challenges, both foreign and domestic. There is a need for strong leadership, and I am very grateful to my fellow senators and representatives for their vote of confidence in my ability to lead. I'd like to take this opportunity to announce that Mr. James Carson will be my campaign manager. Mr. Nelson Keaton will be my treasurer. Someone told me you have to make that announcement for it to be official." There was laughter from the press and those onstage. Jenkins smiled, appreciative that the press got the joke. "We are gearing up for the Iowa caucus, which is just around the corner. So, without any more fanfare, I'll be boarding a plane to Iowa this evening with Jim Carson to join our supporters to kick this campaign off and hit the ground running. Thank you again for coming, and we'll see you Des Moines tomorrow."

More flashbulbs went off, and Jenkins gave a smile and a wave. Mercer, Barker, and Carson moved forward. Nicole stood back and was thankful not to be at the front. Some strategically placed supporters in the room were clapping and cheering. Chris disappeared off the stage and pulled a string that released a cascade of confetti and balloons. The sign behind Jenkins was revealed, showing a red, white, and blue design with stars and stripes. It read: "Jenkins for President."

Nicole clapped and smiled. She watched Jenkins soak up his shining moment. Jenkins turned his head and saw that she wasn't beside him. He reached back, took her hand and brought her forward for another set of pictures. This went on for a few minutes until Carson ushered them all off stage. Just before leaving it, Carson grabbed the microphone. "See you in Iowa!" he exclaimed.

Everyone joyously walked back to Jenkins's office. Mercer and Barker shook Jenkins's hand again and excused themselves to start the business of gathering endorsements. They worked out how they would coordinate their schedules. Carson would be the point person. He would also work with Chris on the senator's schedule back in Washington. Some key votes were coming up, and Jenkins needed to make a stand. That meant flying back to Washington to give some perfectly timed speeches.

"I'm not kidding, Bobby. The plane leaves tonight for Des Moines. You've got two hours before you have to be at the airport," Carson said as he walked out of the office. Chris walked in and handed his ticket to Jenkins, then turned to hand Nicole her ticket.

"What's this?" Nicole asked.

"It's your ticket," Chris answered. "Carson insisted on sitting next to you, sir. Nikki is across the aisle."

"I'm not going to Iowa tonight," Nicole stated. "I have a meeting scheduled at the firm tomorrow and then lunch with Tony on his yacht."

Jenkins stopped ruffling through the papers on his desk and looked at her. "Can't you postpone that?" He closed a folder and threw it into his briefcase.

"No," Nicole returned, shaking her head. "Bobby, this is your thing. I made this appointment with Tony over two weeks ago. I don't know when he is going to be back in his office again. He seems to be spending more and more time on his yacht. I want to get this over with. I got the feeling that he is planning on retiring now that I won't be with the firm any longer."

"I see," Jenkins said dejectedly. "You'll fly to Iowa after that? You'll join me there?"

Nicole handed her ticket back to Chris. "I'm not sure what day, but we'll talk on the phone. Remember, I'm not the important one here. You're the one running for president."

Jenkins closed his briefcase and walked over to her with her coat in his hands. He opened the coat. "Yes, but if you play your cards right, you just might be First Lady." Nicole paused. She turned and looked at

Jenkins. He could tell he wasn't going to like what she was about to say. "It was a joke. Really, I was joking."

"No, you weren't," Nicole said. "Don't even go there and don't even speak like that to the press. Don't even hint at it." Jenkins looked confused. "It's too soon, Bobby. It's entirely too soon."

Jenkins knew she was right. So many things had happened so quickly in the last few months. She had barely got her feet back on the ground when this announcement hit. She needed time, and that was one thing Jenkins could give her.

"Will you do me one favor?" Nicole asked as they walked out of Jenkins's office.

"Anything."

She smiled at how he always wanted to please her. "Don't just accept the party line on things. Stay true to your convictions. Don't change fighting for what's right because you want to be president so badly. Be the change, Bobby, which you have always wanted to be. This election is so important, and we both know we are at a crossroads here. I admire your stances on so many issues. Don't let them manipulate you. If you lose because of big money or lack of support from the voters, then it is what it is, but at least you were true to yourself."

Jenkins smiled at her naiveté. Politics was a world of compromise. If he truly wanted to be elected, he knew he was going to have to compromise, and he was going to have to stroke the egos of big money. "I can only do my best." It was the only answer he could give her. "With you by my side, maybe I can be that strong presence that you think I am."

{V}

The next morning, Nicole talked with Jenkins over the phone. Jenkins informed her of strategy decisions, and Nicole offered her advice before she left for her appointment at the law firm. She was nervous, but she was determined to get what she deserved. She had it all worked out, and in an earlier conversation with Tony, she had made it clear that she expected no problems with the other partners regarding compensation. Tony promised her that she would get what she wanted at the minimum.

As she walked to Tony's yacht carrying a small paper bag containing some bakery bread, assorted cheeses, and a bottle of white wine, she reflected on the meeting. The meeting itself was a difficult negotiation. She never cared for Rosen; she now understood how Tony protected her from the wrath of the other two partners. Pruett was more levelheaded and, in the end, realized it was best to be generous with their offer. She was quite pleased with the outcome.

Tony spotted Nicole and waved. She smiled and quickened her pace to the yacht, stopping just before stepping on the boat. "Permission to come aboard, Captain?" she jokingly asked.

"Permission granted," Tony gladly said. Nicole walked onto the yacht via a little gangway bridge. Tony offered his hand to help her on board. They hugged each other, made awkward by the bag of groceries coming between them. Tony took the bag out of Nicole's hands as they moved inside to the covered and heated living area of the yacht.

They entered the cabin, which was nicely decorated and very comfortable. Tony walked to the galley with the bag of food and began to unload it. "Thanks for stopping for this." He took out the bottle of wine and put it in the little refrigerator. "I want to chill this for a few minutes. How did the meeting go?"

Nicole knew he didn't want all the details. He was only interested in the amount of money she had negotiated. "I would say it went very well. They offered a little over eight hundred thousand, and I settled for one million."

"Woohoo!" Tony exclaimed through a huge grin. "Congratulations!" Nicole smiled as Tony walked over to her to give her another hug. They held the embrace for a moment. Tony softly said, "I'm so proud of you, Nikki."

Nicole truly missed Tony, even though they had had their differences through the years. She never realized until this moment how much he had protected her and helped her with her career. There were not many women in her field who could have accomplished the things she had accomplished without the help of a male mentor championing her. "Thank you, Tony. Thank you for all your help." She pulled away to look at him.

Tony understood why she was thanking him. "It was my pleasure. You are smart and one hell of a lawyer. The firm was extremely lucky to have you. I just wish that I hadn't pushed all those horrible cases on you. If I could do it over, I would have assigned a number of those cases to someone else."

"It's over now. Let's put it behind us." Nicole took a deep breath. "The chowder smells wonderful." She took her coat off and laid it on the corner of a leather couch. "Is it about ready? I'm starving." She moved to the galley. The galley, sitting area, and dining area were all open, a perfect setup for the bachelor standing before her.

Tony retrieved the bottle from the fridge, opened it, and poured her a glass of white wine. "It's just about ready." He handed her the glass. "I'll slice some of this bread while we wait." He took out a cutting board and bowl. He began slicing the baguette and tossing the pieces into it. He then handed Nicole a plate and cheese slicer. "If you would like to arrange the cheeses," he said. Nicole took a drink of her wine and began the task given to her. She allowed the wine to warm her. She took another sip just as Tony returned from placing the bread on the table. "Are you feeling okay?" Tony asked.

"It was harder than I thought it would be to walk into that firm. I don't think that person exists anymore. So many things have happened, and I don't think I'll ever be the same," Nicole explained. "I'm not sure I have the strength I used to have." Nicole paused a moment. "I miss Carol. Being in the office brought back so many memories." Nicole looked down. Whenever she thought of Carol, her heart ached.

"We've certainly lost a lot of friends this past year."

"Amen to that," Nicole said as she raised her glass. Tony brought his glass to hers, producing a little clink when the crystal glasses touched. They simultaneously took a drink.

"This is the first time we've seen each other since you disappeared after Carol's murder. What happened to you?" Tony asked as he stirred the soup.

"Oh gosh, that is a long story," Nicole said as she brought the plate of cheeses to the table and sat. She didn't want to relive the whole ordeal by telling Tony all that had happened. She could tell by the look on his face that she was going to have to do just that. "Where should I start?"

"For starters, what happened at the nightclub?" Tony asked as he retrieved his wine and came over to the table to sit down with Nicole.

"It's a bit difficult to talk about, Tony. We arrived at the nightclub and Carol was already celebrating her victory in court." Nicole began to tell the story. She mentioned how Carol had made eye contact with a man with icy blue eyes who turned out to be the Serpent. Nicole was trying not to divulge too much, but she also knew that Tony would not be satisfied until he had all the pieces of the puzzle. She skipped to the part where Sean had told her she could identify the assassin and that he wanted to use her to set a trap. She had been whisked away to North Carolina where the dashing British agent succeeded in killing the assassin. The trap had worked. She was hopeful the information she provided, which matched the tale spun for the media, was enough to satisfy Tony's curiosity.

Tony stood, walking the short distance back to the galley. He took two bowls from a cabinet and ladled some chowder into each of them. He was trying to determine how much Nicole knew and whether he wanted to continue on this subject during lunch. "What an experience you had. I can certainly see why you don't like to talk about it. How Andrews was assassinated was so horrific." Tony returned to the table with the soup, setting a bowl in front of Nicole before sitting back down. "The papers didn't say anything about a British agent, though."

"No, they didn't." Nicole cringed, knowing she had made a mistake in mentioning the agent. "If you could keep that quiet, I'd appreciate it."

"They didn't mention much about you at all." Tony continued to prod. "Whose idea was that?"

"It was a joint decision. I didn't want to deal with the press and Bobby was kind enough to help draft a press release along with his investigator, Kevin Thompson."

"It doesn't add up, Nikki. Why was Jenkins even involved?" Tony pushed.

Nicole ate some of her soup and reached for a piece of bread. She was contemplating her answer. "Tony, can I trust you? What I mean to say is, if I tell you some things, would you keep it to yourself and not use it or divulge it to your Republican friends?" Nicole asked. "After all, I am dating Senator Jenkins, and there are some things I know that were not disclosed to the press. I don't want to put Bobby in a bad position."

Tony almost dropped his spoon into his bowl. For a brief second, he wondered if Nicole knew about the tape. To find out, he knew he had to put her mind at ease. "I've had a bit of a falling out with my old friends, including Mark Stevens. I plan to sail. I doubt I'll see any of those folks again. I highly doubt I'll be in this port very much in the future. I have one more official meeting as a partner in Rosen, Shafer, and Pruett and then I'm leaving."

"Why? What happened?" Nicole asked. Her confusion was genuine, and Tony could see that. He knew that Nicole wasn't talking about the taped confession.

"Let's just say my eyes have been opened." Tony dodged the question for now. He wasn't lying either. The Norman Sipes confession tape had opened his eyes. There wasn't a day that went by that Tony didn't curse Sipes for having the tape delivered to him upon his death. "What is it that you think could hurt Jenkins?"

"It wouldn't hurt Bobby, but it is something that isn't known. He is a good friend of the British agent. So, the public doesn't know how involved he was in the assassin's death," Nicole explained. "He hasn't closed the investigation into the assassination even though he is under pressure to do so. He isn't satisfied with the scenario that has played out in the press that it was just Sipes acting on his own."

"That's interesting. He planted that scenario on numerous occasions."

"He won't name names until he has the evidence. I can only say that he is actively working the investigation." She finished her chowder. "I tried to get word to you after Carol's death, but Sean, the British agent, would not take the risk for me to do that. Bobby offered to contact you, but Sean wouldn't allow that either. I can only imagine you were worried sick about me." Nicole was trying to change the subject, but with each comment, Tony was becoming more convinced that Nicole didn't understand that she again was at the center of a developing storm.

Tony smiled and finished his chowder. "A lot was going on at that time and, yes, I was concerned about you. Losing Carol and then not knowing what happened to you was disconcerting." Tony stood up, picking up his bowl. "Would you like anymore?"

"No, thank you. It was excellent. Where did you learn to cook?" Nicole asked, once again trying to change the subject.

Tony picked up her bowl and put them in the sink in the galley. Nicole started to pick up the leftover cheese and bread, but Tony told her to let it sit there, and he would get it later. Tony poured another glass of wine for each of them, explaining that he had been spending a lot of time on his boat. Because of that, he had to learn how to cook. He was no longer interested in state dinners at the White House or even dinners with old friends.

"I'm tired. It was hard work getting to a position of having so many favors to call in when I needed them. Most were used to keep Sipes out of trouble. That time took a lot out of me." Tony didn't mention how much he felt used and how much he had not been told. It wasn't the right time to blurt that out. He was wrestling with the idea of telling Nicole all he knew, but he wasn't sure just what that would accomplish. He walked over to the couch and Nicole followed. "So, tell me about you and Jenkins. How serious is it?"

Nicole smiled. "It's pretty serious. He treats me well." She started to blush. "With his schedule on the Hill, I don't know how he finds the time to make me feel special. And now with the campaign..." Tony smiled as Nicole trailed off. She took a deep breath. "Actually, in all honesty, I think he is more in love with me than I am with him at this point in the relationship."

"You always found him attractive."

"Yes, and he is intelligent." Nicole paused. "He is also powerful, and because of his position on various committees, he has his secrets. It's complicated at times."

"And that aggravates you." It was more a statement than a question. Tony knew her too well.

As they sat down on the couch, Nicole could feel a change in the air. She took a sip of her wine and placed it on the table beside the couch. She looked at Tony and could tell he was feeling uneasy. "What's wrong, Tony?"

Tony hesitated. "I have something I want to say, but I'm not sure how to say it."

"My stars, Tony, after all this time you can't just say it?"

"I'm not sure how much I should say or even how to start."

"Are you in some kind of trouble?" Nicole asked, beginning to worry.

"Maybe, in a way, I am," Tony replied cryptically. "You see, I'm holding a secret that only one other person knows. That is evident now. In fact, I'm pretty sure this other person has told you nothing about this." Tony paused as he saw Nicole's brow furrow.

"This other person is someone I know?" Nicole asked.

"Intimately," Tony purposely chose that word.

There was only one person Nicole knew intimately at the moment. "Bobby?"

"Yes," Tony confirmed. "Has he shown you a tape, a VCR tape?"

"No. I mean we watch movies, but I don't think that is what you are talking about." Nicole said.

"No, it isn't a tape for entertainment." Tony paused, wondering if he should even tell Nicole. "It concerns the investigation, or, I should say, I'm concerned with Jenkins's investigation. The tape includes some evidence that should have been given to the committee. I hope he'll give it to the committee."

"You're not making any sense, Tony. I'm sure if you gave him some information, he would have passed it on to the committee."

"I don't think he did, Nikki. This tape…" He paused. "It told him everything he needed to know about the assassination. It is pretty damning evidence and, quite frankly if it had been shared properly, we'd be in the midst of a pretty big shake-up right now."

"Tony, are you saying that Bobby is sitting on this evidence for some reason?"

"I don't know. He hasn't said anything to you about it?"

"I have no idea what you are talking about. What is it? What is this evidence?" Nicole asked.

"Ask Jenkins," Tony instructed. "If he truly loves you and wants you by his side, he should not be hiding this from you." Tony paused. "But then if he wants to use it to bribe people, maybe he wouldn't tell you."

"Bribe people? I think Bobby wields enough power that he doesn't have to bribe people."

"Nikki, this evidence would afford him even more power."

"What is on this tape?" Nicole asked forcefully.

"It identifies who ordered the assassination of President Andrews," Tony answered, still trying to evade the actual contents of the tape.

Nicole was taken aback. "Wait." Nicole shook her head trying to clear it. "Sipes paid off the assassin. It was Sipes," Nicole stated, suddenly feeling more freedom to discuss this with Tony now that it appeared he had some knowledge of it.

"It goes further than that," Tony said. "Think about it, Nikki. Sipes was broke. Do you think he had the money to pay off an international assassin on his own?"

"Are you telling me there is a cover-up and that Bobby is at the center of it?" Nicole asked. She desperately did not want to believe this. "That's a pretty bold statement, Tony." Nicole was starting to feel defensive of the man she loved. She wanted to believe Jenkins would always do the right thing. "Tony, you better have some pretty strong evidence to accuse Bobby of something like this to me."

Tony sat for a moment looking Nicole in the eyes. "I do."

"Why are you doing this? I know you never really liked him. Are you intentionally doing this to break us up or something?"

Tony shook his head. "Sipes is not the only one responsible for the Andrews assassination. My client—my former client, wanted to make sure that fact was known. He didn't want to be the only one going down in history as the person responsible." Tony sat for a moment. "Tell Jenkins you want to see the tape. Ask him what he intends to do with it." He finished his wine and got up from the couch. "I've probably said too much, but something needs to be done. Maybe you can light a fire under Jenkins. If not, then I'll have to do something." Tony was already making plans of what he had to do before he left Washington, DC, for the warmer waters of Key West.

Nicole stood up and put on her coat. She had so many emotions running through her. When she finished buttoning her coat, she frustratingly dropped her hands to her side. "I don't know what to say." Then she recalled the reading at the party and her mind started churning.

"You don't need to say anything to me. Just ask Jenkins to see the tape." Tony replied. "I have no doubt that you will be great counsel to him. Maybe that is all he needs." Nicole was about to say something when Tony walked over to her and gently put his hands on her shoulders. "Good-bye, Nikki. I'm not sure we'll talk again, but I want you to know that I've always had your best interests at heart and I still do. I wish you the best with Jenkins. Here's some advice: Keep your eyes open and don't think that anyone in that circle can't hurt you. They can and they will if you aren't part of the play."

"I don't think Bobby would intentionally cover something up for his gain. I can't believe that, Tony. I know you have always been jealous of him."

Tony dropped his arms and looked directly at Nicole. "Jealousy has nothing to do with this. Time apart has shown me you have always been interested in nothing more than being a friend. Believe me, if I wanted to get Jenkins, I would not have talked to you," he said with no hint of anger. Nicole was skilled at reading Tony, and she cocked her head when she realized that Tony was not angry. His body language indicated that he was calm. That nagging tarot card flashed in her mind again. She could see the Lovers as plain as day. She closed her eyes to try and erase the image.

"I need to go." Nicole turned and walked to the door of the cabin. She turned back around to look at Tony. "If you're upset with the way that Bobby is handling something, then you should go to Bobby directly. Don't expect me to deliver messages or be a pawn in whatever game you are trying to play."

"I'm not playing a game. You should know what Jenkins knows for your own safety. Good-bye, Nikki." He turned away from her and walked to the sleeping quarters of his yacht. Nicole left feeling frustrated with what she thought was just a play by Tony to come between her and Jenkins.

Chapter Two

Early February 1980

"I t amazes me, Kent, that you are walking as well as you are after that surgery," Charlie remarked as he walked with a shackled Kent Chapman down a long hallway that led to a metal door. Outside the door, a prison van was idling, and two guards were positioned on each side of the van's open back doors.

Kent underwent his surgery a few days after Kevin Thompson had shot him at the beach house in North Carolina. A week after his surgery, he was flown across the ocean where the CIA guards released him into SIS custody. Charlie was with the guards who accompanied Kent in the following weeks to and from the prison in London, which was only a temporary home. After Kent was interrogated for his knowledge of the Serpent's network and procedures, he was to be transferred to HM Prison Wakefield. Wakefield seemed like a harsh punishment for someone who betrayed his country. Rated as a maximum security prison and located in Wakefield, West Yorkshire, England, it was home to those who committed the most heinous of crimes. Monster Mansion, as it was called, housed high-profile, high-risk sex offenders and murderers. Kent had protested his eventual transfer to this prison, hoping that his knowledge would lessen the charge and imprisonment. He couldn't have been more wrong.

Kent shuffled down the hallway, still angry about his situation. "I still can't believe that you have the nerve to send me to Wakefield after all the help I have given you."

"Yes, well, you were the one who chose to aid the Serpent. I don't know how you could have looked Sean in the eye all these years pretending to be his friend." Charlie did find this the most distasteful part of Kent's charade. "You went through training together. It is beyond me how you can sleep at night knowing what you were doing to someone who would have taken a bullet for you."

Kent scoffed at Charlie's comments. In Charlie's eyes, Kent had become very bitter. Charlie's eyebrows lowered as he pondered whether the image of the cheery, helpful Kent was a facade and this bitter person was real.

They reached the door and Charlie opened it. The two guards that had been following Charlie and Kent placed their hands on their holstered guns but relaxed when they spotted the prison guards with their semi-automatic rifles at the ready. Kent walked to the open back doors of the van, and the two guards helped him in and to a bench that was heavily bolted to the van's side wall. It was not designed for comfort. The guards strapped him to the bench, a leather strap around his waist. They secured his shackles to the floor with heavy bolts. They yanked a couple of times on the chains to make sure they were secured. Kent grimaced and cursed as the cuffs cut into his skin. There were no good-byes exchanged between Kent and Charlie as one of the guards jumped in the back and the doors to the van were closed and locked. The guard who was the driver sauntered up to Charlie with a clipboard. Charlie looked over the paperwork and then signed it.

Returning to the driver's seat, the guard got in and drove away. With that, Kent was on his way to the infamous prison. Jack Kensington, the SIS director, had no love for traitors. He had lobbied heavily for Kent to be sent to Wakefield and he got his wish. Charlie wondered if it was a gross overreaction, but he also knew that most of information Kent supplied was fictitious. Elliot, who worked closely with Sean, also knew that Kent was lying. Charlie shrugged his shoulders, indifferent to what would or could happen to Kent, and walked back into SIS headquarters.

The van rumbled down the road. No one in the van had any interest in conversing. It seemed like an eternity before they left London behind. Since Kent's transfer happened late on this winter's day, daylight was waning. The guard in the back with Kent seemed to be struggling to stay awake. Kent silently observed both guards and then yawned.

"You wouldn't happen to have any coffee stashed somewhere, would you?" Kent asked, finally breaking the silence.

"This isn't a bloody airplane," the guard sitting across from him shot back.

"No, that's obvious," Kent replied.

The guard driving the van looked in his rearview mirror during this exchange but offered no additional commentary. The van continued to ramble along, each and every bump excruciatingly felt in the backsides of its three occupants. Kent was trying to determine what was worse: the endless rattling over bumps in the road or the foul odor ever-present inside the van.

They were a good hour into the trip when Kent finally nodded off. The guard across from him was finding it very hard to keep his eyes open. He repeatedly looked out the front window hole that separated the back compartment from the driver and its prisoners. Through that hole, the guard could see the rearview mirror surrounded by the darkness of the evening. The whining of the wheels on the road added to the fight to stay awake. The guard shifted his look back to Kent, asleep, with his mouth open, his head bobbing forward in rhythm with the van's movement. It was hypnotizing. The guard started to nod off but re-awoke with a jolt of his head. He then went back to looking out the front window hole.

In a split second, everything changed. The guard in the back had just nodded off when he felt a strange vibration that resonated through the seat. Kent felt it too, and he opened his eyes, confused by it. A loud bang rapidly followed the strange vibration, then a whoosh and both men looked forward to see the driver grabbing the wheel in a desperate attempt to control the van. It swayed right and left as the driver applied the brakes to try and slow the vehicle. Just as the van was slowing, it took a violent swing to the left, the rear of the van seemed to catapult forward, just as a repeated firecracker sound was heard.

The guard in the back looked forward into the rearview mirror to see the driver slumped in his seat and no longer in control of the vehicle. Blood trickled down the left side of his face, and within a second the van started to roll over. Kent tried his best to shield his face. Unable to raise his hands, he lowered his head between his shrugged shoulders. He didn't have to worry about falling out of his seat—he was chained and strapped into the body of the van to ensure he would not escape. The guard who was sitting across from him was not so lucky. With each roll of the van, the sound of his head and body hitting metal made a sickening thud. When the van came to a stop in a field a ways from the road, the guard was unconscious, lying across Kent's chest. The van was on its side. Kent's backside was horizontal with the ground. He lay in shock listening for sounds outside the van.

A few minutes later he heard some whispered voices speaking French, and a smile crept across his face. The van's back doors opened. Five men, whose identities were shielded under black masks, stood outside. Without speaking, two men grabbed the guard and removed him from Kent's chest. Another man removed the keys to Kent's chains from the guard's belt and began to unshackle him. No one spoke. When Kent was free, the men exited the van. Four of the men were already disappearing into the dark.

Kent rubbed his wrists as the fifth man handed him a backpack. He saluted Kent and took a few steps backward before he turned and ran into the darkness. Kent looked around and listened. Did he hear a siren? Was the crash witnessed by anyone other than these five masked men? He heard nothing. He opened the backpack and peered inside. He smiled when he realized his orders had been carried out with precision. He had everything he needed to flee England. He started off to find cover and disappear into the night.

{II}

As Nicole entered Jenkins's condo through the front door, she heard the phone ringing. She hurriedly put her purse and coat down and ran over to Jenkins's favorite chair, answering with a rushed hello.

"I'm sorry. I believe I dialed the wrong number," a man with a British accent said.

"Who were you trying to reach?" Nicole responded.

"I was trying to reach Senator Robert Jenkins."

"You've dialed correctly. I'm afraid he isn't here right now. He's flying in from New Hampshire. I expect him any minute," Nicole said, trying to be helpful. *I'm a sucker for a British accent,* she thought. The man's accent reminded her of Sean.

"How silly of me! I should have realized with his campaign for president that he'd be entirely too busy to help." The man seemed flustered.

"I don't understand," Nicole replied as she tilted her head. "May I take a message and have the senator call you?"

"Well, I'm afraid that depends on who you are," the man answered with a chuckle in his voice.

"I'm sorry. I'm Nicole Charbonneau, a friend of the senator's."

"Nicole? This is Nicole?" The man asked almost in disbelief.

"Yes," Nicole confirmed rather confused that the man seemed to know who she was and seemed excited about it.

"This is Charlie Dawson, Sean Adkins's superior. Nicole, it is quite good to finally talk with you. I was beginning to wonder if we would ever meet."

"Mr. Dawson! It is so very good to talk with you." Nicole sat down in Jenkins's chair. "How is Sean? Is he doing well?"

"Well, I'm afraid that is why I'm calling." Nicole didn't like the sound of that. The smile started to disappear from her lips. "I was wondering if Sean had been in touch with Bobby."

"Not that I'm aware of. What's wrong?"

"He hasn't returned home, and we are all beginning to worry about him."

"He's not in England? Do you know where he is?" Nicole asked, beginning to worry as well.

"Oh yes, we've been in contact. It's just that we expected him home by this time. I was going to ask if Bobby could perhaps drop down to see him since he was very helpful the last time." Charlie was rambling. He rather enjoyed hearing Nicole's voice. "But that was foolish of me. I'm sure with his campaign he will be entirely too busy…"

"You were referring to when the Serpent killed Sean's wife and child," Nicole said, although her voice trailed up at the end as if it was intended to be a question.

"Oh, he told you about that time."

"Sean did, yes," Nicole confirmed. "So, you know where he is."

"Yes," Charlie confirmed.

"Can you tell me?" Nicole prodded.

Charlie was quiet for quite a few seconds. "Nicole," he finally started. "I'd feel much better having this conversation with Bobby. No offense to you, my dear, it is just that I'm more comfortable dealing with the people I'm used to dealing with. If Bobby could find the time to call me, I would greatly appreciate it. I know he is rather busy, but perhaps he could refer me to someone who could help. Could you tell Bobby to call me? I'll be at the office for another hour, and then he can reach me at home."

Nicole was disappointed that Charlie was not going to divulge Sean's whereabouts. "I'll tell Bobby to call you when he gets home. I do expect him any minute."

Charlie could hear her disappointment. "It is nothing to do with you, Nicole. If it is any conciliation, Sean asks about you when I talk to him."

Nicole smiled when she heard this. "If you talk to him again, please tell him I said hello and that I'd be open to hearing from him."

"Oh dear, I'm not sure Bobby would like to hear that," Charlie responded with the hint of laughter in his voice. "From what our papers have to say over here, you two seem to be quite the item."

Nicole laughed. "And I thought following the Royal Family was your favorite pastime."

"Touché'!" Charlie countered. "I have to say that Bobby certainly looks happy with you on his arm. Tell him to call me, and if I talk to Sean, I will pass on your message. Good-bye." Charlie hung up the phone. Nicole thought for a moment and then did the same. Now she had to tell Bobby to call Charlie without sounding too anxious. If Sean was in danger or suffering, she wanted to help him. This was going to be tricky. She needed to think and was hoping Jenkins wouldn't get home too quickly.

Unfortunately, that was not to be. She heard the garage door open, and Jenkins's car pull in. She walked to the bar to pour them both a drink. She poured Jenkins a scotch. Nicole opted for a glass of white wine. Jenkins entered from the garage and saw Nicole at the bar retrieving the opened wine bottle from the small refrigerator under the bar. He walked over to her, took her in his arms, and they kissed passionately.

"I could get used to you living here," he said. Although they were not living together, Nicole had a key to his condo and, discreetly as possible spent, the night with Jenkins when they could. The campaign commitments were grueling, and there were times when Nicole joined Jenkins at events. She thought it best not to be a constant companion, which she hoped would keep the comments about their relationship to a minimum.

Nicole just smiled, relaxing into his hug. She was well aware of the fact that Jenkins loved her more than she loved him. She wasn't sure how she felt about that, and she wasn't interested in pondering that thought any further. She did love Jenkins and was very attracted to him. She just wasn't in the position to give any more than that after all that had happened. Her heart was still mending, and there were just too many questions left to be answered. Not to mention, there was this bond with Sean that she needed to figure out.

Jenkins released her and looked at his watch. Nicole handed him his scotch, and she picked up her glass of wine. Jenkins took a quick swig and put his glass down on the bar. He started to walk away, loosening his tie as he walked. "We don't have much time. The Barkers have invited us over for dinner. It seems there is something urgent that Larry wants to discuss with us."

"Discuss with us? You and me?" Nicole questioned. She took a drink of her wine.

"No. I'm sorry." Jenkins stopped; realizing his eagerness was confusing. "He wants the Phenom Five, as you call us, to meet," Jenkins clarified. "I'm not sure what it is about, but Larry called about a half hour ago and asked that we come over for dinner. Actually, he didn't ask, he demanded." Jenkins headed toward the stairs. "I want to change my clothes—"

"Bobby," Nicole interrupted him with a sense of urgency that caught Jenkins's attention. "Charlie Dawson called here just before you got home. He would like you to call him as soon as possible."

Jenkins ran his fingers through his hair and then looked at his wristwatch. "Did he say what it was about?"

"It involves Sean," Nicole blurted out almost before Jenkins finished his question. *How come I can scheme to win court cases but am terrible at this?* She looked down at her wine glass and rested her body against the bar.

"Did he tell you anything more?" Jenkins asked, becoming a little irritated.

"No. He said he wanted to talk to you directly." Nicole watched as Jenkins wrestled with what he should do. "Bobby, whatever Senator Barker wants can surely wait until we arrive. I doubt this will take very long."

Jenkins looked at Nicole. "Or I could call Charlie in the morning." At this, Nicole gave him a scornful look that he had only seen a couple of times before, including the night that Carol was killed. "Oh, all right. I won't get a minute's peace until I call him." He walked over to his chair and sat down.

"Don't you think you should call from your den?" Nicole asked.

"Why? You won't let me alone until I tell you everything, so I might as well make the call here." Jenkins was not happy at all. The last thing he wanted was Sean back in their lives. In fact, he felt Sean was the reason why Nicole had not fully committed to their relationship. He could feel that slight bit of hesitation whenever he touched her or commented how much he loved her. The tension between them intensified every time she mentioned Sean's name and Jenkins was very aware of the jealousy and resentment that was growing within him.

He picked up the receiver after locating Charlie's office number in a small black book of phone numbers he carried with him. He began to dial the number. After a few rings, someone picked up. "Hello Charlie, it's Bobby Jenkins. Nikki said you called." Jenkins listened as Charlie thanked him for calling back so quickly. "It is my pleasure. What can I do for you?"

"Well, Bobby, it is a favor, really, and off the record. I was wondering if you could take some time to physically check on Sean for us," Charlie began. "While he seems to be fine, he has yet to return to England."

"He's not in England? Where is he?" Jenkins asked, now concerned.

"He is in Tryon, North Carolina. Are you familiar with that city?"

Jenkins chuckled. "I'd hardly call it a city. How on earth did he get there? That is on the other side of the state. What has you concerned, Charlie?"

"We'd like to have him back here as soon as possible. On a rather personal note, he hasn't sounded like himself. I'm afraid that he might be fighting some of those demons he was fighting when you were such a help to him. It is easy to hide what is truly going on when you are talking on the phone." Charlie paused. "There has also been an unfortunate development that requires his services urgently."

Jenkins sat quietly for a moment. "Charlie, I'm not sure how quickly I could get down there. I'm thinking over my schedule with all the primaries and North Carolina's primary isn't until May."

"Oh, dear, that is too long a wait I'm afraid."

Jenkins heard the worry in Charlie's voice. He glanced up to see Nicole intensely staring at him with a look of concern. "I'm late for a dinner meeting now. Can I call you again in the morning after I check my schedule? I might be able to arrange something so that a pass through that small town won't look too conspicuous." Jenkins listened as the hope in Charlie's voice grew. "Is there a concern about bringing Nikki?"

"Not at all, I would expect that Sean would be happy to see her."

"Do you have an address for him?" Jenkins picked up a piece of paper and pen from the end table next to his chair. He wrote down the address, said good-bye, and hung up the phone. Without looking at Nicole, he stood up, placed the paper in his pocket and announced, "Sean is in Tryon, North Carolina."

"Where?" Nicole asked, having never heard of the place.

"It's a quaint little town in the foothills of the Smokies," Jenkins said as he walked to the stairs. Just before exiting the room he finished with, "The Barkers were expecting us at five thirty." It was a few minutes past five thirty when Jenkins finished the call. He walked upstairs to change. Jenkins also wanted to be alone to rein in his emotions.

Nicole smiled as she brought the glass of wine up to her lips. There was a chance that she would see Sean again. She felt a feeling of warmth in her chest around her heart that she hadn't felt in a long time. She was almost tingling with excitement. She took another sip of her wine. She knew she had to hide these feelings from Jenkins. She desperately wanted to see Sean, but if she appeared too anxious, Jenkins might decide to go without her. She smiled at her thoughts. Of course, Jenkins should know he would not be able to keep her from seeing him. She wouldn't let him. If he couldn't fit the trip into his schedule, Nicole might go down to Tryon without him. She took her last drink of wine. She knew she was going to see Sean and it was going to be soon.

Jenkins returned in a fresh suit and grabbed both his coat and Nicole's off the chair. "Are you ready?"

Nicole put her glass down on the bar. She turned to allow Jenkins to help her into her coat. "What's the topic of conversation tonight?"

"I have no idea what you lovely ladies will be talking about." Jenkins smiled as he thwarted Nicole's attempt to find out what the Phenom Five were going to discuss. They exited the house to the garage. There was little discussion between them on the drive over to the Barker's residence.

{III}

Louise Barker walked with Jenkins and Nicole to the great room of their home where the other distinguished guests were enjoying their drinks and discussions. Nicole was taken aback at first by the powerful members of Congress standing before her. She wasn't sure why this happened each time she saw them gathered. Senator Daniel Mercer, the majority whip of the Senate, was standing by the fireplace. His wife was standing beside him and in conversation with the House of Representatives minority leader's wife, Helen Connors. Her husband, Harry Connors, was talking with Mercer. They seemed to be commenting on the weather and the warmth of the fire in a pleasant conversation. Rounding out the Phenom Five, as Nicole referred to them, was the very powerful representative from California, Victor Albareto, who was up for reelection in November but didn't seem to be the least bit worried.

Nicole had accidentally let her nickname for these five men slip in an interview, and now the media was starting to use it, much to the dislike of Senator Barker. The Phenom Five—Senator Larry Barker, Senator Daniel Mercer, Senator Bobby Jenkins, Representative Harry Connors and Representative Victor Albareto—were the most powerful Democrats in the nation, setting the platform for the Democratic Party. While Jenkins and perhaps Mercer could have the trait of modesty attributed to them, the others could not. Jenkins and Mercer didn't like their names associated with anything as vain as being called "phenomenal." They preferred "powerful." They acknowledged their roles in steering the Democratic Party and spearheading most of the legislation on which both chambers of Congress voted. Their relationship with the Republicans was on good terms. While their negotiations could be seen as heavy-handed at times to those outside politics, it was nothing more than good negotiating along with exploiting the person across the aisle's weakness. The power they wielded was also something that these five men did not want to lose in the upcoming election.

"Hello, Bobby and Nikki," Senator Barker called when he saw them enter the room. He walked over to shake hands with Bobby and give Nicole the typical bear hug that she despised intensely. This always seemed to bring a smile and constrained chuckle to Jenkins.

"Sorry we're late," Jenkins said. "We need to figure out how to make Dupont Circle work someday."

"Thankfully, that doesn't fall under our jurisdiction!" Barker said, adding a laugh at the end. "Help yourself to a drink. I think dinner should be ready shortly." Barker then walked off to join Mercer.

Jenkins took Nicole's hand and walked over to the fully stocked bar to their right. A beautiful stained glassed window was behind the bar on an exterior wall. It was an abstract, but if you looked hard enough, you could make out the Capitol building and its surrounding landscape. It was quite beautiful. Very subtle in color and design, it provided a calm, peaceful feeling for anyone who looked at it.

Nicole indicated that she would like to have a glass of wine, which Jenkins poured for her. He then helped himself to Barker's single malt vintage scotch.

Nicole whispered to Jenkins, questioning the topic of conversation among the Phenom Five only to be thwarted again by Jenkins. With a smile, he reminded her that the topic among the ladies was up to them. "You know, Bobby, the year is 1980, not 1880," Nicole said, making a not-so-subtle point that perhaps it was time to include the women in the discussions.

"How time flies," Jenkins shot back as he took a drink of his scotch to drown his sarcasm. "I have to say; I love this 1963 Glenmorangie. Would you like a taste?" He asked Nicole.

She smiled as she knew he was trying to change the subject on purpose. "Do you think that what you men talk about is not discussed with their wives when they get home?"

"Nikki, I don't know, and I don't care. In case you haven't noticed, we aren't married and what the others tell their wives is none of my business," Jenkins affirmed. He could tell his remarks hit a sore spot with Nicole. He also knew he was lashing out at her because of the resentment he was feeling over Sean. His responses to her since the phone call with Charlie had been sharp and snappy. Jenkins realized what he was doing when he watched Nicole's demeanor change; her shoulders slumped slightly forward, and a frown crossed her lips as she looked down at her wine glass. Jenkins sighed and softened his tone. "It isn't that I don't trust you, I do. It is just that what we discuss is meant to occur behind closed doors for a reason. It's like a war room. If the plans get out, then the enemy would be harder to conquer. There are just some things that are better left to just a few."

"So democracy is expendable," Nicole responded, not looking up from her glass.

"What we do is not a threat to democracy. No one took the elections away and no one will. We are here to represent those who elected us, and they expect us to do whatever we can to make sure that we represent them well."

Nicole looked Jenkins in the eye. "Are you naïve enough to believe that this secret plotting is what they had in mind when they cast their vote?"

Jenkins smiled and shook his head in disbelief. "You really think that the Republicans aren't doing the same thing?"

"I didn't say that. I'm talking about the everyday citizen," Nicole returned. "I know the Republicans are doing the same thing."

Jenkins was resentful. "So you want us not to do this so that they can have the upper hand?"

"I didn't say that either," Nicole retorted.

"It's the way it works, Nikki. I'm sorry if that offends you or the average citizen. We have strategies, and we make plans. We have a platform that we work to achieve. They vote for the platform. We plot and discuss how certain legislation will affect the country and that platform. We vote in our constituents best interests, and above all, we negotiate in their best interests as well." Jenkins took another drink of his scotch. "Isn't that what a democracy is all about?"

"As long as you haven't forgotten that the negotiations are done with your constituents' best interests at heart, then I would have to answer, yes," Nicole said, taking a drink. She didn't like losing. "I just don't like closed door meetings," she finished.

Jenkins gave a little laugh, looking at Nicole with a little gleam of love in his eyes. This was one of the things he did love about her. He wondered how she could disarm him so easily. "You don't like being excluded from the discussion. If we invited you into the meetings, you wouldn't see anything wrong with them." He walked out from behind the bar.

Nicole felt a little wounded and perhaps insulted. "I would not," she quietly protested. He gently took her arm as they walked to the center of the room toward the Mercers. He kissed her on the cheek, an action not missed by a couple of the wives who smiled longingly, remembering how their own husbands used to do the same thing. "I hate this little box you are putting me in," she whispered to him. "Look at them all smiling at me. I feel like I've journeyed back to the 1950s or something."

Jenkins stopped and looked at Nicole. "Nikki, we are the youngest people in the room. They are from the 1950s." They both laughed quietly at Jenkins's comment. "We'll talk about your concerns after this evening is over. Don't expect any changes to happen, but I do want to hear why you feel I'm putting you in some kind of box." This truly did concern Jenkins, as he knew Nicole would never stay with him if she felt she was just someone who was on his arm to make him look good. This, of course, was at the root of his conundrum.

How much could he trust her, knowing she had a sharp mind for politics and the law? How much would she put up with before she decided that he wasn't the knight in shining armor that she made him out to be? Would she be able to forgive him for all the times he decided not to disclose information to her, including the confession tape that was securely locked in his safe? That information, she would feel, was something she should be privy to, and yet he couldn't bring himself to let her see it.

Two months after obtaining it, he still wasn't sure who to let in or what he should do with that tape. The power of knowing who plotted to kill President Andrews was seductive. Jenkins had been battling its seduction for months, and the power the tape wielded was still clouding his judgment. Could the country withstand multiple trails of treason? Could he withstand the political wrath if it were discovered that he had been hiding it all this time? It was like a sickness, witnessing how those who committed the act of treason behaved, secure in their belief that the secret had died with Norman Sipes. It was fascinating to watch. Their brashness and egotistic belief that they had literally gotten away with murder enraged Jenkins. Still, he had to keep it to himself until he could determine the best way to use the information. He was bearing the weight of this information alone. *It was better this way*, Jenkins convinced himself. He had forgotten that there was someone else who knew the power the tape wielded and was growing restless in the shadows. Tony's ability to upset Jenkins's plan never entered Jenkins's mind, but Tony didn't forget, and his actions were being carefully planned.

Jenkins was focused on one thing: the power that tape would give him. The timing had to be right, and then he would use it to his advantage. He wanted desperately to start action against Jefferies for the murder of John Spencer. Jenkins's lips curled in disgust when he thought of Jefferies. He hadn't realized he was showing his disgust on his face until Nicole asked if he was all right. Her voice jolted him back to the present. He adjusted his tie with his free hand and cleared his throat.

"What were you thinking about?" Nicole asked.

"It's nothing, darling," Jenkins said. "Shall we join the others?"

"Are you sure you're okay? Where were you?" Nicole pressed.

Jenkins smiled at her concern. "I had a fleeting thought of John. I get a little upset that we haven't put more pressure on Jefferies about the crash. Something I will remedy tomorrow."

"I understand," Nicole said, placing her arm between Jenkins's arm and his body. She rested her hand on the crux of his elbow. They walked over to join the others who were standing by the fireplace. Shortly after exchanging pleasantries with everyone, the Barkers announced that dinner was ready to be served. They followed their hosts to the dining room. The table was lavishly set, reflecting Louise's love for entertaining.

The Barkers certainly exhibited the old school of Washington politics and yet seemed to be able to connect with the younger generation. Nicole couldn't put her finger on the why or how. She thought it was because the Barkers seemed to be able to convince the public that their role was truly a service. Barker, along with Senator Mercer, had a way of calming the Senate and keeping the rogue senators in line, resulting in any drama being eliminated from public view. Nicole had to admit that Jenkins also had that ability, but she chalked that up to his military background more than the charm that the three of them possessed. Jenkins was twenty-five years younger than Barker and seventeen years younger than Mercer. In the four years that Jenkins had been a senator, he had managed to garner the trust of two men who had been in the Senate for more than a decade. Barker made no secret of the fact that he felt Jenkins was his apprentice and Jenkins made no secret that he held Barker in the highest esteem. Barker's support made Jenkins's rise within the Senate possible.

"Let's not sit by our spouses," Louise announced as they entered the room. "But let's do make sure we are boy, girl, boy, girl, please. To start things off, Larry will sit at the head of the table as usual." Her husband gave a little bow as he headed to his seat. Barker always conceded to his wife's wishes when it came to entertaining. "Nikki, you can sit on Larry's right." She pointed to the chair, and Nicole slightly hesitated as she walked away from Jenkins. "Anne, please sit on Larry's left." She finished directing everyone to their seats and discovered that inevitably married couples were sitting adjacent to one another. Sitting down, the hostess declared in a cheerful voice, "Oh well, I did try." Everyone gave a smile and acknowledged that she did indeed try. The Albaretos and Connors were who Nicole considered the lucky ones. They were sitting next to each other. Nicole felt like Jenkins was the farthest away possible. He certainly was far enough away not to be able to save her from any blunders she might make in front of Senator Barker or Anne Mercer. Nicole was not very comfortable with that thought. She looked at Jenkins seated across from her and at the end of the table next to Louise.

"Well, I have to say, I'm very happy to be sitting next to this fine-looking young man," Mrs. Connors said as she took Jenkins's arm, causing him to blush. It was no secret that Mrs. Connors found Jenkins very attractive and sought him out at every party. There was only five years difference between them. Representative Connors had apologized multiple times to Jenkins for his young, second wife's behavior. Connors had divorced his first wife of twenty years, seduced by this young vixen, who had now taken hold of Jenkins's arm. It was no secret there was trouble between the spouses, and neither of them seemed to care that each had found comfort in other people's beds for fleeting moments of satisfaction. The one bed that Mrs. Connors sought but had not succeeded in securing was Jenkins's, and she didn't care who knew it. Jenkins, on the other hand, despised the woman for all her weaknesses and awkward flirting that usually left him feeling tongue-tied. It astonished him that a woman of distinction would behave in such a manner. There was no possible way to always blame it on alcohol as suggested by Connors upon every apology. Mrs. Connors was never drunk when she made her wishes known to Jenkins or others.

Louise took Jenkins's hand that was resting on the table into hers and squeezed it. Nicole would have thought that the two women were making a play if it weren't for Louise's age and, of course, her marriage and position in society. Nicole despised Mrs. Connors actions. She could barely speak with Mrs. Connors and avoided having to do so. Nicole knew Louise's squeezing of Jenkins's hand was Louise's way of apologizing to Jenkins for her placing Mrs. Connors and Jenkins together.

However, Louise did intervene before Jenkins had a chance to pull his arm away or make a statement. "Now Mrs. Connors, while we all just adore this quiet young man, we must remember ourselves or some of us will not be enjoying the pleasure of his conversation." While it was a subtle reminder that she was married and should conduct herself as such, it was a reprimand that she would not be welcome at the table if she did not appropriately conduct herself. The not-so-veiled threat was quietly acknowledged. Mrs. Connors removed her arm, cleared her throat and then placed her napkin on her lap. The comment did nothing to keep her husband from staring her down.

Nicole looked at Jenkins. He gave a quick smile and a wink. Nicole returned his smile, still feeling a mile away from him. It was an awkward moment that seemed to purposely linger on for a few minutes. Nicole noticed for the first time the pangs of jealousy that she felt when she saw Mrs. Connors grab her beau's arm. She had never been one to get jealous before. She wondered if her jealousy was a result of how she felt about him or if it was a fear that he could at any time cheat on her. She acknowledged to herself that she didn't know him well enough to determine without a reasonable doubt if he were that type. She smiled as she thought about the times they had been apart. The campaign trips and long sessions in Congress were the main culprits. Granted he could cheat on her at any time, but she felt that Jenkins wouldn't put himself in that position. She smiled as she realized this and chided herself for her foolishness. It was quite clear to everyone that Senator Jenkins was madly in love with her. He was off the most eligible bachelor list in everyone's mind except hers and Mrs. Connors's.

The Barkers hadn't had time for the dinner to be catered, so Louise prepared the meal herself. She took the quiet moment to announce that she would appreciate a turned eye to the cooking. She hoped that everyone would realize being among friends was the real treat. Waiting for the signal, her staff was at the ready to serve the guests. After her quick statement, Louise gave a nod to her butler who disappeared into the kitchen. A few seconds later their appetizer was in front of them, and all were enjoying pleasant conversation as well as the food.

Nicole was being quiet, listening to the various conversations occurring around her. Jenkins noticed this and caught her eye. He tilted his head with a curious look on his face as if to ask if everything was all right. She smiled and nodded quickly to reassure him. He then returned to his conversation with Albareto. Louise noticed the gesture. She leaned over to Jenkins to start a private conversation with him. "I must say, Bobby, that I am so appreciative of how you fawn over Nikki."

Jenkins took his napkin and tapped it around his mouth hoping that it in some way hid his embarrassment. He wasn't sure what to say. "You've noticed that have you?"

"My dear boy, don't be embarrassed. That is a rare quality these days, especially in Washington," Louise started. "Most of us, meaning the wives, are reliving how our husbands used to treat us before we said, 'I do' and the political life took over." She looked at Jenkins, who felt as if he was being judged in some kind of contest. "You really do love her don't you? This isn't just a game you are playing because she looks good on your arm and her credentials are perfect for the Oval Office."

Jenkins had forgotten that Louise had a way of cutting through the charade that most members of Congress and their wives typically danced around. In a way, Nicole was very much like Louise in that she lived her life the way she wanted to live it. Jenkins sat back in his chair a moment realizing that Louise was a very strong woman, much like Eleanor Roosevelt. He looked at Louise and leaned forward. "I do love her very much." He paused a moment and then added, "If someone were to say to me that I could have my seat in the Senate *or* Nicole Charbonneau, I would walk away from the Senate that instant." He could see Louise was astonished at his answer. "And then I would continue my run for the presidency," he finished with a wink.

Louise couldn't contain herself. She let out a laugh that caught the attention of the whole room. "I'm so sorry. Something the senator said took me totally by surprise. Please, continue with your conversations. It doesn't bear repeating. It's all in the context you see." Jenkins acknowledged her comments with a slight nod of his head. When everyone had returned to their conversations, Louise looked at Jenkins. "I like Nikki. Please do me a favor. No, do us all a favor. Whatever you do, don't hurt her so much that she loses the love she has for you. Friendship is wonderful. But never give her a reason to stop caring." She looked at Nicole and then at her husband. "When you stop caring on the level of your soul, you stop loving in the way that you love her now. You won't know what I'm trying to say until you have lost it. So please, don't lose it. Nothing on this Earth is more important than what you are feeling right now."

Jenkins looked at Louise and wondered what Senator Barker had done to make his wife warn him about losing love. He wondered how Barker had hurt her and what he promised her to make her stay. He knew he stood the chance of losing Nicole. He hoped he could achieve his political dreams and keep these feelings alive. He smiled as he thought about how naïve Nicole was to the devious transactions that occurred behind closed doors. He knew that she had this childlike idea that politics would clean itself up before it passed the point of no return. And yet here he sat with one of the darkest secrets of all time. In some ways, he wished that Tony Shafer had never darkened his Senate office with his visit to deliver the videotape. Jenkins realized that it was like having J. R. R. Tolkien's One Ring in his possession. The videotape had its way of summoning evil and persuading him that maybe it wasn't a bad thing to have this knowledge, which ultimately could be used as power. Maybe he could use it to attain his dreams and then change the country's course to a better path. He shook his head slightly and smiled again as he heard himself say, *Who are you kidding?*

"Bobby?" Louise put her hand on the Senator's arm. "Are you feeling all right?"

The sound of her voice snapped him out of his thoughts. "I'm sorry. Yes, I'm fine. I was just lost in thought. Nikki and I had a wonderful conversation the other day, similar to this and I was recalling something I said." He patted the corners of his mouth again and replaced the napkin on his lap. One of the servants removed the plate in front of him. "Thank you," he said quickly before returning to the thought he was sharing with Louise. "In light of your advice, I wish I had said something different now." He took a drink of water hoping his lie would satisfy her and allow her to prattle on about something else. He was thankful when the conversation was interrupted by Senator Barker at the other end of the table.

"I just can't imagine you not practicing law, Nikki." Barker's astonishment at Nicole's statement raised his voice a little higher in volume than he realized. "Bobby, did you know this?"

"That Nikki is not going back into law? Yes, I knew that," Jenkins confirmed, giving Nicole a smile and a wink for support. "I suppose this conversation was brought on by her sharing that she has left the law firm of Rosen, Shafer, and Pruett." There was that man's name again. Was Tony Shafer going to be his unseen nemesis?

Nicole smiled and confirmed, "Yes, it was."

"So you won't be practicing law at all?" Louise asked Nicole.

"I don't think so. I thought that I might go back to the Department of Justice as a US Attorney again, but I'm not sure I'm up for trying some of the murder cases, if you know what I mean," Nicole said, clearing her throat. She tried to force from her mind the grizzly scene of the Serpent lying dead in his own blood on the beach house floor. She wondered if the feeling of fear the Serpent had brought into her life, which was now her demon, would ever leave her. She picked up her glass and took a quick drink. Jenkins was intently watching her, ready to jump in if she needed him to do so. "So," she started with a more upbeat tone in her voice, "I'm shopping around to see what might interest me as a second career."

Barker looked at Jenkins, who could tell that Barker's mind was racing with possibilities. "I am sure we can think of something for you," Barker said with a smile.

Nicole looked at the senator who was still looking at Jenkins. She looked at Jenkins then back at Barker. The smile on her face began to disappear as she realized that these powerful men wanted to control her life, her decisions. "I'm not cut out for politics as I have informed Tony Shafer on many occasions."

"What don't you like about politics?" Representative Connors asked.

"It's not that I don't like politics or the idea of being a representative or senator…"

"Or president," Louise chimed in with a gracious, encouraging smile.

Nicole acknowledged her comment with a slightly embarrassed smile. "…Or president," she added. "It's that I don't think I could say anything tactful when presented with some of the blatant falsehoods by opponents. I'd be pretty blunt, and no one likes a blunt politician."

"I think that Harry Truman would have disagreed with that statement," Representative Albareto said.

"The whole idea just frightens me," Nicole stated. "I really don't think it's for me."

"There are other ways to be involved without being in the spotlight," Louise added. She took her napkin from her lap and placed it on the table, symbolizing that dinner was complete. "We can talk more about this in the great room, while the gentlemen conduct their business in my husband's study. The staff will serve dessert and drinks in each room. Shall we?"

Nicole watched as everyone took Louise's cue and placed their napkins on the table. They pushed themselves back from the table and stood. Nicole followed suit and waited as the women went in one direction and the men in the opposite. Jenkins reached the end of the table where Nicole was and walked over to her. "Is everything all right?" he asked, standing close enough to kiss her quickly.

"Yes, I think so," Nicole replied. "I feel like I just walked into a scheme concocted by you and Senator Barker."

Jenkins chuckled. "I assure you I have no idea what they are up to."

"And then there is this feminist side of me that wants to be in that study with you, just to prove a point." Jenkins looked at Nicole, who couldn't determine what that look was saying. "What?"

"I haven't seen that side of you in a long time. I missed it. That feistiness and confidence that you had at the White House dinner where we first met have returned. I had forgotten it," Jenkins said. "I hope to see more of it."

"Are you sure? Most men despise us feminists."

"Most men aren't as cocky as I am," Jenkins answered with a smile.

"Now that could be taken a couple of ways," Nicole retorted, meeting his smile.

Jenkins raised his eyebrows and gave her another quick kiss. "See you in a little bit."

"Are you really going to discuss business?"

"Yes. There is an election to win, you know," Jenkins said as he pointed her in the direction of the great room and gave her a little push. "Go on now. Don't make me patronize you," he quipped with a twinkle in his eye and a smile on his face, knowing that was exactly what he was doing.

Nicole shook her head, fighting the urge to laugh and yet feeling a surge of anger. "Don't get used to this," was all she could say as she walked toward what felt like a lion's den: the wives of prominent men who many times in the past couldn't wait to pounce on the opportunity to belittle their own.

Jenkins turned for the study knowing he would indeed pay for his actions. Nicole would not let him sleep until she knew all that went on in the study that evening. He only hoped he could dodge the interrogation.

Nicole entered the great room just as after dinner drinks were being poured. On the coffee table, an assortment of liqueurs sat on a spotlessly shined silver platter, meticulously centered on being just an arm's reach from the pride. Nicole opted for Grand Marnier to go with the torte that was being served for dessert. She sat on the sofa next to Louise, who had motioned her to do so. The other wives were discussing shopping and other activities, which Nicole found boring. It wasn't that she didn't like shopping; she just didn't like making it an all-day affair. She wasn't up on all the fashion news or who was dating whom in society. Nicole was stylish enough, never going unnoticed in a room. Other things, however, were more important and deserving of her attention.

"Now, let's talk about what you should be doing," Louise stated. "If you aren't going to practice law, perhaps then managing a charity or an assistant to an ambassador would be something that interests you." She was wracking her brain trying to determine what would be of interest to Nicole. "It needs to be something that the senator could point to as aiding his campaign. You know what I mean, something that provides both of you with impeccable respect. It has to be something that you could champion as a first lady."

"Whoa!" Nicole exclaimed, trying to restrain a laugh. "We aren't married yet. I think you are getting a little ahead of yourself." Nicole put her dessert plate down. "I mean no disrespect, Louise. It is just that Bobby and I have only been together for a little over two months and that's no guarantee that we are going to marry."

The whole room went silent as the three other ladies gave small, but audible, gasps. Almost simultaneously the women in the room confirmed Louise's assertion that Jenkins was going to marry Nicole much to Nicole's displeasure.

"Oh, my dear," Mrs. Mercer started. "I have never seen Bobby more in love or blindly interested in anyone as he is with you. And as you know, he has had his pick of all kinds of women, from actresses to activists. Oh my stars, do you all remember?" She turned her attention to the other ladies. "Was it his high school sweetheart that he brought to a dinner engagement here?"

"Oh, now Anne, she was a sweet young lady." Mrs. Albareto said defensively.

"Yes, she was sweet and immature and out of her league," Mrs. Mercer retorted, moving her chest forward with each assertion. "That was terrible. It was a good thing that he brought her to the dinner party before he had to take her to an important function."

"Well, she never made it to that function, now did she?" Mrs. Connors chimed in with what appeared to be a coy smile, but Nicole knew there was something vicious behind it.

"No. No, he ended up going to the function all by himself," Mrs. Mercer confirmed. "I almost felt sorry for him, but it would have been a complete disaster."

Nicole sat and listened to the full litany of women that Jenkins had brought to various dinner parties and how each of them didn't measure up to some archaic set of standards that these women had concocted out of some perverted opinion of motherhood. They were more like wolves in sheep's clothing than respectable ladies. She wasn't sure what they were like exactly, except that, given the chance, they could tear any other woman apart. It made her stop and wonder what they thought of her. It wasn't the first time that she had witnessed this behavior. For some unknown reason, women had to belittle other women. It explained why she preferred the company of men. On the other hand, she hadn't kept up with every woman that Jenkins had dated. This afforded her a quick education. Other than the high school sweetheart, the list was pretty impressive.

"And you all believe that after that long list of women you just berated, that Bobby would be interested in settling down with me?" Nicole asked.

There was a small pregnant pause as the subtle insult of the word "berated" hung in the air. Nicole had more to say on the topic but felt that she had made her point with that word. Finally, Louise spoke up. "Nikki, all of us are very much aware of how he looks at you, and even this evening when you talked about trying murder cases, he was ready to jump to support you. He has never done that with any of the women we've been discussing here. He has used dinner parties with us before to test out the women he has been interested in, and we have never uttered a word of approval or disapproval about any of them to him. I believe that most of the women he has been with have fallen short in his own eyes, not ours." Louise took a drink of her cognac. "We are merely saying that we don't think this is going to be the case with you."

Nicole finished her Grand Marnier and placed the glass down on the table in front of her. "I apologize if my choice of words offended any of you. I feel like I should explain something to you. I am sure you are aware that I'm a feminist." She could almost hear the distasteful groan the women were choking back. "I realize we are from different generations. I also realize that standing behind your man is very important to you, and I commend your strength and willingness to do so. What I can't endorse is the need to discredit other women based on some outdated standard. I am not that kind of woman. I believe in our ability to be just as successful as any man. I believe that we should be paid the same wages, granted the same opportunities. And if you think that I didn't bring that belief to the table at my old job, just ask Tony Shafer how many scars he has as a result of not meeting that belief." The ladies laughed. "It is not good for us to attack our own. We should be enabling our own. The women you talk about already knew they weren't approved of before they even left here. I have to say that you have me wondering what you think of me and whether I'll pass the test. But frankly, I don't care what you think or what you'll tell your husbands about me. If Senator Jenkins doesn't want to see me again because I don't meet your standards, well then, he is not the man I want to be with either. I don't know about your lives with your husbands, and I don't know your sacrifices. But if you were given the opportunity and if you have daughters of your own, don't you want their lives to be different?"

"They are different than ours," Louise returned.

"And you are just as proud of them as your mothers were of you I would imagine," Nicole stated.

"Of course we are," Mrs. Mercer chimed in. "Nikki, I think you are wrong not to consider running for office. Yes, you're blunt and honest, and that probably won't sit well with a lot of people, but I think once people get to know you, it could be a blessing for this country."

"I thank you for that, Mrs. Mercer," Nicole said. "But I'm rather interested in hearing about other opportunities." She couldn't resist her next statement. "Besides, if I marry Senator Jenkins, the last thing I want is to oppose my husband for the Senate seat." The ladies all laughed at her comment.

{IV}

The discussion in Senator Barker's study struck a different tone. All five gentlemen were of a serious mind. It was an election year, and one of their own was in the running. Even with the amount of power Jenkins had obtained, he was genuinely admired and liked by the other four men. Jenkins never paid attention to the gossip about him being the most eligible bachelor on Capitol Hill. He prided himself on his honesty and his skill of negotiation. When he entered the study, he honestly thought the topic of conversation would be campaign strategy. He was not prepared to witness what was about to occur: the unsavory display of a Washington power play.

"Connors, have a seat," Barker said as he sat down. "No, sit over here." Barker pointed to the chair with its back to the fireplace, which Jenkins referred to as the hot seat. "Please close the door, Bobby." Jenkins was the last to enter the room.

"Yes, of course," Bobby said as he closed the door. Jenkins saw Connors in the hot seat and at first thought that his wife's flirting with him was the reason. "Larry, if this is about—"

"It's not." Barker cut him off midsentence. He pointed that he wanted Jenkins to sit next to Mercer and proceed to pull his pipe from a drawer. Jenkins sat down where he was instructed and gave Mercer a confused look. To everyone outside the group, Barker seemed to be the most powerful of the five men. The Texan's voice alone could cause anyone's knees to buckle when he turned his attention their way on the Senate floor. Jenkins had watched the spectacle occur numerous times. He admired Barker's patience, waiting for the precise moment to catch his opponent in an indefensible position.

There was an awkward moment as the four men waited for Barker to speak. Mercer, as the majority whip in the Senate, spoke first. "I believe we are gathered here to adjust a breach of protocol for this group. Is that true, Larry?"

Barker fiddled with his pipe, cleaning out the bowl. "There are cigars for anyone who would like one." He was letting the tension grow in the room. No one moved. Barker put the pipe to his mouth and drew in a breath. Satisfied the pipe bowl was sufficiently cleaned, he reached for his bag of pipe tobacco. "Connors, Mercer is correct. We are here to discuss a breach, but not just in our protocol."

Jenkins was confused. He didn't remember a protocol existing between the five men. There were some unwritten rules, a code of conduct, but he would hardly go so far as calling them protocol. Maybe it was his military background that brought about the confusion. Nothing had ever been written down or about these meetings.

Barker continued. "I consider this a breach in ethics, and you had better be glad that I'm not bringing this to the Senate floor." As Barker spoke Jenkins watched the blood drain from Connors's face. He became almost ashen white. "I can see by your reaction you know what I'm talking about."

Connors sat for a moment, trying to formulate his defense in his head. Connors had held and still did a block of representatives in the northern states-the rust belt. These were industrial states with strong unions. Connors, who represented Detroit, Michigan, with its large automotive corporations, was not happy with Jenkins's stance on drilling in the ANWR. Jenkins was heavily backing the new Corporate Average Fuel Economy (CAFE) standards, one of the key platforms in his campaign, using it to defend his stance of no drilling for oil in the ANWR. Detroit wanted the drilling and did not want new CAFE standards. The day after

Jenkins's campaign speech in Maine where he referenced his support for the CAFE standards, Connors appeared on the House floor denouncing the standards and blatantly condemning Jenkins's position. "If you are referring to my speech—"

"That is partly what I'm addressing here," Barker interrupted. "Now Connors, I thought this business about drilling in ANWR was behind us. The bill has been set aside for now."

"Yes, it has been set aside, but our young friend here is pushing a bill with higher CAFE standards, and some of my constituents are not happy about that."

"You mean some of your campaign's biggest contributors, don't you?" Jenkins accused.

"They are one in the same. I represent them, and they expect me to do my job. And they will also be contributing to your campaign," Connors shot back through gritted teeth.

"Sometimes, doing your job is not doing what is good for an industry but is ultimately good for the people and the environment," Jenkins charged. "The standards are not that far of a stretch considering the Japanese are very close to reaching them with their automobiles. And we both know the corporations will give more money to the GOP."

"In case you haven't noticed, hotshot, the American people are not interested in smaller, more efficient cars," Connors shot back, slightly more irritated. "And my constituents work in the automotive industry, so I'm not just talking white-collar jobs."

"You believe that to be true?" Jenkins asked. "If that's the case, then why bother with CAFE standards at all? We'll just let the Japanese enter the market with higher fuel-efficient cars. As oil prices rise because of the impending embargo, we will see how quickly the American car companies see their sales tumble. When they do, they will come begging for a bailout from the government." Jenkins shook his head. His usual southern charm abandoned him as he raised his voice in anger. "For God's sake, man, get your head out of your ass and do these dinosaurs a favor. Tell them to cinch up their belts and get with the program."

Connors could not stand it when someone younger than him thought he had all the answers. "You think it's that easy?" Connors yelled back. "Where do you come off telling an industry how to run its business? They have tons of research showing what Americans want. Just whose head is up their ass? My job isn't telling industry what or how to make their products, and it sure as hell isn't your job either!"

"Bobby's right," Barker interjected, just as Jenkins was about to answer. "The automotive industry is changing, and they better open their eyes to that fact. We are on the brink of another oil crisis, and we have got to end our dependence on foreign oil. I'm sorry, Connors, but your automotive friends need to wake up and understand we aren't impressed with their lack of action."

"And I'm telling you, my friends, if you want their backing for this election; you better kill this CAFE standards bill. You also better delay any discussion of ANCILA until after the election." Connors was adamant.

Barker didn't like being threatened, especially by a junior statesman. He lit his pipe, staring at the representative. He blew the smoke out of his mouth slowly as he contemplated his answer. This was done to calm his anger, although most in the room thought it was to add to Connors's nervousness. "You realize that you are a part of our little cartel because we believed that you were a strong representative who would be able to convey our direction to the automotive industry and not the other way around. It now sounds like they are controlling you. Is that the case? If so, what do they have on you?"

Barker had cut to the chase. Of course, he had heard rumors and withheld this information from the others. Jenkins wasn't even aware of any misconduct. Barker, as well as the other three gentlemen, stared at Connors as sweat beaded on his forehead. "How did you know?" was all he could muster. Connors began to tremble; his white-knuckled fingers wrapped around the arms of the chair as he tried to calm himself.

"Know what?" Barker asked calmly. It was clear to everyone in the room that Barker had something on Connors.

Connors smirked. "You have obviously been told something."

"I have. However, I want to hear it from you," Barker confirmed.

Connors stared at Barker. "I'd rather do this privately," he pleaded.

"As you know, what is shared among us stays among us." Barker gave a quick glance to the others, saying, "If any of you don't want to know, then you may leave and join the women in the other room; however as you know, Representative Connors, to be here is quite an honor. Helping to steer the party's direction is quite an honor. Our behavior should be above reproach," Barker reminded him. "You have a responsibility to tell us."

Connors swallowed hard as he dropped his head in shame. "A few months ago I was treated to a night on the town by the automotive big three. It was quite a night," Connors said as he tried not to laugh. "I need you gentlemen to promise me that my wife never finds out." Albareto put his drink down on the table. He stood, moving away from Barker to lean against the floor-to-ceiling bookcase in the back of the room. "To make it short, I was unfaithful. There are pictures. I had a lot to drink."

"You weren't just drinking," Barker charged.

"No, I wasn't just drinking. There were some drugs, some cocaine," Connors said shamefully. "But I can handle this."

Jenkins looked down at the floor. Mercer looked directly at Connors.

"No, you can't," Barker said. "And we won't handle this for you. You will to check yourself into a rehab program. You are going to confess to your wife what you have done. You will announce tomorrow that you are going into rehab and counseling with your wife." Barker put the pipe in the ashtray on the table in front of him.

"You know that will cost me the election!" Connors exclaimed.

"Larry," Jenkins started. "It is going to be a tight race in the House. I don't think we can afford to lose that seat."

"We'll lose it anyway when this comes out, and we all know it will come out eventually," Barker stated flatly. "It is better for you to do it now and maybe we can tap someone in the party for your seat that may be able to rebound from your mistakes. In any case, I will not have the automotive industry thinking they have you in their back pockets and, through you, control over our actions. That just isn't going to happen," Barker declared standing up. "Am I clear?" He looked at Connors.

"This job," Connors started. "My service means everything to me. I beg you not to make me do this. I'll lose my family—"

Barker gave a small laugh. "Why didn't you think of that before you snorted cocaine and cheated on your wife?" He paused for a second before he yelled, "Damn it, Harry! We stood here in this very room and pledged to be above this type of thing. We didn't want to be in a position where bribes could play into our decisions."

Jenkins looked at Barker. His mind quickly churned up the image of the pledge that was made in this very room three years ago. *Damn that tape,* Jenkins thought to himself. He knew it was only a matter of time before he had to inform Barker and Mercer of its existence. He knew it was the key to toppling the current Republican stronghold. He still worried about its impact on the American people. It was a slippery slope, and no one was going to be the clear winner. Jenkins looked at Connors and swore the man was close to tears. Barker's voice pulled him back to the current situation. "Would you like to tell your wife here, with our support, or alone?"

"Larry," Jenkins was appalled by Barker's question. "Let the man have a little dignity."

"He doesn't have any left in my opinion," Barker returned.

"I have to side with Bobby on this one. Harry, go home with your wife and have the discussion." Mercer commanded.

"Can we trust you to do it?" Barker asked. "Were you ever going to tell us?"

"I was trying to make it go away," Connors admitted, downing the rest of his after-dinner cognac. "I'll leave now. As you can imagine, I'm not feeling so well." Connors attempted to see if there was any support in the room.

"Let me know if you need any assistance," Barker said as he watched Connors walk to the study door. Connors didn't even acknowledge the comment. He walked out of the study to the great room.

Meanwhile, back in the study, Barker had just sat down. The room was still quiet. Jenkins's thoughts were still on what or how he should deal with the tape. As the election heated up, the investigation was going to draw more attention. The silence was finally broken.

"How did you know?" Albareto asked Barker.

"I received a phone call from one of the CEOs. He started talking to me like I had already agreed to something that Connors told him I had agreed to. The details don't matter. I was intrigued and played along. During the conversation, I commented how he got Connors to change his position. He was all too willing to tell me about the evening they had and offered to do the same for me the next time I was in Michigan." Barker adjusted his jacket. "Of course, that won't be happening." There was a short pause. "There is one more concern before we call it a night. Some of us here, myself included, had pledged strong support for Sanford before Bobby entered the race. I think over the coming weeks; we should make it clear that we are backing Bobby."

Jenkins looked at Barker. "That would be much appreciated." He smiled. The gentlemen raised their glasses in a toast and drank from the glasses to seal the sentiment.

"It's been a long night. I think we should adjourn," Barker stated.

"Yes, I think that would be a good idea," Albareto seconded. "This was quite a shock. I'm sure the ladies are wondering what happened."

Jenkins smiled again. "I'm sure I won't get a moment's peace until Nikki knows what happened."

"Yes, well, I think we can let them in on it. Mrs. Connors is going to need some support over the next few weeks. Louise knew what was going to happen, so it would be best if they all knew," Barker said as he walked to the door of the study and opened it. "Just make sure Nikki knows not to make any statements to the press."

"I don't think we have to worry about that," Jenkins reassured Barker. "When she returned from her ordeal in North Carolina, she dodged the press very well. With them constantly hounding her during this campaign, she has no love for them." The men laughed at the comment. Albareto pitied the press. He didn't like strong women, which explained why his wife hardly ever said a word in public. "I hope what happened here this evening won't come back to haunt us. He knows a lot about our strategies, and he could use it to our dismay."

"We've done nothing to be ashamed of or to hide. At least I know I haven't, have any of you?" Barker turned down the hall, not waiting for an answer. Jenkins quickly followed him with Mercer and Albareto right behind.

The gentlemen entered the great room where it was announced that business was done for the evening and that there were some early committee meetings that they needed to attend in the morning. The Albaretos were the first to leave, followed by the Mercers.

Jenkins helped Nicole with her coat and then turned to accept his coat from Louise. "Good night," Jenkins said as they walked out into the cold night air. He put his arm around Nicole as they walked to the car. "That was an interesting evening."

"Yes, it was strange," Nicole replied as they arrived at the car. Jenkins opened the passenger door, and Nicole got in. Jenkins walked around to the other side waving a final goodbye to the Barkers, who waited for him to start the car before they closed the door and turned off the porch light.

Jenkins pulled away from the curb and headed for his condo. After a few minutes of silence, Jenkins finally asked, "Why did you think it was strange?"

"It seemed like they had my next career determined for me without even asking," Nicole replied. "And I had never seen anyone look as pale as Connors did when he came out of the study. I don't think he was sick. He looked scared. I should know. I know what scared looks like."

Jenkins smiled at her last comment. "I won't argue with that. He was scared or, I should say, he is scared." Nicole looked at Jenkins. Without having to be asked, he continued. "Connors will be announcing that he is entering rehab in the next couple of days."

"What?"

"He is no longer part of the Phenom Five—a decision made by Barker that I hope doesn't come back to haunt us." Jenkins paused, and Nicole waited for him to continue. "It seems Connors had a little too much fun at the expense of his automotive backers. They plied him with drinks, cocaine, and women; photos and film at eleven if he didn't do as they wanted him to do."

This was enough for Nicole. She turned her head and looked out the window. "I don't know if I should feel sorry for his wife or wonder if she will even care about him."

"It is going to be difficult for her," Jenkins stated. "Although we know it was not the first time he strayed."

"You seem awfully detached from this," Nicole accused.

"He is not exactly my best friend, Nikki. He was getting a bit too high and mighty. I didn't appreciate his attack last week regarding the CAFE standards. In case you haven't noticed, the five of us don't attack each other in public." He paused. "I should have known something was up. Barker ended up getting a call from a CEO. Connors was being bribed to get us to back off the standards and provide other incentives."

"Are the five of you your own ethics committee?" Nicole asked, implying that they were holding themselves above reproach.

"In a way, I guess we are. This stays between us by the way. When we formed our little cartel, we knew we would have to stay clean, so to speak. As clean as any politician can be these days. I'm not sure how good we are doing with that. What Connors did was way over the line. No one is perfect. We all make mistakes, but we shouldn't have corporations blackmailing us."

"I'm curious, Barker and Mercer don't know everything you know do they?" Nicole asked.

"Like what?"

"Your relationship with SIS, Sean and Charlie, for example, what do they know about that?"

"That I have a couple of sources there. I never name them, and they assume it is part of my duties as chairman of the Intelligence Committee. They don't ask, and I don't tell."

"That's what I mean, though. So you could have all kinds of secrets, and that's OK because it's not a need-to-know thing." Nicole was trying to wrap her mind around what was right and what was wrong when it came to the standards of the Phenom Five.

"Is that a question?" Jenkins asked.

"Sort of."

Jenkins wasn't sure what she was referring to but knew he had to choose his words carefully. "I'm sure I'm not the only one who has not placed all his cards on the table."

Nicole decided she was never going to get Jenkins to tell her all he knew. She wasn't sure she wanted to know. They rode the rest of the way home in silence.

Nicole entered the condo. Jenkins closed the door behind him. She unbuttoned her coat and threw it on a chair by the foyer. "I need to ask you something. Was tonight some sort of test?"

"Test? I'm not sure I understand." Jenkins took off his coat and hung it up in the closet. "Did something happen?" Nicole walked over to the couch and sat down. Jenkins moved toward his favorite chair. "Would you like something to drink?" He asked while he was still standing. Nicole shook her head, and Jenkins sat down.

"Well, I had the honor of hearing about all the other women you have brought to those dinners." Nicole was a bit sarcastic. "The long list included your old high school sweetheart who evidently didn't make the right impression. And I had no idea that you had even dated a few Hollywood starlets."

Jenkins took a deep breath. "It was not a test, and I'm sorry that you had to endure that. It must have been very hard to hear." He paused, thinking about his high school sweetheart. "It is a shame. My old high school sweetheart is just that, a sweetheart of a person. She didn't like it here and, honestly, she never would have liked it here. We both grew up and have gone in different directions. She is married now, and I believe has two children. She is quite happy. She even told me in the last Christmas card she sent that she was glad we split up."

"Ouch!" Nicole said with a laugh.

Jenkins laughed too. "I think I understand why she had to say that to me now."

"It was all so surreal. I mean I am sitting there listening to them list every woman you have ever been with, and I'm thinking, why am I here?" Nicole paused and looked at Jenkins. "I mean really, Bobby if you can be with someone like Jennifer Anders…" Her voice trailed off. Jennifer Anders was a gorgeous Hollywood starlet who had adorned the arms of Hollywood's most attractive and sought-after men.

"We weren't exactly right for each other," Jenkins interrupted. "Don't get me wrong, Jennifer is a very sweet and very beautiful woman, but we just didn't click. I think that's the expression that is used." Jenkins looked at Nicole. "Did they also recall how long I was with each of these women?"

"No, not really, they just said that you were with them long enough to bring them to one of the dinners so that you could seek their approval."

"Nikki, I don't understand." Jenkins's brow was furrowed. "Are you jealous of these women?"

"No, I don't think so. I mean I know you are called the most eligible bachelor on Capitol Hill for a reason."

"Did it ever occur to you…" Jenkins paused for a moment, wondering if he really wanted to say it. He started over. "Did it ever occur to you that these women weren't interested or in love with me because of my missing leg?"

Startled, Nicole looked at Jenkins. "No. Is that true?"

"Some of them, yes, thought I was some kind of freak, and to be honest, I was not exactly in the same place I am now. I had nightmares and was wrestling demons through some of those relationships. Some women can only see the lack of something, whether that be physical or mental," Jenkins explained. "I'm not proud to say this, but my interest back then was to have someone on my arm, like Jennifer, to prove to others as well as myself that I was desirable. So, the reputation of being the most eligible bachelor didn't come from me being the most desirable. It was quite the opposite." There was a long silence as Jenkins worked up the courage to ask, "Does it bother you?"

"Does what bother me, your missing leg?" Nicole wanted to confirm before she spoke. Jenkins for the first time looked vulnerable to her. "No," she replied as soon as he began to nod his head.

"It is perfectly understandable if it does," Jenkins said, still looking at her.

She never took her eyes from his. "It doesn't bother me, Bobby. There is so much that I love about you. Those things by far overshadow your missing leg. I thought those other relationships ended because you dumped them. You never complain about your leg, and aside from a slight difference in the way you walk, no one would even know. There is so much more to you. I was attracted to you for many reasons." She paused. "I never give it a thought."

Jenkins smiled and breathed a small sigh of relief. "Thank you," he said gently. "Now back to your question of why you are here with me. I have to say; I fell in love with you the first night we formally met. You were fearless, intelligent, and I had watched you from afar at previous dinners. I had always wanted to meet you but didn't dare to introduce myself. When we finally did meet, the way you handled yourself in that high-pressure situation made quite an impression on me. Yes, I'll admit that your beauty was what first attracted me to you. I was so nervous when I saw you switch those names at the table."

Nicole gave a little chuckle remembering that moment. "You hid it very well."

"Thank you. I wanted to appear confident. Evidently I succeeded." Jenkins smiled. "When you took on Johnson with your comments about ANCILA, well, that's when you got me. I knew then that you were not only gorgeous but highly intelligent. To me, that is a combination I can't resist."

"So, the fact that I'm a feminist doesn't bother you?"

"It irritates the shit out of me," Jenkins said, not missing a beat. "But I wouldn't have it any other way. I don't see how you couldn't be a feminist. You are far too intelligent, brave, and beautiful to not make a difference for the women in this world. So don't be in such a rush to figure out what you want to do next. Recover from the last few months, and when you are feeling up to it, tackle what you want to do with the rest of your life."

"I know one thing," Nicole started. "I don't want anyone deciding for me what I am going to do."

"I won't," Jenkins declared.

"I'm not talking about you. I'm talking about those women tonight," Nicole said.

Jenkins laughed. "Don't worry. They will be busy supporting Connors's wife and stabbing her in the back when she isn't around," Jenkins retorted flippantly.

"You see!" Nicole almost shouted. "This pisses me off."

"I'm not telling them to do it," Jenkins defended himself.

"I know! We don't need men to destroy us or our confidence. We have other women who do that rather well!" Nicole exclaimed. "It's not Mrs. Connors's fault that her husband was weak and a bit of an asshole, and yet, we'll blame her and tear her apart for her so-called part in it. Of course, her infidelity will only add to all the gossip. They will talk about how weak she is and how she brought this on herself. And then there is this part of me that thinks she is only going to get what she deserves for her part in bringing down his first marriage."

"Nikki, it isn't like men don't attack other men. Look around. Look at the attacks on the campaign trail" Jenkins responded.

"Yes, but you're in politics."

"Oh, so just politicians do this?" Jenkins laughed. "Think again, my dear."

"What do you mean?"

"I've seen it everywhere. It's a feeding frenzy. It isn't just women on women or men on men. I've seen CEOs do it. I've seen best friends all their lives turn on one another. It is a part of human nature."

"It's flawed human nature," Nicole said.

"I won't disagree with that. Regardless of where they are in society when someone feels their power is being threatened or taken away, their first instinct is to fight. They want to injure them, mentally or physically. Show the least bit of weakness and watch out, you are the next victim."

"Wow! Where did that come from?" Nicole asked.

"Too many years being a politician is where that came from."

"Then why stay a politician?"

"Because I truly believe that I can make a difference," Jenkins explained. "The day I believe I can't make a difference is the day that

I'll leave this profession. We have to make some hard decisions, or we're going to lose our country." He looked at Nicole. "The Phenom Five talked briefly about this a few weeks ago. We all can see this happening. We want to stop it." Jenkins paused for a moment, remembering again what he had in his possession. "And I have some very hard decisions to make in the coming weeks," he mumbled to himself.

"What was that? I didn't hear you."

"It was nothing important. It's getting late." Jenkins stood up and retrieved her coat. "I'll call you in the morning."

Nicole stood up and walked to Jenkins. "You saw reporters?"

"You didn't?" Jenkins questioned with a smile.

"Damn them." Nicole smiled and kissed him goodnight. They walked to the front door where Jenkins gave her another kiss. He stood in the doorway as Nicole quickly walked to her car.

"You're breaking our heart, Nikki!" one reporter yelled. "Can't you spend the night just once?"

"Goodnight," Nicole said as she got in her car. "Sorry, you had to wait out in the cold so long." She shut her car door, started the engine, and drove off. Jenkins shut the door to his condo when she was safely out of sight.

{V}

In the darkness of the moonless sky, the pulsing noise of a military helicopter's engine drowned out the peaceful rhythm of the ocean waves. The copter's pilot was checking his radar while the copilot looked through the windows with a pair of binoculars. In the belly of the copter were five Navy SEALs waiting for the command to carry out their orders.

"It's like looking for a needle in a haystack," the copilot remarked to the pilot. "This must be some big name drug dealer to force us out here on a wild goose chase."

"I heard the command came down from POTUS himself. When we wake up in the morning, we'll read about it in the paper," the pilot joked as he did a visual scan. He heard a bleep, and he looked down at the radar. "Check out your three o'clock," the pilot told his copilot. The copilot looked through his binoculars as the pilot turned the copter.

"Vita Mea—that's it!" The copilot exclaimed. "Does any of this strike you as odd?"

"It's not our duty to question orders," the pilot declared, and he called back to the SEAL team to prepare for deployment.

The Vita Mea was a forty-five-foot sailing yacht; in Latin, the name translated to "My Life." The yacht was spotted off the coast of Key West, and as the copter approached, the pilot made an observation he felt he should share. "Copter pilot to SEAL team commander."

"Go ahead," the commander directed.

"Looks like this target has run ashore. Do you want to deploy on land or directly aboard the ship?"

"The order is on the ship."

"Affirmative," the copter pilot confirmed. "Prepare to board."

The leader of the SEAL team gave the thumbs up to his men. They moved into position as the copter hovered above the yacht. The pilot was correct that the yacht had been scuttled onto the small barrier island that had been underwater at high tide.

After boarding the yacht, the five Navy SEALs searched the boat for the captain, finding a dead body on the counter in the galley of the ship. The man's face was bludgeoned with blood soaking his white shirt and hair. There was blood on the counter and the floor. One of the SEALs pulled the dead man from the counter onto the floor. "Sir, making a positive ID is going to be difficult," he said.

The commander walked over and looked at the white-haired man. "That white hair is good enough for me." The commander walked back out to the deck and waved to a crewman on the copter. He lowered a large, fully packed duffel bag. "Let's plant this shit and get out of here." The commander ordered two of his men. He returned to the galley and instructed the two men to ransack the galley and to wrap the dead man's body in the white sheets from the bed. The commander then started looking through drawers and what he considered hiding places, tossing the contents onto the floor. He looked for a safe but did not find one.

When the contents of the duffel bag were securely hidden and the yacht looked even more ransacked, three of the five SEAL members returned to the copter. A few ropes were lowered, one by each of the three men, and were tied around the dead body. The final two SEAL team members scurried up to the copter. The commander ordered the copter pilot to head out to sea. The copter rose, clearing the body from the deck, and turned to head out to sea.

The SEAL team commander peered between the two pilots, looking at his radar. "How deep would you guess this area to be?" He asked the pilot and pointed to a position to the left of the radar screen.

"Pretty deep," the pilot replied, not knowing the depth off the top of his head.

"Head over there," the commander ordered.

The pilot didn't acknowledge the order verbally, but he turned the copter and headed for that spot. The commander watched as the deep water drew near. He walked to the open door of the copter and peered out. "Let him go," he ordered the three SEALs who were holding the ropes with quite some effort. They had braced themselves with special vests and ropes tied to the copter to keep from falling out of the open door.

Upon the command, the three ropes were thrown out the open door, and the body dropped into the ocean with a large splash. "We're done here," the commander told the copter pilot. "Let's return home."

"Returning home," the pilot confirmed, looking at the copilot. The copter turned, heading back to the mainland. Upon returning to the base, the Navy SEAL team commander reported to their superiors that their mission was successfully accomplished. They were then dismissed and ordered to get some sleep. Since this mission was highly classified, they were reminded not to speak a word of it to anyone.

Chapter Three

Second Week of February 1980

T he next morning, Jenkins arrived early at his Senate office and was looking through various reports and memos left by Chris. He dialed the phone of his campaign manager and told him that he was planning to leave the next day to check on the headquarters in Greenville, South Carolina. This was the cover for heading down to check on Sean, as promised to Charlie Dawson. After a fifteen-minute argument, Jenkins finally won by reminding him that the South Carolina primary was only a few weeks away. He then made a compromise, saying that he would meet him in Greenville and travel to the bigger cities to make appearances. That seemed to satisfy Carson. His next phone call was to Nicole.

"Are your bags packed?" Jenkins asked.

"Where are we going now?" Nicole asked, assuming that Carson ordered another campaign appearance.

"South Carolina," Jenkins informed her. "We'll be traveling by way of Tryon, North Carolina."

Nicole smiled. "Thank you, Bobby."

"I have some business to attend to today. We'll leave tomorrow morning," Jenkins told her. "Can we have dinner tonight?"

"Yes, of course," Nicole replied. "Where would you like to eat?"

"I don't yet. I'll call you later this afternoon," Jenkins said as Chris came into his office. "I need to go, darling. I'll call you soon. Bye."

Chris reminded Jenkins that Kevin Thompson, his investigator, wanted to meet with him regarding the investigation. Chris motioned for Thompson to enter. After Thompson reported his findings, most of which were dead ends, Jenkins informed Thompson that he wanted him to look into the death of Spencer as well. He wanted Thompson to find evidence that Jefferies ordered the tampering of the plane so that it would crash. Thompson wrote himself a note.

"I wish I were able to talk with Sean," Thompson said. "I need to know more about how the Serpent operated. That might shine some light on how Sipes got the name."

"Well, you are in luck," Jenkins confided as Chris entered the room to tell him that there was a vote and he was needed on the Senate floor. "Pack a bag and join Nikki and me. We are heading to South Carolina in the morning. We might just run into our old friend." He winked at Thompson, who smiled. "I need to run. Be at my home around six tomorrow morning." With that, Jenkins left for the Senate floor.

The day was packed with meetings, campaign arrangements, and statements made on current affairs, and before Jenkins knew it, it was close to eight in the evening. He looked at his watch and realized that he had not called Nicole. He picked up the phone and dialed Nicole's condo. There was no answer. "Chris, can you call my condo and see if Nikki is there?" Jenkins was looking down at a stack of papers that were spread across his desk. He hadn't noticed that Nicole was leaning against the door frame of his office. "Chris?"

"She's not at your condo, sir," Chris yelled back.

"Damn it," Jenkins said as his shoulders slumped, feeling he had let her down.

"If you take a minute and look up, you might be surprised," Nicole said. She was holding a plastic bag that contained two Styrofoam containers. She had brought dinner for Chris, Thompson, Jenkins and herself.

Jenkins looked up when he heard her voice. He smiled, sat back in his desk chair, and tossed his pen onto his desk. "I'm the luckiest man in the world."

"Don't push it," Nicole said with a smile. "Where in this mess would you like your dinner?"

Jenkins pointed to the conversation area. Nicole walked over to it and set the bag down on the table. Chris stood up from his desk, wiping his hands on the napkin that had accompanied his dinner which he was already eating. "Thanks, Nikki." He closed the door.

"You're welcome, Chris."

"Thank you!" Thompson chimed in as the door started to close. Nicole, in the same lyrical chime, answered Thompson back. She started to unpack the meals as Jenkins left his desk to join her. "I called Chris at about six when I didn't hear from you. He said you were busy, so I thought I'd bring dinner to you. I know much you like Johnny Boy." Johnny Boy Carryout specialized in barbeque ribs. She knew they would all be hungry, so she selected a full slab with coleslaw and French fries. Nicole opted for a rib sandwich.

"I appreciate your understanding. I don't see this slowing down anytime soon." Jenkins sighed and gave her a quick kiss.

"I would imagine it is only going to get worse," Nicole stated. They talked while they ate and Jenkins told her the plan for the campaign stops in South Carolina. "I think that's a good plan. Instead of looking like you are catching up with the late announcement, it looks like you are thinking ahead."

Jenkins stopped eating. He slowly turned his head and looked at Nicole. "Why didn't I think of that?"

Nicole smiled. "Because you were too busy trying to keep from telling people your main reason for heading down to that area."

"I think, my dear, you just gave me the answer to the media question about why I'll be in South Carolina this early." Jenkins put another bite of food in his mouth.

"Anything else I can solve for you while I'm here? I know, how about world peace?" Nicole joked.

"That would be wonderful, but I think it will take a bit longer than I have right now." Jenkins looked at his watch. "I have another couple of hours of work to do, I'm afraid. Thompson is meeting me at my condo at six tomorrow morning."

"He's coming with us?"

"Yes, he has some questions for Sean."

"Oh, I see," Nicole replied.

"We'll swing by and pick you up around six thirty," Jenkins took the last bite of the last rib. "Thank you so much for doing this," he said, pointing to the empty containers.

"It was my pleasure." Nicole was finished eating as well. She stood up and gathered the containers, placing them back into the plastic bag. "I'll see you in the morning then." They embraced and gave each other a long kiss.

"There are times when I don't think this run for president is worth it," Jenkins said. "I miss you."

Nicole sighed. "Well, it's not me who's worried about what the religious right thinks about our relationship." She winked. Jenkins shook his head at her comment and kissed her again.

He let her go and walked her to the door of his office. "Be careful." He looked at his watch. "Kevin, do you mind walking Nicole to her car?"

"Not at all, sir," Thompson responded. He stood up, grabbed his coat, and they walked out together.

{II}

The alarm woke Jenkins at five thirty in the morning. He showered, dressed, and grabbed a quick bite to eat before Thompson arrived at six. They loaded up Jenkins's car, drove over to pick up Nicole, and then headed on their way to Tryon, North Carolina. They had a good seven-hour drive in front of them without many stops. They were thankful for the extra few minutes of daylight each day in February brought them.

They arrived in Tryon around three thirty in the afternoon. The main road took them past all the little shops. Train tracks were on their right along with a small, but precious, community park. Nicole imagined that everyone knew each other and there were no secrets in this town. She couldn't imagine why Sean had picked this place, except for its beauty and quietness.

Thompson sat in the passenger seat navigating as Jenkins drove through the small town. Tryon sat very close to the South Carolina border and just north was the Saluda Grade, which took one up the side of a foothill to another quaint little southern town aptly named Saluda. Nina Simone was born in Tryon. Nicole remembered that fact because while she was working on some civil rights cases, she recalled that Simone refused to start a concert until her parents were allowed to sit in the front row after being removed from their seats so that the white folks could sit there. She recalled thinking how brave Simone was. She looked around at all the white faces along Main Street and wondered just where Simone might have been born. She found herself looking and occupying her mind on various things as they got closer to the border and the road that would lead her to Sean.

They turned right on a road that would hopefully take them to Lake Lanier. Sean was renting a house located on the lake and Thompson was looking for an address to help them along. Nicole caught glimpses of the lake as the road meandered around it. Lake houses and boathouses obscured the view occasionally, but Nicole decided it was a peaceful lake and realized then that it must have been the tranquility of this place that had attracted Sean.

"There it is," Thompson said, pointing, as Jenkins pulled the car into the driveway. Thompson's voice snapped Nicole out of her daydream and set her heart racing. Any second now she would see Sean.

Jenkins turned the engine off, and Thompson got out. Jenkins turned to look at Nicole. She was about to open the door. "Are you all right?" Jenkins asked.

"I'm fine," Nicole acknowledged as she opened the door. Jenkins could feel the cold of the afternoon setting in—or was he feeling her pulling away from him?

Thompson walked up to the door and rang the doorbell. There was no answer. He walked around the cabin, looking in windows where he could. When he reached the senator and Nicole after circling the small house, he announced, "I don't think anyone's home."

"Maybe we should grab something to eat and come back in an hour," Jenkins suggested. "There were some restaurants back in town." They turned to head back to the car. Nicole was walking in front of Thompson, opting for the backseat again. They reached the car, and Thompson waited before opening his door. Movement on the road had caught his eye.

Nicole looked in the same direction as Thompson, which was down the road they had just traveled. She spotted a familiar figure walking with his head down. She had seen the figure when they drove past him but didn't pay him any attention. Her thoughts had been elsewhere. She squinted and looked harder. She knew it was Sean. She dropped her purse by the side of the car and started to run toward him.

"Nikki!" Jenkins yelled as he started after her. Thompson wasn't far behind. "Nikki, wait!"

Sean heard Jenkins yell and looked up immediately to see Nicole running toward him. It was a sight he had hoped for in his dreams almost every night. He began to quicken his pace as he saw her, never taking his eyes off her. He dropped his backpack as he started to run. As they met, Sean lifted her up into his arms and spun her around. He placed one hand on the back of her head, intertwining his fingers in her cinnamon-colored hair. His other arm was around her waist. He buried his face in her neck and took a deep breath. He remembered the scent of her perfume. The very perfume she used to blind the Serpent long enough to allow her to break free. He recalled that scent often. Now the scent and the woman that wore it were in his arms. He was so happy that he had to laugh. He felt a tear reach his now clean-shaven cheek, prompting him to say in his familiar British accent, "Nicole, I've missed you." Nicole responded by hugging him tighter. She couldn't speak. Her emotions were running rampant, and she just wanted to hold Sean.

Jenkins stopped when he saw Sean take Nicole into his arms and spin her around. His heart skipped a beat. He felt the first pangs of jealousy, and he didn't like it. He stood and watched the woman he loved in the arms of a very good friend. He felt utterly helpless.

Thompson walked up alongside Jenkins. He looked at the senator and then at Sean. "You know that doesn't mean anything, Senator. It's no different than the bond you shared with John Spencer."

"I never hugged John like that," Jenkins bitterly responded as he started to walk toward Sean and Nicole.

Thompson looked down at the ground. He smiled for a second and then mumbled to himself, "This is going to be fun." He started after the Senator. When they reached Sean and Nicole, she was holding his face with her two hands and batting back more tears. Sean was staring into her eyes.

Nicole finally found the strength to say something. "Are you feeling all right?" Her voice cracked. "No more nightmares?" That was the second question. Sean tried to look down, but Nicole would not let him. "Sean, please, I need to know." A tear started down her cheek but was intercepted by Sean's finger.

"No more nightmares of Sarah," he said as he wiped her tear away. He saw Jenkins walking up with Thompson, and his eyes looked at them both. He backed up a bit from Nicole whose hands started to leave his face in a slow, very hesitant breaking of the caress between them. "Bobby, Kevin," he greeted them. "Is this some kind of intervention called for by Charlie?"

Jenkins laughed. "You guessed it. He called asking me to come down and check on you." When Nicole heard Jenkins's voice, she started to turn to face him. Sean managed to keep one arm around her while he offered his other hand to the senator. Nicole wiped her eyes and cheeks to dry them. Sean shook Thompson's hand last.

"Good to see you, Kevin," Sean said as Thompson took his hand.

Thompson noticed Sean's arm around Nicole. "The Three Musketeers back together again," he said with a laugh. Sean and Nicole joined him. It couldn't have made the senator feel anymore removed from them. "It's a bit nippy out here. You are renting a house I hope," Thompson said in an attempt to break the tense moment.

"I believe that is your car in the driveway. Let me get my pack, and we'll head on in," Sean said as he turned back to retrieve his backpack that was a few feet away. "Sorry to say that I don't have much to eat or drink. I wasn't expecting company. I just picked up a few essentials." When Sean turned back around, he saw Jenkins's arm around Nicole's shoulders. He had slipped his arm around her now that she was free of Sean's hold.

"Are you doing all right, dear?" Jenkins asked in his southern drawl that would melt the heart of any women, let alone the woman he loved. He slid his hand down her arm and took her hand. Nicole answered with a smile and quick nod of the head. "Shall we?" He said when he noticed that Sean had grabbed his pack. They all walked up to the house together.

Sean knew by Jenkins's actions that they were indeed a couple. But Sean also knew what he felt when he saw her again. As everyone suspected, he had fallen for Nicole. He had never seen a woman as brave as she was, nor as beautiful.

Once inside the house, everyone removed their coats and took a seat in the living room. Sean was the last to walk in and seemed a bit baffled. "I'm afraid I don't have anything to offer you to drink except some gin, scotch, or just water from the tap."

Thompson was the first to speak. "Scotch sounds good to me."

"I'll just have a glass of water," Jenkins replied.

"I'll give you a hand," Nicole offered. She followed him into the kitchen. Sean was already taking the glasses down from the cabinet. "How long have you been here?"

"I've been here for a couple of months," Sean replied. "When I left the beach house, I just started walking, and when I was tired, I'd find a hotel and sleep. I hitchhiked and caught some rides with a few truckers." He put the glasses down on the counter and started to retrieve some ice for the drinks. "What would you like to drink?"

"Water, please. Charlie is pretty worried about you."

"Yes, I figured that out from the last ring he gave me," Sean said as he turned the tap on. He filled Jenkins's glass with water and then Nicole's. He filled the third glass.

"You're not drinking?" Nicole asked.

"No."

"Were you drinking heavily?"

"Yes, I was hitting it pretty hard for a while. It's time to let everyone know I'm doing all right now." Sean said as he watched her fix the drink for Thompson. "I'm sorry that Charlie caused such a fuss and had Jenkins come all the way down here. But I have to say; I'm so very glad to see you, Nicole."

She looked at Sean when she heard that last sentence. "I don't understand why you felt you had to isolate yourself. It was horrible trying to figure out where you were and whether you needed help." She looked down at the glasses, which were now ready to be taken into the other room. "I would have been happy to help you, Sean."

Sean gave her a quick smile and a wink. "We better get in there, or your boyfriend will become even more jealous." Sean picked up two of the water glasses and walked into the living room. Nicole watched him leave before she picked up her glass and Thompson's scotch. Once all the glasses were distributed, and everyone was sitting down, Sean decided to get the conversation started. "I understand that Charlie was concerned and asked you to come down to check on me, but what I don't understand is why it took three of you to do this. Did Charlie paint some picture of me being a total mess?"

"He wasn't sure. He was very concerned," Jenkins replied. "And you know Nikki would not let me have a moment of peace until I said she could come. Kevin, well, he has some questions for you." Nicole shot a look his way with the permission statement and decided to let it slide.

"It is awfully nice to see you all again," Sean said. "There isn't much new with me. I needed time alone to work through some things. One of them, of course, is figuring out what I want to do next. I'm not thrilled with the idea of being out in the field any longer. I certainly don't want a desk job. So I've been trying to wrap my head around that."

"I'm sure Charlie would be able to help with that decision," Jenkins responded. "I'm sure your father would be happy to hear you don't want to be in the field any longer. And I'm sure he or your brother wouldn't mind your help in their offices."

"Work as one of their aides?" Sean was almost ready to laugh. "No thank you. I think I'd rather slit my wrists than have to deal with my family on a daily basis."

"As Kevin can tell you, there are a number of times having a good investigator comes in handy," Jenkins asserted.

"It's not a bad gig," Kevin said with a smile.

"No. I'm very serious, that isn't the job for me," Sean replied. "So, there you have it. The big decision in front of me: Just what will Sean Adkins do next?"

Nicole was looking at Sean the whole time while they were talking. She could identify with his dilemma. She also didn't know what was next for her. "I suppose these kinds of turbulent episodes have a way of turning the world upside down."

"Yes, they do, don't they?" Sean paused. "Are you going back to practicing law?"

"No," Nicole said. "Like you, I'm between professions." Sean smiled at the feeling of having a companion hanging in limbo with him.

"How long are you planning on staying here, Sean?" Jenkins asked. Sean's eyes shifted to Jenkins, and for a second Sean couldn't tell if

Jenkins's question was coming from genuine curiosity or if he was feeling threatened by his presence near Nicole. Jenkins made no attempt to commit to either through his body language.

"I should probably head back in a few days since he sent a posse for me."

"So soon," Nicole said disappointedly.

"It's not that soon," Sean said touched by her disappointment. "Besides, I'm sure my family wants me home. Charlie has been deflecting the wrath of my family long enough. It's time to start anew as they say."

"You have everything you need to get home?" Jenkins questioned.

"Bobby!" Nicole started. "You are practically pushing the man out of the country."

Jenkins looked at his love. The words stung. "No, I'm not, Nikki. I want to make sure he doesn't need some help to get back home. I'm offering my services. I'm not kicking him out of the country." Jenkins's tone, although seemingly reserved to most everyone else, was strained and showed a hint of anger toward the accusation. Nicole picked up on the tone and looked down.

Sean caught Nicole's reaction, and it told him that his presence was quickly influencing their relationship. In one way that pleased Sean; it let him know that Nicole might have some feelings for him. However, he didn't want to be the reason they broke up. If he and Nicole were to be together, she would have to decide that on her own without him coming between the two of them. "There is a problem with my passport," he said.

"What problem is that?" Jenkins asked.

"I don't have one. I left in such a hurry from your beach house. My passport was in the bedroom with some clothes. I only had my wallet on me and my gun." Jenkins gave a concerned look. "No need to worry, mate. I didn't rob anything. Charlie's been sending me money." Jenkins seemed to breathe a sigh of relief. Sean looked at Thompson. "You didn't happen to clean out the rooms before you left."

Thompson smiled. "I did. I didn't want to leave anything behind that could tie you to that beach house. Your passport is in my luggage out in the car."

"Ah! Well, that problem is solved," Sean said. "Thank you, Kevin." Sean took a sip of his water. "I don't know much about the restaurants here. I've been eating in all the time. Should we go get a bite to eat?" He stood up. "There is one open bedroom. I believe that couch turns into a bed somehow, so if you want to stay here, you are more than welcome to do so."

"I think that sounds like a good plan," Jenkins confirmed. "Let's go get something to eat."

They grabbed their coats and headed out to the car. Thompson was the last person out of the house and smiled at the tension that was growing between the other three. He was hoping he was nowhere near when all hell broke loose.

It was becoming quite clear to Nicole that Jenkins was not about to trust her alone with Sean. There were things that Nicole wanted to discuss with Sean. She didn't deny to herself or even to Jenkins that she had feelings for Sean. She felt a conversation with Sean would help to clear the air and they could be friends. She started a relationship with Jenkins, and she had made promises to him. She was committed to their relationship; however, the behavior Jenkins was exhibiting started to make her begin to question those commitments. He was overreaching in his protection, and for the duration of the drive to the restaurant, he answered questions either directed to her or her questions to Sean. She made up her mind that she would talk to Jenkins about it this evening when they were alone in their room. She wanted to make it clear that she did want to spend some time alone with Sean so they could talk things over once and for all.

They chose a restaurant in the center of the main strip. It was a little family-owned place with a good variety of home-cooked fare. To say dinner was awkward would be an understatement. Thompson wasn't much of a talker, to begin with, but Nicole and Sean weren't in the mood to talk either—well, not with others present. Jenkins tried a number of times to get the conversation going on various topics including the different times he had visited Sean in the past. Sean wasn't interested in discussing the past, and after the third or fourth attempt by Jenkins, Sean made it clear that those days were over.

"Sean, as you know, we are conducting a special investigation into President Andrews's assassination," Jenkins finally started. "Is there any reason why I should call you to testify?"

Sean looked at Jenkins confused. "I'm not sure. Is there something specific you'd like to know?"

"Chapman has been supplying some information on the Serpent's network and the Serpent himself. Do you think it would be wise if we debriefed you in a closed session? For example, did any of your intelligence point to who possibly hired the Serpent to perform the assassination?" Jenkins took a bite of his steak. "Of course, don't answer that here. But that would be the type of information we'd be asking you to provide—details about the Serpent if you have any."

"I'm willing to meet with your committee if you like, Bobby. I'm sure Charlie would provide answers to any questions you have. I've not been watching the news, so I have no idea how your investigation is going. I just figured you would have pinned that whole ordeal on Chapman and the Serpent and call it closed." Sean took a drink from his glass of water. He was just about finished with his meal.

"No. We're still investigating the whole ordeal. We haven't found out yet who hired the assassin. Also, you may remember my friend, John Spencer?" Sean nodded his head. "He was killed in a very suspicious plane crash. We have reason to believe that his death is somehow tied to all of this as well."

"I know nothing about that," Sean replied.

"Wait," Nicole started quietly. "Are you saying that this whole thing with Sipes illegally drilling in Alaska has something to do with Andrews's assassination?"

"No," Jenkins answered quickly. He felt his cheeks start to warm. He took a drink of his wine and cleared his throat. "I didn't mean to implicate that connection at all. There is still a lot we don't know."

Nicole looked at Thompson, who had been doing the investigating. Sean followed Nicole's eyes to Thompson.

"So, you are handling the investigation?" Sean asked, looking at Thompson.

"Yes. There isn't much to go on. It's like all the evidence just disappeared," Thompson explained, showing his frustration. "People are not talking. We know Sipes was killed because he made the payoff."

"It's a little hard when key suspects are buried," Sean confirmed.

"I know you didn't have a choice, but if we were able to capture the Serpent alive, would he have talked?" Thompson asked. Nicole put her fork down and rubbed her upper arms as if she had caught a chill. It was a thought she didn't want to think about. Thompson saw her reaction. "I'm sorry, Nikki."

She just waved her hand, unable to say anything.

Sean cocked his head, unsure why she reacted the way she did. His nightmares had ended. Now he was wondering if hers had ended as well. "I don't think that matters now, Kevin. Other than Sipes, who made contact to pay him off, he would not have known any of the others, if there were indeed others involved. He only dealt with the person who would pay him."

"Was an actual written contract signed?" Thompson asked.

"Really, can this be done some other time, like, when I'm not around?" Nicole pleaded. She brought her hands up to her forehead and rubbed her temples.

Jenkins put his arm around her and brought her to him. "Yes, perhaps when you two get back to DC."

"I'm sorry, Nikki," Thompson said again.

Sean didn't answer. He just continued to look at Nicole. It wasn't like her to get a queasy stomach or be upset at just questions. Here was a woman who had held her best friend after she had been murdered and didn't flinch. Sean wanted even more to have some time alone with Nicole. Now he wanted to help her get past whatever she was experiencing.

They finished their dinners, Jenkins paid the bill, and they drove back to the cabin. All of them were oblivious to the fact that the townspeople were now gossiping that this stranger had ties to their senator. Just who was this man? That was the question circulating around town like a whirlwind. Since they would never find out, the tall tales would begin with the wildest imaginations fanning the rumor mill.

It had been a long day, and the travelers were ready for bed. The dampness in the air was bothering the senator's leg—the phantom pain always seemed worst before a storm or in damp weather. Jenkins was hoping that they would have a sunny day for the drive to Greenville. A sunny day to start off the campaign would be perfect. They watched the local news for the weather report and then all said their good nights. Thompson was on the couch and opted to have the television on for a while longer. He turned the sound down and was watching the images.

Jenkins turned to Sean. "Sean, Nicole and I have some campaigning to do in Greenville tomorrow. The plan is that Kevin will drive us down to Greenville where we'll meet with Carson, my campaign manager. You and Kevin can then drive my car home, and Kevin can debrief you before you leave for England."

Nicole shot a look at Bobby with fear in her eyes that she might not get to see Sean before he departed. Sean caught the look out of the corner of his eye. "When will you return to DC?"

"We are hitting some towns here and won't be back until the end of next week," Jenkins replied.

Nicole bit her lip. It just became obvious to her that Jenkins had planned this all along. This was it. This was the last time she was to see Sean. Furious, she turned, walked through the bedroom door and slammed it shut.

"What time do we need to be in Greenville?" Sean asked.

"I have an appearance scheduled at ten," Jenkins replied. He looked at the now closed bedroom door wondering if it was safe to enter.

"I'll be ready," Sean responded as he watched Jenkins reluctantly walk toward the room that Nicole had entered. Part of him hoped she had locked the door. She had not. Sean was dismayed to see that Nicole was sharing a room with Jenkins, signifying their relationship was further along than he had hoped. Sean said goodnight again to everyone before he disappeared behind his bedroom door.

Jenkins entered the bedroom and shut the door. "We need to be in Greenville around ten, so we'll need to leave here no later than seven forty-five. That will give us enough time to stop for breakfast."

Nicole didn't answer him. She had already dressed for bed and was pulling the covers back. "Good night." She climbed in the bed and turned over on her side facing away from Jenkins.

Jenkins stood for a moment, hesitating to say anything for fear of triggering her wrath. He started to undress as he walked to his suitcase to retrieve his pajamas. After changing, he walked out of the bedroom to the adjoining bathroom. When he returned, Nicole was asleep or at least pretending to be asleep. He slid quietly into bed, hoping he didn't wake her. He turned the light off on the nightstand and settled in for some much-needed sleep.

Nicole did finally fall asleep, but not after a few tears ran down her cheek when she thought that she would not be alone with Sean. She didn't allow herself to sob as she didn't want Jenkins to know how much he had hurt her. She'd have that good cry when she was back home, alone in her condo. Sleep finally came when she promised herself that, however, this sleep was not peaceful.

Within a few hours, Nicole was dreaming. She was sitting at the table of the fortune-teller again. It was not at the party but in a black room. It was a room she had never seen before. A single candle flickered on the table between her and the fortune-teller. Suddenly, the Lovers card appeared, and Nicole looked closer. The eyes of the man on the Lovers card turned to the icy blue eyes of the Serpent. The eyes that Nicole had tried so hard to forget were now in her dream as if he was reaching out of the depths of hell to get to her. As she stared at the card, the eyes strengthened and grew larger, their piercing quality attempting to hypnotize her. Her heart began to beat faster, and she was engulfed in fear. She couldn't catch her breath. She frantically looked around, but she was alone. Branches of the tree behind the image of the man on the Lover card began to extend outward toward her. The branches wrapped around her wrists and arms, pulling her toward the piercing blue eyes. She screamed, but no one heard her. As she got closer and closer to the icy blue eyes, she tossed in bed, finally startling herself awake. She was breathing hard, not fully awake. She forced herself to sit up. Her violent, quick movement woke Jenkins.

Nicole was trying to catch her breath when Jenkins rolled over and placed his hand on her back. "Are you all right, Nikki? What is it?"

Nicole took a few more deep breaths. "I'm sorry," she whispered, still a bit breathless. "It was a bad dream. Go back to sleep; you have a long day tomorrow. I'm going to get a drink of water."

Jenkins started to throw the covers back. "I'll go with you, and you can tell me about your dream."

"No, don't be silly," Nicole said, now out of bed and putting on her robe. "You have to be on top of your game tomorrow. Go to sleep. It was just a weird, scary dream. I don't want to talk about it. It's nothing."

Jenkins hesitated. "Are you sure?"

"Yes. I'm just going to get a glass of water, and I'll be back before you know it." Nicole walked to the door and, before opening it, looked at Jenkins. He was already dozing off to sleep. She envied that about him. She determined he adapted to the habit of sleeping when he could at boot camp training for the SEAL program. She quietly opened and closed the door so that she didn't wake Thompson or Sean.

She quietly tiptoed to the kitchen and retrieved a glass from the cabinet. She turned on the faucet and filled it halfway with water. Moonlight was streaming through the window in the breakfast nook, and it was glimmering on the lake. She turned to look out the window, just when a burst of wind shook the tree branches, and Nicole felt the grip of fear from her dream surge again. She slumped to the floor, still holding the glass in one hand. She brought her knees to her chest, holding them with both arms, her hands holding the glass. She was trying desperately to rid the fear from her body. She hadn't felt this scared in weeks. She lowered her head to her knees in an attempt to hide.

Suddenly, a hand gently wrapped around her arm startling her. She tried not to scream, but a small gasp escaped as she took in a breath. Her head sprung up from her knees and water leaped out of the glass as she recoiled instinctively.

"It's Sean," he whispered and repeated. "It's Sean." Nicole looked at him and saw that it was him. She relaxed as soon as she saw his face. "I heard the door open, and it was a sound that I hadn't heard before. I came out to check on it and found you here. Are you all right?"

"Yes," Nicole answered. Trying to control her shaking hand, she brought the glass to her mouth and took a drink.

"Nightmare?" Sean asked concerned.

"No, it was just a bad dream." Nicole tried to reassure him.

Sean sat down facing her, his legs parallel to hers and never letting go of her arm. "I'm not buying it." He smiled as he whispered to her. "I know about nightmares and bad dreams, remember?" Nicole tried to smile. "They are one in the same. Was it the Serpent?"

Tears formed in her eyes. "Not really, it was his eyes, but it was more this whole tarot card thing." Nicole looked at Sean who had the strangest look on his face. She could tell she wasn't making sense. "It starts with a tarot card and the Serpent's eyes blazed through it, and the tree grabbed me and started to pull me to him."

"He's dead, Nicole," Sean whispered. They were sitting so close that they could whisper and both notice their breath caressing their body when doing so.

"I know. I hadn't seen those eyes until tonight."

Sean frowned and looked down. "Sorry." He hated that he brought back that memory to her.

"No, it has nothing to do with you," Nicole countered. "It doesn't matter. You needed to be there during the reading to fully understand."

Sean was still confused. "I didn't think you would go for that kind—"

"I don't. It was a party at Larry Barker's, a senator and friend of Bobby's. They forced me to do it."

"Are you still frightened?"

"I don't think so. I don't know." Nicole took another drink. "Maybe I suppressed everything too soon. Maybe everything just happened so fast that I just pushed it aside and didn't deal with any of it." She looked at Sean. "How does one deal with this kind of thing?"

"You're asking me?" They both laughed quietly, and Sean brought his head to hers. Their foreheads touched, and their eyes met when he pulled away. "Are you really okay?"

"Most of the time," Nicole replied. "I don't dream that often. I had panic attacks for a few weeks, and I had one the night of that damn party," she recalled. "And then this. I suppose that's progress. What about you?"

"I don't have nightmares of Sarah anymore," Sean offered, trying to dodge her question.

"But you still have nightmares?"

"Yes," he confirmed. "And I sleep lightly."

"Who do you dream of? Or should I say what do you dream?"

Sean smiled. "Maybe I'll tell you someday." Sean didn't see the point in telling Nicole that he dreams of her being in trouble, especially since she already had a nightmare this evening. Sean's hand on her arm was very close to her cheek. He raised his index finger and stroked Nicole's cheek. Nicole moved it closer to his hand. They sat and looked into each other's eyes. Sean madly wanted to kiss her.

"I've missed you," Nicole said. "I've missed you so much."

Sean smiled. "You know I missed you."

"Why didn't you call or try to get word to me?"

"Nicole I was in a very bad place when I left that beach house. And you don't know me. You know that crazed man who was after revenge and who emptied an entire clip into the bastard who murdered his wife and child. How could you possibly care for me?" Sean pulled back from her. "I had to work through all those layers of hate and..." He shook his head trying to find the right word, but couldn't. "Anyway, you think of me as a knight on a white stallion. I'm not." Sean looked away and toward the bedroom door, still closed with Jenkins sleeping on the other side.

"You saved my life. Doesn't that count for something?" Sean didn't look at her. "You tried to save Carol's life. Sean, these things have to count for something. I don't make it a habit of going around looking for..."

Sean looked at her. "For what?"

Nicole smiled. "Well, British agents for one thing and people with licenses to kill for another."

Sean laughed. "We aren't your average, run-of-the-mill sort of people, are we?"

"No."

"I'm sure when I'm not around, Bobby treats you very nicely." Sean looked back toward the door. "And I don't think he would be very happy to find us here." Sean paused for a moment. He was about to ask a question when Nicole interjected.

"Don't ask it."

"Do you?" Sean looked at her. "I need to know."

"I don't know. I thought I did. He was there for me when I got back to DC. He was everything I was looking for before my life changed before I met you." Sean looked away from her. "Sean, I care for him, and I have a lot of respect for him. Yes, we are in a relationship." She could see the words were hurting him. "You have to understand. I thought you left me and returned to England. I had no idea you were here suffering, or I would have come to help you. Bobby helped me work through the darkness; I guess just like he helped you." She looked away. "I never stopped looking out windows wishing I would see you walking up the sidewalk to my front door. But when you didn't, Bobby found me and calmed the storm." She put her hand around Sean's arm. She tugged it a little to get him to look at her. "But I never stopped looking for you out those windows."

Sean smiled as he broke their eye contact again. "Well." He shook his head not sure what to say. "I think we better get back to bed. Bobby's going to wake up and wonder where you are." He stood up and offered a hand to Nicole. She first handed him the empty glass. Sean placed it on the counter. She took his hand, and he pulled her to her feet. She moved toward him. She wanted to hug him. Sean stiffened his arms and stepped back. "There's a man in there who loves you and he is a good friend of mine. We'll never know, Nicole. I won't come between the relationship of two people I care for very much. So, I think we better be good friends."

Nicole's lower lip quivered. "Don't go home to England until I can see you off."

Sean shook his head. "I don't want to see you crying in the airport."

"Oh, you'd rather see me crying here instead?" Nicole said as tears rolled down her cheek.

"I'd rather see you happy. Bobby makes you happy, doesn't he?"

"Sometimes he does."

"That's better than never," Sean said. He squeezed both her hands in his, which he hadn't let go of since they stood up. "Good night." He finally let go and walked back to his room. He disappeared inside. Nicole stood for a few minutes longer, brought her hand up, and touched the cheek he had stroked earlier trying to recall their conversation. She bit her lip gently as she admitted to herself that she was more confused than ever when it came to which man she loved more. She returned to her bedroom where Jenkins was fast asleep. She slipped into bed without waking him and secure in the knowledge that her conversation with Sean would be her secret to keep.

After breakfast, they all left for Greenville. Jenkins was driving with Thompson in the passenger seat navigating and looking at maps to determine exactly where Carson wanted to meet. Sean and Nicole were in the backseat. Nicole was well aware that Jenkins could see her in the rearview mirror. Nicole felt he was checking the mirror constantly. Sean was sitting across from her, and she wasn't taking advantage of this time. Before too long, they were at their destination.

Jenkins parked the car in its designated spot. Crowds were already forming for the event. Jenkins opened the trunk and removed his and Nicole's suitcases. Two staffers appeared, shook their hands, and disappeared. Carson emerged from behind the stage and walked toward Jenkins.

Jenkins handed the keys to Kevin. "You might as well get started. Have a safe journey back. Sean," he said offering his hand. "It was good to see you and thank you for all your help."

Sean shook his hand. "Take care."

Jenkins turned to Nicole. "I'll see you in a few minutes?"

"Yes," Nicole said. Jenkins turned to head off Carson whom he didn't want to introduce to Sean.

Thompson opened the driver's side door. "I'll see you back in DC."

"Thanks, Kevin." Nicole looked down at the ground and took a step forward. While looking down, she said to Sean, "Please don't leave until after I get back to DC."

There was little space between them, just enough that Sean had to reach to take Nicole's hand. "Only if you promise to take me to the airport by yourself, then I'll promise to stay."

Nicole looked up at the reversal of Sean's stance. "I promise."

Sean smiled. "Then I'll stay until you get back to DC."

Nicole smiled back. "Thank you." Nicole was well aware of the photographers forming along a temporary fence put up to keep them away from what was considered to be a private area. "Be careful heading back."

"I might persuade Kevin to hang around a bit," Sean said. "I'll see you soon."

"Nikki!" Jenkins yelled as he started to walk away with Carson to the backstage area. He waved for her to join him. He looked over to the fence indicating that the photographers were gathering.

"What's he afraid of?" Sean asked.

"Honestly, that we'll hug in front of the photographers, and then I'll have to explain who you are and why I was hugging you."

"Well, that almost sounds like a dare," Sean declared with a devilish grin on his face.

Nicole smiled and then laughed. "Let's not push our luck. He'll be surprised enough to find out you are still in DC when we get back." She extended her hand. "I don't know what to say. 'Thank you' sounds redundant and 'I'll miss you' sounds like—"

Sean took her hand and raised it to his lips. He kissed it gently and then smiled without moving his lips away from her hand. "I'm going to enjoy listening to how you explain this one."

Nicole laughed even more. "Thank you—thanks a lot." She laughed as she removed her hand from Sean's but not before he snuck another kiss. Nicole just shook her head, with a huge smile on her face as she walked away. How was she going to explain that scene? She looked up to see Jenkins glaring at her as she walked toward him.

"What?" Nicole asked as she reached his side.

"He needed to do that?"

"Oh, relax. He wanted to hug me, so you got off easy." Nicole kept walking so she didn't catch the scornful look on Jenkins's face and he didn't see the smirk on Nicole's.

Sean watched her walk away from him, her swagger seeming to have appeared again. He remembered seeing the sway in her hips the day they walked on the beach and before that night in the nightclub after he literally ran into her.

Thompson walked up behind him and started, "We better get on the road."

Sean gave him a quick glance. "Why don't we stay and watch his speech?"

Thompson thought for a minute. "Something inside me says I should force you into that car, but then there is this side of me that says, 'Oh what the hell, let's stay.'"

Sean turned his head and looked at Thompson. "Well then, let's go get a prime viewing spot."

Thompson shook his head. "Do you always cause this much trouble?"

Sean turned his head away from watching Nicole to look at Thompson. "You have no idea. I was much worse actually." Sean gave a sinister smile, winked, and started to walk to the front of the stage.

Jenkins prided himself on his ability to hide his anger in most tense situations. He had learned from Senator Mercer, the master of hiding emotion, and to a lesser degree from Senator Barker. But no one had prepared him well enough for the situation he walked into onstage. He fully believed that Sean and Thompson were on the road back to Washington. Onstage, before a loud, yelling crowd, was the chairman of the Greenville Democratic Party. He had the honor of introducing Senator Jenkins. Jenkins was off stage left, unable to see half the house, so to speak. He was straightening his tie while Nicole brushed away some lint from his shoulder. When he finished fidgeting with his tie,

Nicole shook her head and straightened it for him. The speaker was doing his duty, raising the fervor in the crowd as he built up the introduction.

Sean was fascinated by all the noise and chanting. With a confused look, he turned to Thompson who was standing stone-faced and unimpressed. Thompson turned his head noticing Sean's confusion, and he laughed. "I take it you've never been to a political rally?"

"Not one like this. He's that well liked?" Sean asked sincerely.

"You think they let people in who don't like him?" Thompson smirked.

The thought that the crowd was handpicked surprised Sean. "All of them?"

"Yep," Thompson confirmed laughing. "When he gets to the larger towns there may be a contingent of Sanford supporters who will manage to sneak in or stand in the back far away from the stage."

"Amazing," Sean replied.

The speaker ended with a high emphasis, a shout really, of Senator Robert Jenkins. The crowd went nuts. Sean scanned the crowd and noticed that the majority of them were women, about his age or younger. The last time Sean had been among screaming women was at a rock concert. As soon as Jenkins was visible, a woman standing behind Sean let out an ear-piercing scream. Both Sean and Thompson quickly covered their ears and turned to look at the woman. They were surprised to see tears coming from her eyes. They looked at one another in utter disbelief. The woman ignored their looks and started screaming "Bobby! Bobby!!" The two men looked at each other again, Sean rolling his eyes and Thompson stifling a laugh. Jenkins was holding hands with Nicole, now without the coat, she had worn all morning, not allowing anyone to see the dress underneath. Jenkins stopped and waved to the crowd.

Sean turned back around, and his eyes went directly to Nicole, standing no more than twenty yards in front of him and up on the stage. His mouth literally dropped open when he saw her. She had turned to greet a small contingent of Democratic nobility that had gathered on the stage while Jenkins waved to the crowd.

The dress that Nicole had chosen for the affair was stunning: violet in color, with a V-shaped opening in the back that gathered at the waist. The satin-looking material was loose and hung from the shoulders like the soft folds of drapery. The skirt, while not form fitting, hung elegantly from the waist to just above the knee, swaying playfully against her legs with each movement. Sean was mesmerized and waited for her to turn around. Jenkins had turned at the call of her voice to shake the hands of the people behind him. When he did, like clockwork, she turned to the front to wave to the crowd. A few whistles and catcalls were heard. Jenkins turned at the sound of them and teasingly waved a finger. Jenkins couldn't blame the men for whistling—he also had noticed that she was absolutely radiant in this dress.

The front of the dress gathered at each shoulder, the gentle drape of the material forming a U-shaped neckline. What the back playfully alluded access to, the front only hinted at, leaving the rest to one's imagination. It was then that Sean realized just how beautiful Nicole truly was and how skillfully confident she was in displaying her sexuality. It made him want her even more.

Jenkins had finished shaking the hands of the dignitaries and was about to head to the podium, reaching for Nicole's hand, when the woman behind Sean and Thompson screamed once again. Jenkins's attention was pulled in that direction, and that is when he saw Sean. Just a flash of anger came across his face, and Sean saw it. Jenkins shot a quick look at Thompson, who Jenkins felt had failed him. Jenkins quickly covered up his anger, forced a smile, and waved to the woman who was losing the last semblance of her composure. She was now jumping up and down using Sean's and Thompson's shoulders for assistance. Sean couldn't help but laugh at the whole scene. Jenkins was still staring at Sean when Sean turned his attention back to the stage. Sean gave a devious smile and started to clap slowly. Sean's action clearly sent a message to Jenkins. Sean had no intention of backing away from his care for Nicole.

Nicole knew something was wrong when she felt Jenkins's grip on her hand strengthen. She was looking the other direction, waving to the crowd. When she felt his grip tighten up, she turned her attention, with a smile on her face, to see Jenkins's fleeting glance of anger. She followed his stare to Sean, who was in a stare down with Jenkins. Nicole, keeping her wits about her, waved to the crowd on that side of the stage and then gently, with a hint of playfulness, pulled Jenkins with her as she walked toward the podium. The crowd caught the subtle playfulness, and a genuine laugh roared throughout the crowd. Nicole graciously smiled at the crowd and gave a playful shrug of her shoulders as if to say, "What can I do?" The crowd laughed harder.

Jenkins went to the podium, now with a smile on his face, and said into the microphone. "Good morning Greenville!" The crowd gave a loud cheer. "Thank you so much for that warm welcome that only we southern states know how to give." Nicole stepped back away from the podium so that Jenkins could give his speech. She shifted her eyes over to Sean, who was staring at her. She allowed a little smile to cross her lips as she blushed from his gaze. She looked down, her curled hair falling to cover her reddening face. When she felt in control again, she shook her hair from her face and placed her attention on Jenkins, still feeling the unrelenting gaze of Sean.

When the cheers died down from Jenkins's greeting, he started into his speech laying out his platform. The speech was to be short and sweet, reminding them of Jenkins's roots in the South. "We are at a crossroads. Strong leadership is needed and a strong voice to represent our positions to the world is long overdue. Clear objectives need to be defined and negotiated, not just with the rest of the world, but even here at home. They need to be conducted so that America can thrive and lead the world into a prosperous future." Jenkins's voice rose on the last words to the delight of the crowd. The applause and cheers were deafening. "I have the credentials to do this. I will stand up to the Soviets and our other enemies, not just with weapons but with diplomacy before we deploy any of our courageous men to fight. I have led men in battle, and our resolve will not dwindle at a time when it should be strengthened. I will call on the Soviet Union to withdraw its armies and stop thrusting a civil war upon the people of Afghanistan. Soviet aggression needs to stop!" More cheers rose from the crowds. Jenkins turned to look at Nicole who was clapping calmly. She knew this rhetoric would do nothing to stop the war that was escalating in Afghanistan.

Jenkins transitioned to the hostage crisis. "In Iran, fifty Americans are being held hostage, innocent victims of the unrest in these neighboring countries. It is time we bring these Americans home!" Thunderous applause rose from the crowd again.

Sean furrowed his brow and leaned over to Thompson. "He didn't say how he was going to do that."

Thompson laughed. "Welcome to American politics."

Jenkins quieted the crowd using his hands to calm them. "We will negotiate from a position of strength, but we will not yield to blackmail. Never should Americans shudder at the feet of any nation. Iran needs to understand that the real threat to her existence is from the Soviet Union and the Soviet invasion of Afghanistan. The Soviet invasion poses a serious threat to peace not seen since World War II. Iran should tread carefully in making an enemy of the United States when the Soviet Union is perched on her doorstep." The crowd cheered again. Nicole, however, clapped her hands out of courtesy. The speech was sounding like a call for war, something Nicole could not support.

"These actions have placed the world in a precarious situation. Any attempt by any outside force to gain authority in the Persian Gulf region should be viewed as an assault on the vital interests of the United States, and it will not be tolerated! As chairman of the Intelligence Committee, I see a need for the gathering of information provided to our government, allowing us to make confident decisions to avoid the calamitous steps to war. This is why, as a senator, I am introducing a bill that will remove some of the restraints on gathering intelligence. These restraints, if they were in place before the fall of Iran, would have prevented the capture of these brave Americans." There was more applause, and Jenkins turned quickly to look at Nicole. She smiled, but also made a little motion with her index finger, one quick rotation, indicating that Jenkins should wrap it up. Jenkins took a quick look at the next point on his note cards. He started to improvise.

"This is a time when America faces many obstacles. These obstacles are not just in our foreign policy. They also affect our natural resources, our economy, and our civil liberties." Jenkins paused a moment, looking down at his note cards again. Nicole's message was clear. He was talking too deeply on one subject, a very worrisome one at that. He raised his note cards so the crowd could see him thumbing through them. He moved his head slightly from side to side as if he was reading them quickly to himself. A few people chuckled. He then threw the cards over his back, saying, "That's enough of that." The crowd shouted and laughed. It made Jenkins look like he was his own man. They loved this little gesture. "Our challenges are formidable, but I am here today to tell you that I have never witnessed more resolve and unity than I have these past three months. Yellow ribbons wrapped around the trees that I drive past remind me that this nation consists of people whose strength and unity is unwavering. I have never been prouder to be an American, and it is because of you that this nation will remain strong and free. Thank you for your support!" Jenkins stepped back from the microphone. Nicole stepped forward to him. Jenkins couldn't resist hugging her, not only because he found the dress she wore as exciting as Sean did, but also because Sean was there staring at them.

"Nice ending," Nicole whispered in his ear. "You got them with that impromptu gesture. That's the Bobby Jenkins I know."

Jenkins placed his hands on her waist so he could look her in the eye. He gave her a quick kiss. The crowd's cheers increased in volume at this display of affection. They both waved to the cheering crowd and walked off the stage as a marching band, which had been late and missed the beginning of the rally, began to play. When they reached the end of the stage and started down the steps, Jenkins saw the scowl on Carson's face.

"How many times do I have to tell you to stick to the script?" Carson had no trouble showing his anger.

"Until you get tired of telling me that, I suppose," Jenkins shot back. "Where is the bus parked? We better get going to the next stop, don't you think?" Jenkins and Nicole started walking in the direction indicated by one of the campaign staffers.

Carson fell in behind them. "We'll talk about this on the bus."

Jenkins stopped. "No, we won't. You need to quit trying to make me something I'm not. They—" Jenkins pointed toward the crowd. "The American people will either like me or hate me, but it is me that they will be seeing, not some fake political puppet. If I lose, I lose—but at least I'll have my dignity. I'll write my own speeches from now on, do you understand that? You are not writing my speeches any longer. End of discussion." Jenkins unleashed on Carson some of the anger that he wanted to give Sean. He stormed off, and Nicole had to scramble to keep up with him. She couldn't have been prouder of Jenkins than she was at that moment.

Carson, on the other hand, was even more enraged. Behind Jenkins's back, he motioned for his personal aide to approach him. When he arrived at his side, Carson pulled car keys from his pocket. "I want you to find the nearest phone. Call Barker and tell him that I am sick and tired of Jenkins going rogue. Either he gets this jackass in line, or I'm walking. Got it?" The aide nodded. "Now get out of here. I'll see you at the next stop." Carson, red-faced and anger still brewing started to walk to the campaign bus. He clenched and unclenched his hands as he walked hoping it would calm him down. It didn't.

Chapter Four

Middle to End of February 1980

No one paid much attention to the lonely man walking down the meandering road, which led him through the vineyards of the Cahors appellation in the Lot Valley region of France. He walked quietly, only waving if someone called out to him. His mismatched attire was not fancy and led the locals to believe he was possibly a lost tourist down on his luck. Kent ignored their comments and actions. He just continued walking.

He arrived at his destination, the little village of Puy-l'Eveque, at dusk. On the edge of this small town sat an old château, which had been meticulously restored by its former owner. The château sat on the hillside overlooking the Lot River. Vineyards surrounded the village, and the château sat regally above them. Kent walked around the relatively small, yet ornate building looking for a way to enter. He did not have a key, but after he gained entry, he could remedy that situation. Surely, there was a raised balcony, a traditional feature of the châteaus in this region of France. Spotting a balcony adorned with a dental type of architectural design—teeth of large chiseled limestone with spaces between them—Kent determined entry might be gained through the wooden door at the back of the balcony. After searching around, he found a rather old rope obviously left behind by a work crew. He made a lasso of sorts (knot tying was not his specialty) and after several attempts, managed to throw and anchor the lasso around one of the upward stones of the balcony. He lapped the rope around one of his arms and tugged on it to make sure all was secured. He let out a sigh and started to climb the rope, reaching the bottom part of the raised balcony. He winced as the rope tightened around his wrists as he brought his feet up to the wall. He could now walk up the wall and was thankful that his feet bore some of his weight relieving his injured wrists. He climbed over the top of the balcony and landed on his feet.

He was pleased to find a wooden door and small window. The door was not new, and he thought that he might be able to break it down. He gave it a good run, ramming his shoulder into it, but the door barely moved. Grimacing and moving his aching shoulder, he decided this approach would not be the best way to enter this building. He tried a firm kick and nothing. He turned his attention to the window. He looked around to see if there was any possibility of being seen before attempting to shatter the glass. No one was in sight. The château was barely visible from the road. On the balcony floor were some rocks. He could only imagine that kids had made a game of throwing rocks up there to try and break the window. Or maybe they tried to break in as he was attempting to do now. The sun was setting lower, and it would be too dark for him to see what he was doing if he waited too much longer. He decided that a more direct, albeit loud, approach should be taken. He took out the gun he had tucked in his back waist. The gun had been in the pack he received from the masked men back in England. He pointed the gun at the window and shot it. The bullet went through the glass, causing a spiderweb-like pattern. It would be easier to break the glass. Removing his shirt, Kent wrapped it around his hand and lowered arm several times. He then started to punch out the glass. Within a few minutes, he was inside.

He wandered around the house looking over its plush furniture and elegant interior design. He could see the Serpent had lived an extravagant lifestyle. He switched on the lights. He walked to the kitchen and realized how hungry he was. Life on the run didn't provide many eating opportunities. He found the kitchen to be very modern despite the age of the building. He opened the refrigerator and found it sparsely stocked. The vegetables were rotten, and the milk was sour. There were a few jars of some kind of canned vegetable and some condiments. The cheese had not aged well in the Serpent's absence. Kent's nostril flared as he caught the smell of it. He opened the freezer and found it well stocked with various meats. The Serpent did not eat out much. He searched through the cabinets and found various packages of food. He was so hungry it didn't bother him that the crackers were stale. The nuts left a lot to be desired as well. The man examined his aching wrists while he ate. The handcuffs had left bruises and some swelling. The ropes had irritated them again. He smiled knowing that Charlie was now beside himself with worry. Kent couldn't have planned a better escape. The Serpent's informants—the informants that he brought into the Serpent's network—had served him well.

After satisfying his hunger, Kent walked around the château looking for the Serpent's office. Kent knew he had to find whatever paperwork the Serpent had left behind in order to assume his identity. The quicker he found the office, the better. Even as he walked around the house, Kent's team of informants was spreading the news that the United States' version of the Serpent's death was contrived. The Serpent was alive. He had never left the undisclosed location of his château in the Lot Valley and was available for hire. Kent finally found the study, sat down behind the desk, and started to open the drawers. Lots of papers were in them, and all of them would need to be read. Kent knew just as much about the Serpent's background as Sean did. He just never told anyone he knew, even during the interrogations. He knew when Sean came back that he would be revealed a fraud for all the lies he had told. There was only enough truth in what he divulged to keep him valuable and alive. He was now ready to become the Serpent, just as he and the Serpent had arranged many months before his death. The only part not planned was Sean killing the Serpent.

The Serpent had been growing tired and wanted to retire from his profession. If the Serpent's plan, which was to have Kent kill Sean at the beach house had succeeded, the Serpent had promised Kent that he would finish the training that they had begun earlier. There were times when the Serpent wondered if Kent was smart enough to carry on the legacy. But the Serpent couldn't deny Kent's sniper aptitude and his desire to be the Serpent. Kent was tied more to the Serpent than anyone ever knew at MI6, including Sean.

The distant rumble of thunder caught Kent's attention. He looked out the window into the darkness. *What a perfect night to announce the Serpent's return. But how should I do that?*

He rifled through the desk looking for clues. He couldn't just kill someone and leave the Serpent's trademark. The Serpent was selective when choosing his victims. At least he was after he had established himself in the realm of evil. Kent knew he couldn't be careless in setting himself up in this charade. He shouldn't move too quickly. He needed to quell his impatience. It would all come together. He would make Sean pay. A smile crept across his face with that thought.

{II}

"It seems that we don't get to spend much time together," Nicole remarked as she and Sean were walking to Sean's departure gate at the airport. "It's like we're always saying goodbye too soon."

"It hasn't been a typical friendship," Sean said smiling at Nicole.

It felt like they were having the conversation they should have had on the day that Sean had killed the Serpent. "It feels like it just happened yesterday." Nicole looked at Sean. "You said you are still having nightmares?"

"Not the same one. Sarah and Kate left me that day. Strangely, I had a feeling they were still around me the entire time I was tracking the Serpent. Almost like I could feel their presence at certain times, but now I don't have that feeling anymore." Sean paused. "I would relive their deaths in the nightmares. It was me discovering their bodies in our home. Now they involve…" Sean's voice trailed off. He dropped his gaze to the floor. He wondered if he should tell her.

In a low voice, Nicole coaxed him on. "What do they involve?"

"You," Sean whispered, looking at her. Nicole was shocked and not sure how to respond. "I see you."

"Me? Am I in danger?" Nicole asked calmly. "You said it is a nightmare."

"I'm not sure. I know that I wake up and that I feel like you've been threatened or that you feel unsafe. It's so hard to describe. There aren't many clues for me to decipher," Sean misstated. He didn't want to tell her that some of the nightmares were of her being shot.

"Maybe it's because we didn't have a chance to have a proper goodbye? All of this happened so quickly," Nicole offered. "You were holding me, and then you were gone. We never really had the chance to make sure each of us was okay."

"That could be it, and it could be my mind just trying to process everything. Just do me a favor and be careful." They reached Sean's gate of departure and stopped walking. "These are really powerful men you are associating with, and they don't need a gun to injure you," Sean added. He was now facing Nicole.

"I thought you trusted Bobby."

"I do. Bobby doesn't worry me. It's the others that do." Sean said with a concerned look. "One thing is for certain. You can trust Kevin. If something happens and you need help, Kevin can help you. I mean if you discover that Bobby can't be trusted." Sean sighed. "I sound like a maniac again." They both chuckled. "Just chalk it up to gut feelings." Sean paused as he looked over at the gate. "I guess I'll always have those instincts." The moment became tense. Sean was searching for something else to say. Nicole was nervously looking around the area, wondering if there were any reporters following them.

"I hate goodbyes." Nicole finally said.

Sean smiled and took her hand. "Then let's say that we'll see each other in the near future. I can't thank you enough for helping me catch the Serpent."

"It's nice not having to look over my shoulder," Nicole stated. "When I heard those gunshots downstairs I thought that Kent had succeeded in his mission to kill you."

"Well, those days are in the past now. We have bright futures ahead of us and all that rubbish." Both of them laughed. They both felt the awkwardness of the moment. Nicole started to back away, but Sean refused to let go of her hand. He wanted desperately to kiss her. He had to kiss her. He desired to know what it would feel like. Their eyes met, and each acknowledged the want and their ache silently to themselves, but it was betrayed in their eyes. He gently brought her into his arms, their eyes never straying from each other. There was no awkwardness now. There was no resistance. Sean pulled her closer to him as their lips touched. Sean had forgotten what love had felt like for the last ten years. He was happy that it was Nicole that brought those feelings back to him.

It was what Nicole had wanted as well. There was a bond between them that would never vanish. The kiss cemented that bond and gave them a curiosity if there could be more. When the kiss ended, the question remained. They looked each other in the eyes. The awkwardness returned as Sean continued to hold her close. Should they acknowledge their feelings? Sean took the lead. "A proper thank-you for such a beautiful woman," he whispered as he released her.

Nicole was still trying to process her feelings. She didn't immediately pull away from Sean. As she started to release him, moving her hands from him, seductively caressing his sides, she gave a quick kiss on his cheek. Sean placed that cheek to Nicole's giving her a quick kiss in return.

"Our flight to London is now boarding." The gate attendant's voice shocked them back to the present.

A tear began to form in Nicole's eye. As one started down her cheek, Sean wiped it away. He shook his head as if to say, *Don't cry.* "I told you I hate goodbyes," Nicole said as she looked down, taking Sean's hand in hers.

"I'll see you later," Sean responded as he took a step back.

"Will you?" Nicole asked. The hope was evident in her voice.

"I believe I will. I really do."

Nicole smiled at Sean's attempt to console her. She was with Jenkins, and the only time she would see Sean would be if Sean's and Jenkins's paths crossed again. That was what Nicole believed. She gathered her strength, trying to keep the smile on her face but failed. As her voice cracked with heartbreaking emotion, she replied, "I'll see you later then."

Sean smiled, nodding his head in agreement. He desperately wanted to grab her up in his arms and steal her away to England with him. He knew that if she were to be with him truly, she would need to end the relationship with Jenkins. He quickly kissed her forehead and turned to board his plane. He only looked back once when the gate attendant checked his ticket. He gave a little wave before he walked down the gangway to his plane.

Nicole waved and smiled as best she could while holding back the tears. When he disappeared, she turned, wiping away the tears that were now running down her cheeks. She wanted to just curl up in a ball and get it all out. *Why do I feel this way?* She started thinking about all the reasons. He had saved her life, and that would have a profound effect on anyone's feelings. Like catnip to a cat, he was virtually irresistible to her. His dark hair and emerald-green eyes were striking. She found this conundrum of someone who could take a life and yet have this sweet, gentle, loving side appealing.

She began her logical processing of the situation. She didn't know him all that well. In fact, she knew very little about him. This reasoning was helping her move on. She, at this very moment, believed she would never see Sean again. She wiped the tears away for what she promised herself would be the last time. She checked her watch and noticed that she was going to be late for her next appointment: a fundraiser at a downtown hotel for the campaign. She quickened her pace, putting Sean in the back of her mind with each step. She did love Jenkins, and the life she was living was a good one. She tried to reassure herself. She did love Jenkins. She did.

{III}

Nicole entered the hotel lobby and went directly to the restroom. She needed to freshen up her makeup before entering the lavish party. She wasn't looking forward to rubbing shoulders with the lobbyists, big-name CEOs and super PAC chairmen. This was the part of politics she despised. She knew if Jenkins was to stand a chance with his campaign, he needed to get in bed with these people. No matter how hard she wished for it not to be, there was some selling of Jenkins's soul that was going to occur. She despised that most of all.

She looked in the mirror and started to wipe the mascara stains from under her eyes with a damp cloth. It felt good to have the cold water dampen the irritated redness under her eyes. She had prepared herself, bringing with her a large purse containing her makeup, knowing she would not be able to hold back the tears when saying goodbye to Sean. She washed her face and quickly applied new makeup. When she was finished, she took a deep breath, fluffed her hair, and pursed her lips one more time. She smoothed her dress, brushing off lint from her winter coat. She slung her purse over her shoulder, picked up her coat, and walked out of the bathroom for the den of lions awaiting her at the fundraising party.

She handed her coat to the coat-check girl, who gave her a tag. Jenkins was greeting folks as they entered the conference room door. When he saw Nicole, he walked out to meet her. They kissed.

"How are you doing?" Jenkins asked. The fresh makeup didn't hide anything from Jenkins, and there was a feeling of emptiness to her kiss.

"It's hard to say goodbye to friends," she replied.

Jenkins hugged her. "I'm sorry. I know you don't like these things and for it to be right after saying goodbye, well, I know it isn't easy."

"Thank you for that," Nicole said. "I'm sorry I'm late."

Jenkins offered his arm, which she accepted, and they walked to the conference room. "Would you do me a favor?"

"Of course." She was puzzled at the tone in his voice.

"Would you get me a scotch from the bar?" Jenkins asked.

She chuckled. "And I thought I was the only one who didn't like these things." They continued to walk to the room. "How's Barker?"

"Still pissed off at me about what I said to Carson in South Carolina and then telling him off as well." He shrugged, reassuring Nicole that he didn't care how Barker felt in the long run.

They reached the door, and Nicole took a quick glance around. "You have a huge turnout. No wonder you want a scotch." Nicole was trying to look at the bright side. "You know that Barker has little to do with all these people being here, don't you?"

"I suppose I do." Jenkins and Nicole continued into the room. Most of the guests were enjoying appetizers and drinks. There was a podium at the front where Nicole discerned the typical pep rally speeches would be made. Behind the small stage and podium was a screen where pictures of campaign rallies were being projected. Jenkins's campaign banners flanked the screen. In the corner, television sets were turned on, and some of the guests were watching the local news.

Nicole walked to the bar and ordered a scotch for Jenkins. Gin and tonic was her choice. She was handed the drinks and turned to find Jenkins in the crowd. He was standing in front of the stage talking with a small group of lobbyists. Just to the side was a larger group that was watching television. Nicole started on her way greeting those who said hello to her, many of them she had never met and was surprised they knew her name. She reached Jenkins's side and handed him his drink. He acknowledged it with a smile and a quick nod but was engaged in a discussion. Nicole turned to watch the images scrolling across the television with a little interest. She took a sip of her gin and tonic through the mixing straw.

The local news anchor was introducing the next story when a picture of a scuttled, ransacked, and a very familiar-looking yacht, caught Nicole's waning interest. She took a step forward, her eyes squinting as she zeroed in on the yacht. A new photo of the boat appeared, and Nicole's mouth dropped open in disbelief. There, on the television screen, was the Vita Mea, Tony's yacht.

"Nikki," Jenkins called to her. "I'd like you to meet…" his voice trailed off as he watched her drop her glass to the floor. He moved quickly to her side. "Nikki, what's wrong?"

"That's Tony's yacht," she said in disbelief. She turned her head and looked at Jenkins.

"What?" Jenkins asked, looking at the television.

They moved closer to the screen. "I'm sure of it. It's the Vita Mea—My Life. I was with him when he christened it. I've sailed with him on that yacht." The photos switched again to a portrait picture of Tony. Nicole looked at Jenkins, who returned her concerned look. He had his arm around Nicole's waist. Below the portrait of Tony were the words "Presumed dead." Nicole buried her head in the crux of Jenkins neck and shoulder. "Not Tony too," was all she could say. Jenkins put his other arm around her and just held her for a few minutes. Chris noticed

Jenkins and Nicole embracing and quickly moved to them. Jenkins handed Chris his drink and then motioned for him to clear a way to the chairs that were sitting along the walls of the room.

Jenkins walked with his arms around Nicole, leading her to a chair. He guided her into the chair as Chris left to get her some water. Jenkins sat down next to her. "I'm so sorry, Nikki."

Nicole tried to wave her grief aside. "What a way to bring down a party," she said, trying to laugh.

Jenkins smiled at her attempt. "Would you like Chris to take you home?"

Barker came barging through the crowd. "Are you about ready, Bobby?"

"In a minute, Larry," Jenkins shot back, irritated.

"We've got to hit them while they're hot, my boy," Barker said, trying to urge him into movement.

"Do you mind?" Jenkins asked. "Nikki has just received some terrible news, and I would like to make sure she is okay before we do this."

"She's fine," Barker insisted, grabbing Jenkins by the arm. He started to pull Jenkins up from the chair.

Jenkins resisted, pulling his arm from Barker's grip. "I will be with you in a minute." Jenkins pronounced each word slowly making sure that Barker took his meaning seriously. Chris returned with the glass of water and handed it to Nicole.

"Go ahead, Bobby," Nicole said as she placed a hand on his shoulder. "I'll be okay. I'll be right here."

"Oh no," Barker interjected. "You have to be onstage with him. You have no idea the complimentary comments I've been receiving all night about you, Nikki. You need to be there as well."

Nicole looked at Barker. "I'm not up for that." She took a drink of water. "This election, his election," she looked at Jenkins, "is all about him, not me." Barker shot her a disapproving look. "Let's see, how did you put it to me? I'm the one who could wreck his campaign, the problem that could cost him this election." Nicole took another drink of water.

"What?" Jenkins asked in surprise. He looked at Barker.

Nicole never broke her cold stare, looking Barker in the eye even when she took that drink of water. "Weren't you the one who told me he would be better off if I just disappeared?" Nicole asked with her head tilted to the right, feigning confusion.

"When did you tell her that?" Jenkins demanded.

"That was you a few days ago in South Carolina, right?" Nicole added.

Barker ignored Jenkins while maintaining his stare down with Nicole. His blood pressure was rising. Barker's jaw was thrust forward, and you could almost hear the gnashing of his teeth.

Nicole felt their altercation was gaining some attention in the room. Nicole drank the rest of the water, handed the empty glass to Chris, and stood up. She faced Barker toe to toe. "You can't have it both ways, old man." She leaned sideways, not breaking the contact with Barker, and took Jenkins by the elbow. Jenkins stood up. Nicole's lips were only a few inches from Barker's jaw. Through clenched teeth, she whispered, making sure the anger she was feeling was not lost, "As I told you in South Carolina, you have no power over me. You don't intimidate me. You don't know me, so don't think that you can manipulate or threaten me." She turned to look at Jenkins, who was now standing. She took Jenkins's elbow and started to walk to the stage, presenting him as if he were the perfect gentleman that he proclaimed to be.

Jenkins was stopped on his way to the stage to shake hands with a number of people, but he never made a movement that would have caused Nicole to remove her hand from the crux of his right elbow. They reached the stage, music started, and the lights were brought up, shining on the podium. Senator Mercer introduced the couple. They stepped up onto the stage and headed to the podium. Mercer shook Jenkins's hand and sidestepped for Jenkins to walk past him. Mercer then greeted Nicole with a smile, kiss to the cheek, and a quick hug. He gestured with his arm for her to move to the other side of him so that she would be closer to Jenkins.

Barker and Carson had written out index cards with the things they wanted Jenkins to say, but Jenkins did not remove them from the pocket his suit jacket. He motioned for the music to stop and for the crowd to quiet down. He thanked everyone for coming. He paused as he formed his next sentence. "In my view, we have been single-mindedly focused on our individual needs. It is time now to have a leader who has the ability to join those individual needs by creating a larger purpose. I believe I can be that leader."

Nicole smiled at Jenkins's double speak and the applause of the crowd. She was always amazed at how these men could say so many words without saying or committing to anything.

Jenkins continued for a few minutes more, stating how he was interested in hearing their concerns which was the purpose of the evening. He ended with, "I have worked with many of you over my several years in the Senate. You know what I stand for and what I am committed to achieving. I look forward to talking with you further, and if you agree with my vision, I hope that I can count on your support. Thank you!" Jenkins waved and turned around to Nicole who smiled at him and walked up to take the hand he offered. Some in the crowd chanted her name.

"Nikki! Nikki!"

Nicole's cheeks blushed as she waved to the crowd. The chant grew stronger, and she waved, shook her head, and waved again. It was becoming clear the crowd wanted to hear from her. Nicole had made it clear to Jenkins, and to Barker too, she thought, that she would never speak at the rallies or fundraising events because she officially had no legal tie to Jenkins. She felt if she remained outside the limelight, the campaign would sidestep the many unanswered questions about their relationship.

Jenkins leaned over to Nicole and whispered, "Are you up to saying anything? You don't have to, and we will walk off this stage right now."

Mercer leaned in, hearing what Jenkins had said. "Nikki, it would be very nice if you said a few words."

Nicole smiled again at the crowd, covered her heart, and waved as a gesture showing she was touched.

Jenkins squeezed her hand. "It is totally up to you, my dear." Jenkins waved to the crowd who was still chanting her name. Jenkins looked at Nicole, who nodded her head. Jenkins escorted her to the microphone to resounding applause.

Nicole stood at the microphone waiting for the crowd to settle. "Never give a lawyer a microphone," she joked. The crowd laughed. "I'm touched by your show of support, but let us not lose our focus. My country, our country, needs change. Bobby has said a number of times that we are at a crossroads in regards to our foreign policy. Equal and civil rights continue to be ignored, and our economy is teetering on the brink of several adversities. If you know, as I do, that the strong leadership this country deserves and desperately needs, can be found in this man," Nicole turned, gesturing with her open hand to Jenkins, "then I strongly suggest that you work hard to make that happen. I know Bobby will listen to your concerns and I have seen him remain faithful to the causes that he has time and time again fought for in the Senate. I know he'll continue to do so. Thank you for your support. The defense rests." She gave a big smile when she said the last three words. The crowd loved it and cheered. She quickly stepped away from the microphone and took Bobby's hand. They walked off the stage together with Mercer right behind them.

Nicole stopped Jenkins at the bottom of the steps. "I need to leave. I need to find out what happened."

"I know," Jenkins assured her. "You were marvelous up there, but I know you are upset. Do you want Chris to take you home?"

"No, I have my car." Nicole gave him a quick kiss. "Call me when you get home."

"Thank you for what you said," Jenkins responded. Nicole smiled and gave him another kiss. "Be careful. Chris—" Jenkins yelled. "Please walk Nikki to her car for me."

Chris acknowledged the order and walked with Nicole toward the exit. She was stopped a few times on her way out. Her tone was pleasant and upbeat, yet all the while her insides were churning. Her mind was racing with questions. Chris ushered her out of the room as quickly as he could, knowing the reason he was sent on the errand was to do just that. Chris walked her to her car, and Nicole dropped him off back at the hotel entrance before heading for home.

Upon arriving at her front door, she discovered a parcel under the welcome mat. She bent down, picked it up, and replaced the welcome mat before unlocking the front door. She walked into the foyer, collecting the mail that had been shoved through the mail slot. She didn't bother to look at the mail or the parcel, and instead tossed them on a chair and threw her coat on top. She clambered up the stairs to her bedroom where she fell onto the bed, completely exhausted. In one day, she had lost two men; one was her mentor and the other, someone who had saved her life. It was almost too much to bear.

Chapter Five

The Next Day

S ean's plane arrived at Heathrow airport on time. He was finally home, and he wondered if anyone would be at the gate to greet him. He gathered his courage and exited the plane with the other passengers. As he walked into the terminal, he was surprised to see Charlie waiting for him.

Charlie smiled when he saw Sean and moved forward in the side-to-side wobble, his cane leading him toward Sean. The two greeted each other with a quick hug. "Hello, Charlie," Sean said as he released him. He smiled, relieved to see Charlie's friendly face. This would give him time to gather intelligence on what the family mood was.

"It's been a long time, Sean. It is so good to see you." Even though Sean was one of his agents in the field, Charlie had always thought of Sean as a son. He had been through so much with Sean that their relationship had grown beyond work. "Your father wants me to bring you by his office. He had a committee meeting that he chairs, and it couldn't be canceled. I'd like to meet with you as soon as you are up for it as well. Did you get any sleep on the plane?" Charlie asked as he began to walk toward the exit.

"Yes, a little, the fella next to me snored the whole way." Sean knew Charlie's question was more about nightmares than how much actual sleep he had gotten. "I've been sleeping much better lately." He wasn't lying. After seeing Nicole again, those nightmares had vanished. The circle had been completed, and Nicole was safe with Jenkins. As much as Sean wanted to see Nicole again, he knew deep down that would not happen. "It's time to get on with things," he said as they exited the terminal.

"Any thoughts to what you want to do next?" Charlie probed as they reached his car.

"I don't want to go out in the field again, Charlie. That has to be over for me," Sean said getting into the car. "I think I've paid my dues."

"And more," Charlie confirmed. "Honestly, I'm relieved to hear you say that, Sean."

"Probably not nearly as relieved as Father will be," Sean said with a laugh. "And no more getting your arse chewed out by him, either."

Charlie laughed. "Well, I'm not sure that is entirely true. I'm sure there will be other opportunities for that." There was a pause before Charlie asked, "Are you thinking of a desk job with SIS?"

"I don't know," Sean answered honestly. "I don't think I'm ready to rush into that decision yet. Nothing interests me right now. I know SIS wants to be debriefed, and I'll be happy to do that over the coming weeks. I suppose that is the next step."

"Yes, we do need to do that. I have a lot of news to tell you as well. Let's not make any decisions until we have a chance to catch up on the latest intelligence." Charlie didn't want to break the news of Kent's escape in the car on the way to his father's office. "I have to say that I sense an air of peace around you, Sean."

"Yes, well, I suppose killing the man who murdered your family can be quite cathartic." He turned his head and looked out the window at the cityscape. "Although that shouldn't be the answer for someone who doesn't have a license to kill; it could get a tad bit messy."

"Yes, indeed," Charlie confirmed, with a droll smile on his face.

The rest of the drive was uneventful, and Charlie dropped Sean off as close to Parliament as he could. Charlie headed back to SIS headquarters knowing the Adkins family would be celebrating Sean's return. He told Sean to call him in the morning to set up a time to meet. Sean thanked Charlie for meeting him at the airport and for the lift to his father's office.

While Sean loved his family, he didn't love the pressure his father and brother could place on him. He knew in a few days he would feel suffocated and be looking for a way to get out from under them.

Sean walked into the Parliament building and greeted security. He told the guard his name. The guard checked a list of prearranged guests for the day. When he found Sean's name, Sean was told to sit down, and they would notify Lord Peter Adkins's office of his arrival. Sean did as he was told, waiting only five minutes before an elderly female, Peter's personal secretary and close friend of the family, walked quickly into the lobby.

"Sean!" Margaret said as she approached him, arms wide open to hug him. "Oh, Lord Adkins is going to be so happy to see you." Sean gave her the hug she sought.

"It's good to see you, Margaret." In some ways, Margaret had assumed the role of surrogate mother after Sean's mother had been killed. While his brother, Geoffrey, accepted this role almost immediately, Sean was always a bit resentful that she had swooped in so quickly. Over the years, he realized that his father had asked for her help, which she had graciously given. "Is Father still in his committee meeting?"

"Yes, but only for a short time more. I've alerted Geoffrey's office, and he will be joining us momentarily." Margaret took his arm. "Come now, let's get a move on. We don't need to stay here in this drafty old lobby."

Sean chuckled at the motherly tone. "Still mothering us, I see," he said chiding her.

"My boy, I still mother your father at times. He's the most punctual representative among us," Margaret declared proudly as she led Sean by the arm to his father's office.

Nothing made Sean more anxious than being with his family. It had not been like this before his wife and child were murdered. He had to admit that the tension started when his hunt of the Serpent intensified. He stood in his father's office and wondered how their meeting would go. Would there be a stern talk about his being away for so long or would his father just accept it was over? Sean wanted to put everything behind him. But before he did that, he wanted to visit the graves of his wife and child to mourn them properly. Sean needed one more good-bye. He was looking out the window when the door opened, and his father walked through it.

"Sean," he said as he walked up to Sean with his arms open expecting an embrace. "I'm so happy that this is over." Peter hugged Sean like he had never hugged him before. "It is so nice to have you finally home."

"Thank you," Sean said, a bit shocked and embarrassed at his father's reaction. He looked past his father to see Geoffrey, whom he then approached to embrace him.

"Are you all right?" Geoffrey asked Sean.

"I'm better," Sean replied. "It was a rough few months. The last ten or so years haven't been all that fun," he continued with a hint of sarcasm that evolved into a sardonic smile. "But, it's over now."

Geoffrey nodded his head in agreement. "Elizabeth wanted me to tell you both that she is expecting you for dinner tonight to celebrate your return, Sean."

"That sounds lovely," Peter declared.

"It does," Sean confirmed. "What time should I be there?"

"I expect that we won't be done here until after seven, so let's say seven thirty," Geoffrey suggested. "I need to get back. I just wanted to see you with my own eyes. We've missed you so much, Sean." Geoffrey gave him another quick hug. "I will see you tonight." With that, Geoffrey left to return to his meeting for which he had granted a twenty-minute recess to say hello.

"Any plans?" Peter asked after Geoffrey had left Peter's office.

"In what respect?" Sean countered, unsure if his father meant immediate plans or future plans.

"Between now and seven thirty," Peter replied. "I don't expect that you have any idea what you want to do after that."

"I'd like to get some sleep," Sean offered with a hint of laughter in his voice. "To put your mind at ease, I don't want to go back out in the field. I have accomplished what I wanted to accomplish. Charlie informed me that I have some debriefings over the next few weeks. I'll get through those first." Peter acknowledged his son's comments with a quick nod. "Right now, before dinner, I'd like to go visit Sarah's and Kate's graves."

Peter smiled. "I thought that might like to do so. I can have my driver take you. When you finish there, he can drop you at your flat so you catch some sleep before we met at Geoffrey's." Peter rang for his car and driver. "I'll see you at Geoffrey's then. I'm sorry that I have to run. This Olympic thing is blowing up, and we're in discussions about whether we'll participate or not."

"Don't worry about it. Go on and get back to work," Sean said. Peter hugged his son once more before he headed back to his committee meeting. Sean left to meet his father's driver.

Sean rode in the backseat to the graveyard, apprehensive about what he would feel when he stood before the headstones. He had not been there in ten years, and while he knew that his wife and child were not there, he felt he needed some kind of closure. As they sat in traffic, Sean saw a florist shop and asked the driver to pull over so that he could buy some flowers. After purchasing a bouquet of red and white roses with a sprinkle of Baby's Breath, he returned to the car, and they made their way to the cemetery.

Sean walked to the graves with the flowers in his hands. He stood looking at the names on the headstones and placed flowers on each one. He touched their names as tears escaped his eyes. "You can rest in peace now, my dears." He stood up, still looking at the headstones. He looked up at the sky, cloudy and gray. "You're free now. I felt you leave me that night when I shot the Serpent. I've loved you with all my heart, and you are now free." He paused a moment, trying to imagine himself releasing them before he took his eyes from the sky. "And so am I." For a fleeting moment, he thought of Nicole. Sean felt a pang of guilt when his feelings for Nicole intruded on his farewell visit with Sarah. He started to walk away, stopped, and looked up again. He thought he could hear Sarah giving him her blessing. "You don't miss a thing, do you?"

He wanted to believe that Sarah would approve of Nicole. "Goodbye Sarah. Goodbye Kate." Sean then looked down, wiped a tear from his cheek, and walked back to the car.

{II}

Sean arrived at Geoffrey's home before his father and brother were finished with their work day. When he rang the bell, there were only a few seconds before, Geoffrey's wife, Elizabeth, swung the door open and threw her arms around him. Sean was surprised by the reaction, but he should not have been. While Elizabeth had married Geoffrey, she was always attracted to Sean. When she found out that Sean had married Sarah, she stopped talking to Sean, avoiding him for months, acting as if Sean had spurned her in some way. Sean knew Elizabeth had always been interested in him and often wondered if she married Geoffrey just to be in Sean's life. He never expressed his concern to Geoffrey, who adored Elizabeth, worshipped her actually. If Elizabeth didn't love Geoffrey as much as he loved her, it was not Sean's place to point that out to him.

It became clear to Sean that Elizabeth was not about to break off the hug. He gave her a quick squeeze and then tried to back away. She felt him starting to pull away, and tightened her grip on him. It was then that Sean felt a tear on his cheek, which brought back the memory of having Nicole in his arms back in Tryon when she ran to him. For a few seconds, he held Elizabeth, pretending he was holding Nicole. Then, realizing that he was holding his brother's wife in his arms, not to mention sending the wrong impression, he forcibly separated himself from her.

"Sean," Elizabeth started when he removed her from his arms. "I am so happy you are home."

"Thank you. It is good to be home," Sean said. "Sarah and Kate can rest in peace now." Sean hoped mentioning his wife's and child's names would jolt Elizabeth back to the reality that he never had any feelings for her. "Have you heard from Geoff or Dad?"

She stepped inside the flat and waited for Sean to enter before closing the door. "They are on their way."

They walked into the living room of the flat engaging in small talk along the way. Sean felt uneasy being alone with Elizabeth, but that was nothing new. Even Sarah noticed Elizabeth's flirting and tolerated it because she knew Sean had no interest. Sean had always chalked it up to the fact that Elizabeth's childhood home was cold and sterile when it came to receiving any attention or love. In fact, her parents left the raising of their only child up to the nanny. Geoffrey had married well, into a noble family, and inherited all that came with that family's dysfunction. Elizabeth moved to the cocktail cart to pour herself a drink. Sean had noticed the alcohol on her breath when she hugged him and wondered how long she had been drinking and if it was an everyday occurrence. "What can I get you to drink?"

"Nothing for me, thank you. I'll wait for the others," Sean said, hoping his abstinence would persuade her to not pour a drink for herself. It didn't work. When Elizabeth finished creating her latest concoction, which consisted of a few different liquors and a splash of soda water, she moved to sit next to Sean. He had strategically placed himself in a chair. Elizabeth sat on the arm of his chair. Sean looked around the room and politely as possible said, "There are plenty of other places to sit, Elizabeth."

"I'm perfectly happy here," she responded. "You know I missed you, Sean." She looked at him longingly. In her eyes, Sean could see her desire. She started to play with a lock of his hair.

"Elizabeth, nothing has changed." Sean removed his hair with a quick swipe. "I thought we had this discussion years ago. You are my brother's wife and will always be my brother's wife." Sean saw the tears well up in her eyes. "I'm sorry Elizabeth, but I could never hurt my brother."

Elizabeth stood up. She walked over to the window and looked out. "Your brother doesn't feel the same way." She waited for Sean to inquire. "You know that he and Sarah had an affair, don't you?"

Sean looked down at his shoes. He knew for a fact that Geoffrey never had an affair with his wife. "Elizabeth…"

"It's true! Ask him. He'll admit it now that this is all over. Ask him why he was at your house the night Sarah was murdered."

Sean stood up. He wasn't going to stay if this was how the evening was going to be. "He was at my house that night because SIS called him. He arrived at my house shortly after I did. As he and I have told you a million times, Geoff did not have an affair with Sarah." Sean started to walk to the door of the room when Elizabeth turned from the window.

"Don't leave. I'm sorry, but you need to know that Geoffrey has cheated on me." Elizabeth placed her drink on the table next to the window where she was standing. "He has had many affairs."

"And that is your problem to work out with Geoff. It is not mine." Sean started to leave the room. "Tell my father and brother…" At that moment, the door to the flat opened, which explained why Elizabeth was hiding her drink on the table.

"Tell us what, Sean?" Geoffrey asked as he greeted him with a hug.

"Nothing," Sean replied.

Geoffrey looked at Sean with suspicion. He whispered to Sean, "Oh dear God, not again."

Sean confirmed what his brother was thinking. "I thought we straightened all this out years ago. I think that she is a bit tipsy," Sean whispered.

Geoffrey sighed as he realized that things were quickly becoming undone. Elizabeth's desire for Sean was not a secret. The only dark secret Geoffrey kept was that Elizabeth had a drinking problem. "Any new piece of gossip I need to know about?"

"You have evidently cheated on her many times. I believe that is a new twist."

"Not that new, unfortunately," Peter chimed in as he hugged his son.

"Give me a moment, please." Geoffrey walked into the room where his wife now sat. She was putting on a sober face as best she could. She greeted him cheerfully, but the words were slightly slurred. When Elizabeth drank, she drank quickly, and the drinks were always three or four liquors combined with a splash of soda. Geoffrey never understood how she could drink something he found so revolting, but she preferred her concoction, perfecting it over the years. There were times when she would try to stay sober, only to fall off the wagon in a matter of weeks. When she was sober, Geoffrey was reminded why he had fallen in love with her in the first place. He was blinded by the fact that Elizabeth was using him to get to Sean. Geoffrey smiled when he remembered how happy he had been when Sean announced he was marrying Sarah. The smile quickly faded when he also remembered how Elizabeth carried on that evening, making her desire for him known to Geoffrey. Things were never the same between them, and the drinking started shortly after that incident. Geoffrey knew one day soon an intervention was going to be needed. He also knew in her fantasy world that when Sean came back, Elizabeth wanted to leave him to be with Sean. Although Geoffrey knew that Sean had no desire, he was afraid of what Sean's denial would do to her. Geoffrey knew that Elizabeth believed that the moment Sean arrived back in England, he would go straight to Elizabeth, providing her with a way to end their marriage. When Sean didn't show up after Geoffrey's phone call to her, she couldn't handle it and started drinking.

"I see you have started the celebration a bit before us," Geoffrey said as he reached her side.

She smiled coyly as if to suggest something had indeed happened between them. "Stop it, Elizabeth! I know Sean was about to walk out the door. Your behavior is thoroughly disgusting and so unbecoming. I suggest you head up to your room before you make an even bigger fool of yourself." Elizabeth was shocked, not by what Geoffrey had said to her, but more that she couldn't pull off the charade that she and Sean had made love, starting their imaginary affair up again. "I suggest you take the back stairs to your bedroom and sober up a bit before we see you again." Geoffrey forcefully helped her out of the chair to her feet.

"I suggest you ask Sean about the hug he gave me, which was seen by all the neighbors," she said. Geoffrey started toward the kitchen pulling her by the arm as they walked. He called one of the staff members to help her up the stairs.

Sean heard her remark about the hug and felt he owed his brother an explanation. Sean and Peter walked into the living room. "The neighbors might misinterpret the hug, Geoff. I apologize for that. You see, I was thinking of someone else—the thought triggered by one of her tears hitting my cheek—and, well, I'm afraid I held your wife a bit too long."

Geoffrey was puzzled. "It was just a hug, correct?"

"Oh yes, just a hug," Sean confirmed.

"I'd rather hear about the 'someone else.' You weren't thinking of Sarah were you?" Geoffrey asked.

"No, it wasn't Sarah," Sean confirmed as he looked down and began to blush.

"Well," Peter started. "Dare I say that it looks like our Sean has fallen in love with someone?"

This always irritated Sean. His father had an annoying habit of thinking he knew everything about him. Peter always assumed that he knew what Sean was feeling, whom Sean liked, or what Sean would do in any given situation. It was no surprise that the irritation shone through in Sean's response. "No, Dad, I'm not in love, and even if I were, it wouldn't matter. She's with someone else. Can we change the subject?" All three sat down as Sean asked, "How long has Elizabeth been drinking like this?"

"It's been a while now. It goes in waves. Some days are better than others. You know it started in earnest right after Sarah's death." Geoffrey looked at Sean. "It rather hurts to say this, but I think she expected you to sweep her off her feet after that. When you disappeared to Kensington's manor and then on your journey to bring the Serpent to justice, it hit her pretty hard."

"I don't know what to say, Geoff," Sean responded. "I've never fancied her. I've never given her any reason to believe that I was in the slight bit interested in her. I'm afraid she finds me too enchanting. You know, being a British agent and all that."

"I know. I am sure it's the secret agent lifestyle that she finds attractive. You know, dashing off to Monaco and sipping champagne on yachts," Geoffrey joked.

"I can assure you, I have not lived that way these past ten years," Sean responded.

"I know. She has always been in love with you, Sean. I knew what I was walking into when I married her. I could see in her eyes that she loved you."

"Then why did you marry her?" his father asked.

"I love her, Dad. You have to admit that, back then, she was stunning and she looked good on my arm. I thought that she would eventually forget about Sean, especially when she saw how, shall we say, Sean was married to his work." Geoffrey looked down at the floor. "That never happened and things got progressively worse when she started drinking."

"It doesn't sound like you have had the best marriage," Peter stated. There was a hint of a question in his comment. Peter wondered if Geoffrey had strayed during this time. Geoffrey knew what his father was insinuating, and he wasn't about to answer it.

"That is enough of this talk. I'll handle it, and I think it is time for Elizabeth to get a handle on this drinking problem, and end this infatuation. What are your plans, Sean?" Geoffrey asked, trying to shift the attention to Sean.

"The next few weeks I'll be debriefing at SIS. Elliot has some new software or something he wants to try out. He wants to use the data we have on the Serpent and some other profiles to try to predict certain movements. I'm not sure what all that means. Charlie mentioned it in the car ride over to Parliament. After that, we'll see what comes. I haven't given it much thought."

Geoffrey had hired a servant to help Elizabeth with the duties around the house since it was apparent that Elizabeth had no desire to lower her perceived standing to perform those duties herself. The servant entered the room to announce dinner. The three men moved to the dining room. The conversation centered on Sean's opportunities, all of which he listened to but announced his desire not to enter into at the present time. He stated he rather fancied taking a bit of a vacation before deciding. As the three men prepared to part ways for the evening, Geoffrey and Peter again expressed their joy that Sean had returned home safely, and they were thankful for all he had achieved. Sean was driven home by his father, who gave him an awkward hug just before he exited the car.

Sean was surprised that his body now required so much sleep. The years of little sleep must have taken their toll, and he gave into it now. He could afford to give into it. Without turning on a light, he walked up the stairs to his bedroom and collapsed onto the bed. Soon he fell into a deep sleep, and he was thankful for sleeping in his own bed.

{III}

Nicole awoke the next morning. Jenkins had called her the previous night as she requested and they spoke about various things regarding the campaign and touched briefly on Tony. She got out of bed, deciding that a cup of tea sounded good. She threw on her robe and headed down the stairs.

When she entered the foyer, her eyes caught the package that she had tossed onto the chair the night before. She walked over, picked it up, and flipped it over and back. She was looking for a return address, but there was none. She gathered up the rest of the mail and walked into her living room. The curiosity of the package had made her forget about the tea. She sat down on her couch, placing the mail beside her, and opened the box. A videotape was inside with a letter. On the label of the tape, the name Tony Shafer was followed by the words, "For your eyes only." She gasped when she saw Tony's name. She then recalled her conversation with Tony on his yacht.

"What are you up to now, Tony?" Nicole asked. Nicole reached for the letter that accompanied the tape. It had slid off her satin robe on to the floor. She opened the envelope, removed the letter, and began reading.

Dear Nikki,

Remember that day on my yacht when I mentioned a tape? Here it is. I have now sent it to you for safekeeping. I have no idea what will happen now. But I want you to know that this tape is real—it is the original. I received the tape right after Sipes's murder. His butler, David delivered it. I mention this because there have been some really strange things happening since I met with Stevens the day before I left DC. I had a meeting with Stevens and Engle to read Sipes's will. I lost my head, and I made a threat. The threat doesn't matter, but I may have tipped my hand. Sipes Oil Company isn't dead. Sipes left no provisions on what should happen. It looks like Engle is going to find someone to run the company. They want their investment back. Again, that doesn't matter. I'm rambling. For the first time in my life, I'm really scared. I hope your clear head will figure something out.

You'll find enclosed a sworn, notarized statement that states how I received the tape and from whom. I got upset with Stevens before I left. I wish I didn't say what I said. I may be paranoid, but I think someone is following me. I'm heading out to sea and not sure what port I'll be in next. I always wanted to sail around the Caribbean. Keep the tape safe, Nikki. Make Jenkins do something with the information. Use all you have to make Jenkins do something. He adores you. He'll listen. I'm sorry to get you involved after all you have been through, but you're the only one who can make Jenkins listen. Please be careful, Nikki.

Nicole removed the top handwritten note to find the notarized sworn statement on how Tony acquired the tape. She walked to her study and sat at her desk. She read through the letter once more, realizing how distracted Tony seemed to be. Then she shredded the handwritten note. Since Tony did not sign the letter, she knew he wanted it destroyed. It was a code they used in the office.

She walked over to the VHS player, turned it on, and inserted the tape. She turned on the TV, turned the channel to three, and walked back to her desk chair. She turned around to see the TV screen showed the scene of a den. Then, suddenly, Norman Sipes walked into the picture and sat down at his desk. Nicole was shocked. She sat down, waiting to hear Sipes's voice.

Sipes picked up the microphone and, looking directly into the camera, he raised his scotch-filled glass in a salute and said, "Tony, if you are viewing this, then I'm dead." Sipes continued. "If you are not sitting down, my friend, I suggest you do so. I have a lot to tell you. You may need some paper, so I'll wait until you get your typical yellow pad. I've always wondered if you were doodling on that paper."

Nicole's jaw dropped open as she realized this was Sipes's confession tape. She looked again at the package. The postmark was from a few days ago. How long did Tony have this tape? This is the tape that he was referring to on his yacht when they had lunch—the tape he encouraged Nicole to ask Jenkins about.

She looked up as Sipes laughed. "Go ahead. I'll wait." Sipes paused for a few seconds. "Hold on, my friend! What I'm about to tell you is going to really rock that puritan world of yours. A lot has happened over the last few days. A lot has happened with my oil company, too. You know that I'm broke, and, well, I started drilling in ANWR before the legislation was to be signed. I wanted to get a jump on the others who no doubt will be setting up shop the day after Andrews signs that bill. In fact, I know two companies that have equipment staged. But all that doesn't matter now. Stevens told me that he thought Andrews was softening on the bill and that he was going to put a little more pressure on him to make sure he signed it. The only ones not surprised to hear he wasn't going to sign that bill were myself, Stevens, Davis, and Jefferies. Yes, that's right. The three of the four largest stakeholders in my company were not surprised by his announcement at the state dinner."

Nicole thought back to that state dinner. That was the night that she met Jenkins for the first time. She also recalled the strange glances exchanged by the men that Sipes just named. She remembered how it confused her then and now it gave her chills.

"All three of them were pressuring me to make the company profitable. Joseph Engle then decided Sipes Oil should start drilling. Honestly, we knew that Andrews was changing his mind and our plan was already put in place by the time of the announcement at the state dinner. What plan?

We devised a plan to remove the only barrier that would keep me from drilling legally in ANWR. With the help of others, I secured enough funds to hire an assassin to kill the president of the United States. You heard me right. I and four others provided funds to hire an international assassin to kill President Andrews. The reason I'm taping this is to take those four other bastards down with me." Sipes took another drink of his scotch. Nicole swallowed as she released the precarious situation in which Tony had put her. "You see, there's an FBI agent in front of my mansion who just gave me a subpoena to appear before Jenkins's Investigation Committee. I'm sure that little prick has all the information he needs to put me in jail for the president's murder. And yet, the agent out front seems to think I won't live that long. So, I made this tape to name them as co-conspirators in case I don't make it to Jenkins's committee meeting in the morning. Who were my co-conspirators? Let me state this clearly: Mark Stevens provided the most money, followed by Congressman Davis, Joseph Engle, and, surprisingly, Matthew Jefferies."

Nicole wanted to jump out of her seat to exclaim that she knew Stevens was involved. She knew that man was no good. She returned her attention to the tape.

"We needed Jefferies to make the initial contact with this assassin. Stevens promised Jefferies he could bail on the plans after the contact was made. Jefferies made contact through a number of phone calls. My phone number was given to the contact, whoever they were, and the assassin took over from there. Seems that little bastard Jefferies didn't tell me if I could identify the assassin, I wouldn't live long after the payment. Nice way to tie up loose ends for those bastards, don't you think? I can now see the plan was to pin this all on me so that they could go free. So, Tony, now you know. What you do with this information I leave in your hands. I hope that you give it to someone who can do something to bring those associated with the assassination to justice. It seems that I will have gotten my punishment. You've always been a good friend. I may not have liked what you said or did when it came to representing me, but I knew you always did your best and you were honest. I couldn't have asked for anything more." Nicole noticed that Sipes struggled to end his confession. Sipes took a breath and let it out. "Good-bye Tony." He stood up from the desk and walked to the camera. A few seconds later the tape ended.

Nicole sat in her chair for a few minutes. Her mind was racing in so many directions. Was Jenkins aware of this tape? Of course he was. Tony said that he had given Jenkins this tape. Was this one of the topics of discussion at the dinner party when Connors was booted from the Phenom Five? Nicole wondered who else knew about this confession. And if they knew, why were the coconspirators not arrested for treason? It had been over three months since the president's assassination. Surely if Jenkins's committee had this tape, they would have acted on it. Nicole stood up and walked over to the VCR. She ejected the tape and put it back in the package.

She opened her safe and placed the tape inside. Suddenly she remembered the reading the fortune-teller gave her at the New Year's Day party at the Barkers. In her mind's eye, she could see the Lovers card clearly as if it had scorched itself into her memory. She recalled the fortune-teller's warnings that someone close to her was hiding something from her. Could this be it? Was this the secret that could hurt her?

She sat down at her desk and turned her desk chair to look out the window. Why did Tony mail her the tape? Tony knew that Nicole would not be able to cover up what that tape revealed. She recalled Tony's words about "being good counsel" to Jenkins. Nicole swung her chair back around to the desk and leaned forward. She put her hands to her head and ran her fingers through her hair. "I need to think of my options here," she said. She slumped down in her chair and rested her head on the back of it, staring at the ceiling. She could go to Jenkins's condo and start the discussion about the tape. She could go directly to the police with the information. That would not look good for Jenkins, considering that he had a copy of the tape. She smiled as she realized that would give Jenkins an out to say he had never seen the tape. They could even devise a story that would discredit the tape. Is the tape credible in the first place? Stevens would certainly deny any association or knowledge. Davis, well, Nicole and Sean saw him give an envelope to Sipes at the nightclub. Nicole closed her eyes as she realized she again was at the center of something potentially dangerous. Did Sean tell Thompson that he saw Davis at the nightclub? Thompson knew already. Did Sean tell anyone else? The questions seemed endless. Jenkins was sure that Jefferies had John Spencer killed. Nicole sat up as she realized that Jefferies did have Spencer killed. Spencer had the evidence that proved it was Sipes who was going to drill in Alaska. Nicole went through her Rolodex to find Ahnah's number. She picked up the phone and dialed, not realizing the time difference.

"Hello, this is Nikki Charbonneau. Is Ahnah available?" Nicole waited as she heard Ahnah's mother call for her. "Hello, Ahnah. It's Nikki."

"Hello, Nikki. How are you?" Ahnah said. "It's so good to hear your voice even if it is the middle of the night here."

Nicole looked at the clock on her desk. "I'm so sorry—I didn't think. Ahnah, I have a question. It has to do with John Spencer. The night he left Alaska, did he have evidence that it was Sipes Oil Company that was trying to drill illegally on your land?" Nicole asked.

"Yes, he had a photograph of the logo. In fact, the logo is stored away with the other equipment. We've cleared the site the best we could with the snow." Ahnah paused for a moment. "Nikki, are you aware that strangers have been up here in the last few days?"

"No. What strangers?"

"Some men were here asking us if we have seen any drilling equipment. Naturally, we told them we have not. They had maps to the exact place. I thought with Sipes dead that this was over."

"I thought so too, Ahnah. You better call Chris on Monday and let him know about this."

"Can't you tell the senator?"

"I don't know if I'm going to see him this weekend," Nicole replied. "He will be on a campaign trip. I'm not sure I'm going to join him on this one." Nicole wasn't sure what she was going to do in the next five minutes let alone the coming days. "When we are on the campaign trail, it gets so hectic and crazy. I'll try to remember to tell him. Thanks for answering my question, and I'm so sorry to have called you in the middle of the night. Keep the senator, I mean us, informed. Bye," Nicole hung up the phone.

Jenkins had enough evidence to subpoena Jefferies. Through his questioning, the tape, her testimony of seeing Davis give Sipes money, he would be able to subpoena Stevens and Davis. Why hadn't he done so? She sat for a few more minutes trying to decide what to do. She didn't want to believe that Jenkins would look the other way and not bring these men to justice. He owed it to the country he served. He declared his candidacy for president relatively late. Nicole had believed that Jenkins wasn't going to be a candidate in this cycle because he was so young. Did he use the information, the tape, in some way that allowed him to persuade Barker to permit him to run? Nicole didn't believe that was possible. But it could be used to keep Stevens from winning if it just happened to be disclosed around the election. Nicole closed her eyes when that thought rang through her mind. "Oh Bobby, how could you?"

She didn't want to jump to conclusions, and she felt she needed to hear from Jenkins what his intentions were. Just as she made her decision to get dressed and head over to Jenkins's condo, the phone rang, startling her out of her thoughts. She calmed herself before answering. "Hello?"

It was Jenkins. "Good morning. Will you be over soon or would you like to meet for breakfast?" Nicole didn't answer. "Nikki? Are you there?"

"What? I'm sorry. I'm a bit distracted with Tony's death," Nicole replied.

"Have you seen the paper?" Jenkins asked.

"No, I haven't. I don't get it delivered," Nicole replied.

"I have it. You can read it here. It looks as if Tony was involved in some kind of drug deal."

"That's absurd!" Nicole declared. Was Stevens framing Tony? Nicole looked out the window to calm herself. "Bobby, Tony was a wealthy man. There was no reason for him to be a drug dealer. He never touched the stuff. In fact, he despised anyone who had anything to do with it. Don't you recall the drug council he founded?"

"Yes, now that you mention it, I do." There was a silence that gave Nicole the chills. What was Jenkins thinking?

"Bobby, I need to talk to you about something." Nicole looked down at the phone to see she had four messages on her answering machine. "Can we eat breakfast at your condo?"

"Sure. Is there something that I can start here while you are on your way?"

"I'll be there in a little bit. I have a couple of things to finish here. It shouldn't be too much longer." She looked down again at her phone's answering machine. Jenkins repeated his inquiry about starting to cook breakfast.

"Nikki?" Jenkins asked. "Did you hear me?"

"I'm sorry?"

"Well, whatever has your attention seems to be important. I will talk to you when you get here." Jenkins responded.

"I'll see you shortly," Nicole said. She hung up the phone and decided to listen to her messages. The first two messages and the last were solicitations, but the third message was from Tony. His message was short and alerting her to the package he sent. He also stated that he was sure he was being followed and that he was taking serious precautions. Nicole wondered what those precautions were. Whatever they were, obviously they didn't work. She closed and locked the safe before heading upstairs to shower and dress.

{IV}

Jenkins was waiting for Nicole to arrive at his condo. He was in his office preparing campaign speeches for his stops in the coming days. He was reading through one of them when he heard his front door open. He stood and walked from his office to greet Nicole in the foyer; however, Nicole wasn't there. She had moved to the living room and was placing her coat on a chair just inside the room. When Jenkins approached, she allowed the hug he offered but turned her cheek when he tried to kiss her. This was Jenkins's first inkling that something was wrong. "What is it, my love?"

Nicole smiled at the "my love" and wondered how many men used that expression today. "Bobby, there is something I need to talk to you about."

"You mentioned that on the phone. I'm not sure I like the sound of it. Let's sit down." Jenkins led her to the couch.

"You know you can tell me anything," Nicole started, hoping he would take a hint and tell her about the tape. She was so deep in her current situation that the meaning of her comment, while clear to her, was lost on him.

"I'm afraid I don't understand."

"Bobby, I don't know how to say this. I know there are things that you have to keep from me. I know there are things that I can't know; national security and all that bullshit."

"I'd hardly call it bullshit." Jenkins chuckled to try and lighten the air in the room that was filling with tension. "Are we discussing what happens in Barker's study again?" He added. At first, he had thought that Nicole was going to express her desire to be with Sean. This conversation was taking him by complete surprise, even though he was relieved that it seemed to be going in a different direction—but a direction he wasn't sure he liked better.

Nicole ignored the Barker comment, although it would make sense to her now why she would not have been invited to join them if the Phenom Five knew about the tape. "I know something that you have known for a long time. And if that is true, I have to add that it will cause me to lose a lot of respect for you. It already has me questioning your motives. I hate that—I hate that this is causing me to think this way. I don't want to…" her voice trailed off as tears began to well up in her eyes. She was frustrated at that; she was angry. If this were true, Jenkins was withholding information. She wanted to yell. She wanted to accuse him. Instead, her eyes were filling with tears, and Nicole regarded that as a weakness. Why was she crying?

"Nikki, tell me what it is. I don't want you to lose faith in me. Let's address this head on. It's worse if you keep it all bottled up." Jenkins couldn't fight an invisible foe. He knew that from all his training. He was used to face-to-face combat. He was good at leading the way out of danger. What he didn't expect was the bombshell that Nicole was about to drop on him. He took her hand in his and turned to face her. His other hand was placed on the back of the couch. He wanted his body language to show her he was open to anything she had to say.

"Bobby, I forgot about this, with the excitement of seeing Sean again and then all the campaign stops. I meant to talk to you then but the days just got crazy." She paused a moment, trying to find the right words. "Remember when I had lunch with Tony?" Jenkins began to withdraw from her. He didn't want to hear what came next. "He told me then that you had something that was important to the investigation of Andrews's assassination. He wanted me to ask you about it, and he hoped that I could be counsel to you." Jenkins withdrew his hand from Nicole and stood up turning his back on her. "He said it was a tape he gave you. He asked me if you had shared that with me." Jenkins turned slightly to look at her. He felt like a trapped animal. He turned his back on her again and walked to the bar. He picked up a glass. "Bobby, I've seen the tape…"

Jenkins dropped the glass he was holding. He caught it just as it hit the top of the table ensuring that it would not break. "What?" He asked calmly.

"I said I've seen the tape," Nicole replied confidently.

"What tape?" Jenkins asked coyly, wondering how she could have seen it. His copy was locked in his safe. He needed to pull himself together. Could Shafer be so stupid as to show Nicole the Sipes confession tape? His mind was racing. What other tape could Tony have that would upset Nicole? He wanted to believe it was something else entirely, but he knew deep down that this was the moment he had been dreading. "I'm sure Tony has a number of interesting—"

"Bobby, don't," Nicole interrupted him. "You know what tape I'm talking about." His attempt at lying irritated her. "I know you have it. Tony told me he delivered a copy to you the day after Sipes was murdered. I have a sworn statement from Tony stating just that." Nicole paused. "Tell me you have Kevin Thompson working on supporting evidence and sworn to secrecy. Tell me you aren't hiding this tape so that you can use it when the time is right."

Jenkins stood there for a moment. She provided him with an out. He could tell her that, and all would be forgiven. He could keep her in his arms, by his side, and only the two of them would know about the tape. He was silent, his back to Nicole. His mind was racing. He wanted desperately to keep her. If he confessed that he had the tape and had not discussed it with anyone, he knew that Nicole would be furious. He knew deep down that Barker would want to use the tape to topple the Republican Party. On the one hand, they deserved to be toppled. They assassinated a president, their president, and committed treason against their country for their own greed. They used Sipes, and they continued to think they got away with it.

"Bobby, please talk to me. What are you thinking?" Nicole asked.

Bobby poured himself a scotch. "Would you like something?"

"It's a little too early in the morning for both of us," Nicole replied. Jenkins didn't heed her unspoken suggestion that he not have a drink.

Jenkins walked back to the couch. Before sitting down, he took a drink of his scotch. He ultimately knew that being honest with Nicole would be the best approach, but he didn't want to tell Nicole the truth. He didn't want Nicole to know that there was a side of him that wanted to use the tape to acquire more power. "It's unfortunate that Tony showed you that tape," Jenkins started with a sinister tone to his voice. Nicole's brow furrowed. Jenkins seemed cold to her, and she didn't like it one bit. "It puts me in a very difficult situation. Yes, I have the tape Tony gave me. I've viewed it several times." Jenkins paused. He couldn't tell her everything. He just couldn't do it. He thought back to Connors's experience at the dinner party. He decided at that very moment that he couldn't go any further in this discussion without informing Barker and Mercer first. "We are indeed trying to find supportive evidence that all the men implicated in Sipes's confession were a part of the assassination." Jenkins took another drink of his scotch. There, he had done it. Then he started to justify his cover-up, his lying to Nicole. He was indeed trying to find evidence. He'd been directing Thompson to search for evidence. Even though that was a delaying tactic, he was telling a version of the truth.

Nicole studied Jenkins's body language. She watched him down the rest of his scotch. She knew Jenkins was hiding something. She studied him further. The sinister tone told her that he didn't like her questioning him. Jenkins fidgeted under her scrutiny. "You're lying," Nicole accused him. "You aren't doing anything, are you?"

"That's not true," Jenkins declared quickly.

"Who else has seen the confession?" Nicole questioned, right on the heels of Jenkins's denial.

"No one," he confessed. Nicole stood up. "But that is going to change." He quickly continued before she could walk away from him.

"For Christ's sake—" Nicole yelled at Jenkins as she turned away from him.

"That's an interesting comment coming from someone who isn't the least bit religious," Jenkins interjected trying to throw Nicole off her game.

Nicole turned and intensely stared at Jenkins. She calmed herself before finishing the comment that Jenkins had interrupted. She assertively asked her question. "What in the hell are you waiting for?"

"Waiting for? I'm not sure I follow you," Jenkins responded. "We are in an investigation. I'm under no obligation to provide any evidence until the investigation is completed."

"You have all the evidence you need!" Nicole yelled. "Mark Stevens is a murderer and a traitor. Jefferies killed John Spencer, your best friend. Dear God, Bobby, can't you see what you have here? Don't you know how strong a confession tape is in the court of law?"

"There you go again—" Jenkins interjected in a typical politician way.

"Knock it off, damn it!" Nicole shouted, infuriated that Jenkins was using his political games on her. "Answer me!"

Jenkins didn't like where this is going, and he was quickly losing his patience. "Watch it, Nikki." This was all he could manage to say. He stood up and walked to the bar.

"'Watch it, Nikki?'" Nicole repeated, broadening her stance and folding her arms. She watched him walk to the bar. "That's all you are going to say. You have a taped confession that states that Sipes, Davis, Jefferies, Engle, and Stevens plotted to kill the president of the United States. You have had this tape since November, and all you can say to me is 'Watch it, Nikki'? What the hell is wrong with you? You should be out there telling—"

"Saying what?!" Jenkins interrupted, slamming his glass down on the bar. His reserved, patient southern accent was no longer apparent. His reaction startled Nicole, and she jumped at the sound of the shattering glass. Jenkins quickly looked at his hand to see if any of the glass shards had cut him. Luckily for him, none had, but it didn't stop his anger from rising as he had hoped. He turned to her and yelled, "Stop badgering me, Nikki! I know what you want me to do. You are like a coon dog on the scent of some escaped convict. You won't stop until it kills you, will you?" Jenkins was just as surprised as Nicole at what came out of his mouth. There was an eerie, awkward silence between them.

Nicole cleared her throat. She looked down and then at the wall forming her next question. "Are you threatening me?" She looked Jenkins in the eye. "I just want to be clear."

"I'm not threatening you," Jenkins pleaded. He replaced the lock of hair that had fallen onto his forehead while he was yelling at Nicole. It was an attempt to regain his composure. "Nikki, there isn't an easy solution to this evidence. There is so much to consider. A sitting president has committed murder and treason. The ramifications of that and the interpretation by foreign nations—"

"I don't give a shit how this looks to other nations," Nicole shot back. "I only care what this says about you, Senator Robert Jenkins, the man running for president. I only care what this says about you, as a person. You can't cover this up at any cost. Do you understand me? You can't do it."

Jenkins studied Nicole, his nostrils flaring. He didn't like being told what he could and could not do. He had the power to do whatever he felt was best. He had convinced himself that keeping this information from the American people was the best course of action. He was under the disillusioning power of the tape. With a hint of anger, he responded, "You and I disagree on that point. Thousands of decisions are made each day without our constituents having the knowledge we have at our disposal to make that decision. This is just another one of those decisions. I will not be forced into this public confession to appease you. The breadth of what you don't know..." There was a part of Jenkins deep down that was yelling *'No!'* It was as if he was outside his body. Some perverse power had taken over his existence, and he could see this whole ugly scene unfolding before him. He could do nothing to stop the evil from taking control, from acting in a way that was so different from the man he thought he was.

Nicole's eyes filled with tears and she swallowed hard. "I thought you were different," she said quietly. A single tear escaped and ran down her cheek as her upper lip quivered. She turned, walking over to the chair to pick up her coat.

Jenkins watched her retrieve her coat, and he feared he was losing her. "Nikki, don't give up on me. There are so many decisions to be made.

I'm just asking for you not to badger me and to stand with me. At this point, I'm not sure where—"

She turned to look at him. "I know where this is going." She started to walk to the door as she said, "And I can't go there. I thought you would be strong enough to lead this nation in a new direction. I thought you were a better person than this." She quickly left the room, and stormed out of the house, slamming the door behind her.

Jenkins moved to the door and opened it. Before Nicole was too far down the walkway, he said, "Nikki, I can't protect you if you aren't with me! Come back!" Nicole didn't pause when she heard his threat to her life. He closed the door as she drove off.

Nicole drove around for hours before returning to her home. She knew that Jenkins would be calling her and she didn't want to hear the phone ringing or his voice through the answering machine. She drove to the harbor and parked the car. She tried to gather her thoughts. What would she do next? Would Jenkins have her killed? Who killed Tony? Was it Stevens as Tony alluded to or was it Jenkins to cover up that he had the confession tape? Her last question made her hold her breath. Was she safe?

She knew the dirty little secret now, and she knew she would never be accepted into the circle. She was a threat to their plans. She knew too much. She sat back in her seat placing a hand to her forehead when she realized, out of all involved, she was the most expendable. She was their biggest threat. She could stay with Jenkins and hope that she could in some way influence the process, living in a constant state of fear. Or, she could disappear as Tony did. She couldn't help but shake her head when she reminded herself of Tony's fate.

She started her car and drove home. There were messages on her answering machine, but Nicole had no desire to listen to them. She knew they were from Jenkins. She continued to explore her limited options. She sat down in the desk chair in her office.

In frustration, she hit the play button on her answering machine. The messages were indeed from Jenkins. Three messages just asked her to call him. The last message was left thirty minutes prior, and Nicole could hear the anger in his voice.

"Nikki, I'm not kidding. What you know can be very dangerous to you, but not nearly as dangerous as what you don't know. There is one thing that remains constant through all of this. I love you, and if you are with me, I will do everything I can to protect you. No one but us needs to know about this. Come back over and let's talk this out. If you do anything else, I can't promise anything."

Nicole felt helpless, just as she did the first time she was in Jenkins's condo. She looked over at the safe, bit her upper lip, and made her decision. She rescued the tape from the safe and ran up the steps to her bedroom. She grabbed a suitcase and began to pack. The thought of fleeing Washington made her feel that she could somehow get control of her life again. She chuckled when she thought that this was the same way Tony had felt. After some errands to put a hold on her mail and stopping at the bank, she left for the airport.

{V}

Sean slept in, or what he considered was sleeping in, rising around eight in the morning. He had a leisurely breakfast before showering and heading to SIS headquarters. He arrived in the midmorning, at about half-past nine. He showed his badge and walked down the hallway to Charlie's office. He greeted Charlie's secretary and was announced before he entered. Charlie informed Sean that Elliot was anxious to get on with some new work that involved extracting all the information he could from Sean about the Serpent. Sean knew this was coming and perhaps his leisurely breakfast was really procrastination. It was work that needed to be done, and the sooner Sean got to it the quicker it would be over.

Charlie fidgeted in his chair. "Sean, sit down." It sounded more like a command, a tone that Sean had not heard in a long time.

"What is it, Charlie?" Sean asked as he sat down across from Charlie's desk.

"I'm afraid I have some bad news." Charlie sat forward. "It concerns Kent Chapman."

"Okay, what about Kent?" Sean asked. His curiosity was now piqued.

"He escaped, and we have reason to believe, intelligence really, that he's in France. He's living in the Lot Valley." Charlie waited as the realization hit Sean.

Sean's facial expression changed from someone who felt his whole life was in front of him back to the stern look of a man who had a license to kill. His eyes became angry. "Escaped to France?" he questioned. Disdain was evident in his tone. He shot out of the chair. "You know what this means, don't you?"

"Yes," Charlie confirmed. "Unfortunately, we do Sean."

"I need to tell Nicole," Sean stated. "Do we have any other intelligence on Kent?"

"No. He landed outside of Paris and boarded a train for Nice, but he never arrived in Nice. We can only assume that he got off somewhere in the Lot Valley since that was the base of operations for the Serpent," Charlie informed him. Sean was standing next to Charlie's desk. He picked up the telephone on Charlie's desk and hesitated. "What is it, Sean?"

"I'm afraid I don't know Nicole's phone number," Sean said, feeling helpless.

"Shall we call Bobby?" Charlie asked.

"I'd rather talk to Nicole directly."

"Well, let's hope her telephone number is listed publicly. While I'm getting her phone number, you get to work with Elliot." Charlie ushered Sean out the door. "I'll bring you the number as soon as I have it."

Six hours later, Elliot opened the door to the top-secret conference room. Charlie entered with a slip of paper in his hand. He had secured Nicole's phone number. Sean took the number, thanked Charlie, and returned to the work at hand. Charlie left them to their work. A few hours later, Elliot and Sean decided to call it quits for the evening. Sean headed back to his flat, Nicole's phone number in his pocket.

He arrived home, flipped on the light in his living room and walked directly to his phone. He dialed Nicole's number and frowned when it went to her recorder. "Nicole, this is Sean. I need you to call me back. I have something to share with you." Sean paused. "Call me, please." Sean left his phone number and added he could be reached at SIS headquarters through Charlie. He hung up the phone with high hopes that he would be talking to Nicole very soon. But that call never came.

Chapter Six

March 1980

Sean and Elliot were five days into their debrief—five days since Sean had called Nicole. He had called Nicole each day, sometimes twice a day, hoping to catch her. He was following Jenkins on the campaign trail and didn't see her. He couldn't help but wonder why she had not returned his calls. He was beginning to believe that Nicole didn't want to talk to him because she chosen Jenkins and couldn't have him in her life at the same time. He laughed at that thought, knowing that Nicole would always talk to him if he approached her. So, why wouldn't she return his calls now?

He arrived at Elliot's office by midmorning, knocked on the door, and entered when it opened. Elliot greeted Sean as he walked back to his desk. Upon it was a huge monitor, which Elliot disappeared behind. It was the beginning of a new age, and Elliot was at the forefront of a technology that would revolutionize intelligence gathering. In Sean's eyes, Elliot was a genius. He was working to prove his theory with some computer system that would be able to predict movements of terrorists or enemies with statistical probabilities. Sean couldn't begin to describe the program or what Elliot was typing into it. He just answered questions. Sean's answers all pertained to the Serpent's behaviors and actions. It was interesting and boring at the same time.

The walls of the room had large maps taped to them. On the maps in numerous places were thumbtacks connected with twine. These thumbtacks and twine traced a route taken. Notes were taped to the maps next to the thumbtacks. The twine had different colors, each color representing an assassin or paramilitary group. It was quite extensive and overwhelming to look at all at once.

Sean walked to the table in the center of the room. He looked over the maps trying to recall where they had left off the night before. Elliot looked at Sean who was now following the twine that was color coded for the Serpent. He was taking his time with each stop and Elliot was wondering if he was reliving each moment. Sean's body language was quiet. He didn't move on to the next thumbtack until he took in all the information.

Sean didn't get all the way through the timeline. In fact, he stopped before the fateful night that Sarah and Kate were murdered. He sat down and looked at Elliot. His trusted coworker could almost see the hurt in his eyes. After a few minutes, Sean said, "I think we better take this in small chunks of time."

"I think that would be best," Elliot confirmed. "I don't think I've captured where you first met the Serpent?"

"That would be 1964, but he wasn't calling himself 'The Serpent' then. His name was Saverio, which means savior in English," Sean explained. He sat back as he lifted his left leg, placing his ankle on his thigh just above the knee.

"Was he a religious man?" Elliot asked as he wrote down Sean's answer.

"His family was very religious. He was too, in a rather perverted way. He was bloodthirsty and seeing people suffer was an aphrodisiac for him. I'm not very religious, but this suffering bit seems to be a common thing among..." Sean's voice trailed off as he tried to come up with a word for the people he was describing. "The people I associated with back then. They all seemed to think that suffering brought not only themselves but the people they killed closer to their God. It was a rather sick notion really. Saverio was no different from that and his obsession with suffering heightened through the years. His suffering didn't heighten but causing the suffering of others did. At some point in time, and I'm sure as we go through this we'll determine just when that was, he decided that he was no longer going to be the one who suffered, but that he would cause the suffering."

Elliot listened intently to Sean's statements. "What makes you say that?"

"Because he saw himself as someone who would grant life as well as take it," Sean responded.

"But he never let anyone live who saw him."

"Yes, he did. Me," Sean said. "Why did he let me live? Was it so that he could point to me and say he granted me life? Was sparing my life some perverted way for him to tie himself back to God?" Sean stood up. "Strange isn't it? Besides the thrill of the cat-and-mouse game for all those years, had he killed me, or rather if Kent had carried out his orders to kill me, the Serpent might still be alive today."

"So that night in North Carolina, the Serpent would have killed Kent?"

"I have no doubt Kent would have been killed as well. We know he wanted Nicole and he wanted me dead. Unless Kent ran from the beach house, he would have had a showdown with the Serpent. That didn't happen." Sean shrugged his shoulders. "That's just conjecture. But now we know that Saverio was training Kent to take over for him."

"So Kevin Thompson played a very important part in that night," Elliot stated flatly.

"Kevin was my ace in the hole. He was fantastic and so sneaky." Sean laughed at his last sentence. "It was kismet that we met."

There was a knock on the door. Charlie opened it and walked into the room. Elliot and Sean looked at him as he walked up to the table. "What is it, Charlie?" Elliot asked with concern. Charlie's face showed the confusion he was feeling.

"Well, I'm a bit confused, but I promised that I'd get a message to Sean."

"A message to me?" Sean reiterated. He looked at Charlie, and he thought about Elizabeth. "Please tell me that Elizabeth isn't up to her old tricks."

"No, it's not from Elizabeth," Charlie declared. "It's from Nicole Charbonneau."

Sean shot out of his chair and walked to Charlie, who was holding a piece of paper in his hands. "Nicole? What did she say?"

"She said to tell you she is at Park Plaza Hotel," Charlie replied.

"She's here in London?" Sean questioned in disbelief.

"Yes, it appears that way. She wouldn't tell me what brought her here, but she said if you could stop by when you get a chance, she would like to talk with you."

Charlie watched Sean. Sean tilted his head, just as confused as Charlie was. "Is Bobby with her?"

Charlie shook his head as he handed him a slip of paper that contained Nicole's room information. "No."

"That's all she said?" Sean asked again.

Charlie confirmed once again that she would not give any details.

"How did she sound?" Sean asked.

"She was putting on a grand front, but I could detect that something has her rattled," Charlie informed him. "In fact, I'd say she was choking back tears."

That last remark caught Sean's attention and he looked at both Charlie and Elliot. "I'm sorry, Elliot, but I haven't been able to reach her via the phone for the last five days. She isn't one to hop on a plane for no good reason. I should check on her."

"It sounds like you should," Elliot said with a hint of a smile on his lips.

Sean shook his head at Elliot's assumption. "She didn't fly all this way to be with me. Trust me."

Charlie smiled. "It's all right if she did, isn't it?"

Sean began to grin, admitting to himself that it would be grand if she had returned to him. As he started toward the door, he retorted "I know her better than you do." He stopped at the door, turning to look at his two colleagues with a serious look on this face. "You two need to get out more." Charlie and Elliot laughed as Sean disappeared down the hallway.

{II}

Nicole had vanished after her disagreement with Jenkins five days ago. She boarded the first available flight to Paris, France. She checked into a hotel in Paris. She posted her checkout date six days later paying her bill in advance. Nicole did not stay long at the Paris hotel. She rarely stopped at the front desk during her short stay. If she had, she would have received the message that Jenkins had called. She boarded the train ferry the following evening.

The train ferry, which ran from Paris to London, was exactly as it is described in its name. Passengers paid for passage to London from Paris, boarding a train at the Gard du Nord station. Nicole purchased a first-class ticket with cash, which meant that when the train stopped at the port, she would not have to leave her compartment. The first-class cars would roll onto the train track-fitted ferry to cross the channel. She was sad to learn from the train crew that this once considered luxury crossing was about to halt operation within the next four months. She had to admit that the compartment and train had seen better days. She felt a bit nostalgic knowing that this mode of transportation was being eliminated. Flying across the channel was now faster and affordable. The train ferry provided Nicole an escape without detection. She hoped.

When she arrived in London, she checked into the Park Plaza Hotel, literally exhausted. Nicole was lying on the bed, thinking about Tony. She wondered how anyone could order someone's life to end all the while acting as if nothing had happened. In the days during her travels, she began to wonder who decided Tony should die. She wondered if Jenkins ordered it, how he could keep a straight face and could love her while plotting to kill a friend of hers. She turned her head and looked at her suitcase realizing the reason Tony was killed was sitting in it. She wondered which side of Jenkins was his true side: a ruthless killer or the powerful, gentle, and caring man. He commanded attention on Capitol Hill and did so with such charisma—which was image and which was the real Jenkins?

A knock on her door startled her awake. She must have dozed off. She got up from the bed, wiping the sleep from her eyes. She ran her fingers through her long hair as she walked to the door. "Who is it?"

"It's Sean."

Nicole quickly unlocked the door and opened it. At the sight of Sean standing there, she couldn't help herself and flung herself into his arms. Sean returned the hug, lifting her off her feet as he walked them into her room. He shut the door behind him. Nicole's hug was like a boa constrictor, smothering as she held onto him tightly. He could tell that this hug was coming from fear. "Nicole, sweetheart, what's wrong?" Nicole didn't answer. She wanted to be in his arms. After a few seconds, Sean repeated his question. "Please talk to me."

Nicole lessened her grip, and he nudged her away from him so that he could see her face. He took her hand and led her to the small, elegant couch in the sitting area of the room. They sat down, and Nicole started into her tale. "I'm afraid Bobby Jenkins isn't the man we thought he was."

Sean looked at Nicole with some suspicion. "What makes you say that?"

"I don't know where to start." Nicole looked away from him.

"How about with what happened that started you down the path that brought you here," Sean replied.

Nicole began with the lunch she had shared with Tony. She informed him how she had forgotten all about it and how she thought Tony was just jealous of her relationship with Jenkins. She then told him that she received a tape from Tony in the mail and confronted Jenkins about it. She said it was a terrible exchange and explained how Jenkins reacted with what she perceived were threats.

Sean sat and listened to Nicole tell her story. He tried to decipher how much were her emotions and how much was the truth. "I left for my condo because I needed to think and to be away from Bobby..." her voice trailed off. This was the first time she had to say it out loud. Somehow that made it more real. "The night before, the news showed images of Tony's ransacked yacht. They didn't find a body, but there was blood everywhere. Before I left my condo, Bobby called. I didn't answer it, but he made it clear in the message that if I didn't stay with him, he couldn't protect me. I flew to Paris and then came here. Every bone in my body told me to flee."

"What does Sipes confess on the tape?" Sean questioned. Nicole hesitated. Sean frowned. "Really, Nicole, after all we've been through, you don't think I can protect you?"

Nicole smiled. "Obviously I think you can. It's why I ended up fleeing to London. He identifies his co-conspirators." Nicole paused, looking at Sean. Sean's face conveyed that he was waiting to hear the rest. "He names Stevens, Davis, Engle, and Jefferies."

Sean blinked his eyes as he questioned if he had heard Nicole correctly. "President Stevens and the FBI director were involved? That's quite an accusation."

"I wouldn't put it past Stevens. With all the infidelity and corruption in his background, he would have never been president without first being vice president. I haven't stopped to think about all the motives for his involvement, but my gut tells me he is capable of it."

"May I see the tape?" Sean asked.

Nicole retrieved the tape from her luggage, handing it to Sean. "I don't have a VCR here."

Sean examined the tape and then looked at Nicole. "Well, I know where there are plenty of these machines. Get your coat. I want to see this tape with my own eyes."

Nicole and Sean left the hotel, Nicole not sure where Sean was taking her. As they approached SIS headquarters, she asked Sean where they were going and when he told her, she replied. "I'm not very comfortable with this, Sean."

"Trust me." They exited the car and headed into the building. Sean was holding Nicole's hand as they walked up to the desk so that Sean could obtain a visitor's pass. He assured the guard that she would be under his supervision. After receiving the badge—colored red so everyone would know she was a visitor—they walked through the doors and into the world of the Secret Intelligence Service. Sean led her down the corridor to Elliot's office. He knocked on the door, and Elliot opened it a few seconds later.

"Hello," Elliot said, surprised to see Sean with the cinnamon-haired woman standing next to him.

"Elliot, this is Nicole. Nicole, meet Elliot," Sean said. Nicole and Elliot greeted each other. "I was wondering if we could watch this tape somewhere private."

"Sorry, Sean, not in here," Elliot said. "But, I believe Charlie has a VCR in his office."

"Right," Sean said as he turned for Charlie's office.

"Was that tape recorded in the UK?" Elliot called. Sean and Nicole turned back around to face him. "If it was recorded in the US, you'll need a US machine to play it on. The tape isn't compatible."

"Are you serious?" Nicole questioned.

"Quite," replied Elliot. "Mind if I tag along? If Charlie doesn't have a player, I know where I can snatch one," Elliot offered as a bribe.

Sean looked at Nicole. "I don't think we're quite ready to let everyone in on the secret just yet." Speaking of secrets, Sean still hadn't told Nicole about Kent.

Elliot was disappointed but truly wanted to help. "I understand. I have a machine in here." Elliot walked away from the door, which started to close slowly. Nicole couldn't help but try to peek into the room. Sean placed the tape in her field of vision. She frowned as she took it from Sean. Elliot returned with the VCR unit and its associated cables. He explained quickly to Sean which cable went where. They were then off to Charlie's office.

When Sean and Nicole entered Charlie's office, over the protests of Charlie's secretary, Sean was surprised to see Jack Kensington, director of SIS, sitting across from Charlie. "I'm sorry," Sean said, still holding the VCR player. Nicole was standing by his side. Jack stood up as did Charlie.

"Good afternoon, Sean," Jack said. "And who might this be?" Sean made the introductions.

"Charlie, I know this is a rather strange request, but I was wondering if it would be possible to borrow your office for about…" Sean's voice trailed off as he hadn't the faintest idea how long the tape was.

"Approximately twenty minutes." Nicole filled in when Sean looked at her.

"Is there something we need to know Sean?" Jack asked.

"I don't know yet," Sean replied. "And until I do, I'd rather watch this in private." Nicole frowned as she now realized three more people knew about this tape. Her worst fear was becoming realized. Sean caught her look. "It's rather important, and we really would prefer that its existence be regarded as top secret." That didn't placate Nicole. She didn't care how covert the intelligence world was supposed to be, Nicole always felt that it was safer to have as few people in the loop as possible. That thought made her wonder if Jenkins felt the same way. *Could it be that Jenkins felt it best not to discuss the tape with anyone because his fear of it leaking out to the press before the government was ready to act?*

"Well, it is most unusual, Sean. Sir, would you mind if we finished our conversation in your office?" Charlie asked his superior with as much respect as he could. Jack agreed since Charlie was willing to accommodate Sean's request. The two gentlemen left, and Sean started looking over the equipment in Charlie's office. There was a television, but there was no VCR. Sean hooked up the machine and, after a failed try, finally got the machine to work. Sean sat down behind Charlie's desk just as Norman Sipes walked into frame.

"That's Norman Sipes," she told Sean. "He was the president of Sipes Oil Company…"

Sean raised his hand indicating that he wanted her to be quiet. Nicole turned her head to watch the tape once more.

Sipes picked up the microphone and, looking directly into the camera, he raised his scotch-filled glass in a salute and said, "Tony, if you are viewing this, then I'm dead. If you are not sitting down, my friend, I suggest you do so. I have a lot to tell you. You may need some paper, so I'll wait until you get your typical yellow pad. I always wonder if you were doodling on that paper." Sipes laughed. "Go ahead. I'll wait."

Sipes paused for a few seconds. In the silence, Nicole added quickly, "Tony is Tony Shafer. I worked for him, and he's one who sent me this tape."

"Nicole," Sean said with a quick glance. "Please, I'm trying to listen." Sipes's confession played once again. Nicole almost had it memorized.

Sean's jaw dropped in shock as Sipes named his co-conspirators. He didn't know what to say. Sipes's body language confirmed that he was telling the truth. There was no hesitation, no frequent blinking of his eyelids. When the tape ended, Sean stood up and walked over to the VCR. "Bobby knows about this tape?" This was the only question he could manage. His mind was racing as he tried to create a timeline. He wondered if Jenkins knew about this tape when he was putting the plan together to trap the Serpent. He knew it would not have mattered if Jenkins did know at that point—Sean would not have changed his plan in any way.

"Yes," Nicole confirmed. "Tony sent me the tape just before his death. Tony knew he was being followed. Sean, Tony sent me the original tape."

"How do you know that?"

"The tab on the back has been removed so that nothing can be taped over the confession. Either Sipes knew it might be erased so he broke the tab out, or Tony removed it after he made the copy for Bobby so that there would be no mistaking that Tony had the original." Nicole didn't want to say this, but she quickly blurted, "Sean, I think Bobby had Tony killed."

"What? No, Nicole, Bobby wouldn't do that." Nicole looked at Sean with contempt. "I have known Bobby for quite some time, and he has always been forthright."

"Then explain to me why when I confronted him about this tape, he took on this whole different personality? He threatened me, Sean. He said he couldn't protect me if I didn't stay with him. He's worried that I'm going to go public just as he worried Tony would go public."

Sean studied Nicole for a moment. He did not doubt that Nicole fled Washington in fear. He removed the tape from the VCR and walked back to Charlie's desk. He handed it back to Nicole who took it with a surprised look on her face. "For a lawyer, you jump to judgment pretty quickly." He sat down across from her.

Nicole was shocked by Sean's comment. Beyond shocked, she was surprised to feel hurt by the tone in his voice. She never considered herself to be judgmental. In fact, she always felt that she took great lengths to gather facts. She mustered as much strength as she could to ask, "Why do you say that?" She almost cringed when she realized that her hurt feelings seemed to shine through in those five small words.

Sean noticed Nicole's tone but decided not to acknowledge it. "Well, first of all, four other people are holding the same secret as you, Tony and Bobby. Maybe Tony let it slip to them that he had the tape. Maybe Sipes sent them a letter that told those four other people that he recorded the tape. Maybe Bobby is protecting you from the same fate as Tony. Mark Stevens seems like a pretty cold-hearted bastard. He killed a sitting president for drilling rights. If Tony let it slip that he knew Stevens was involved, I would bet Stevens would have no problem having Tony killed. Secondly, you did exactly what Bobby didn't want you to do. You ran with the evidence to another country. You didn't give him the opportunity to gather the information he needs to charge a sitting president." Sean paused a minute while he watched his words affect Nicole. "In any case, it doesn't matter because we can't help you."

"What?"

"I can try and protect you, Nicole. You are welcome to stay here. But I, MI6, and the British government can't interfere with our strongest ally's government."

"Sean, this is basically a coup!" Nicole protested. "This has to be exposed!"

"Put yourself in our shoes. If something like this happened here, and if a taped confession fell into the hands of the US, do you honestly think that we would welcome the US government's involvement in our affairs? You know we would not." Sean watched Nicole. "They are our ally, and while I find this particularly horrifying, we can't interfere. We might inform certain individuals in our government about it, but I don't see us doing anything else." Sean paused. "I suppose you haven't thought for a moment about the danger Bobby is in, have you?"

"Bobby?" Nicole looked at Sean with confusion. "All he has to do is show that tape to the American people."

"That is his last resort."

"No—"

"Yes, it is his last resort!" Sean shouted over Nicole's objection. "It is the last thing he wants to do. The uncertainty and chaos that would cause would be catastrophic." Sean lowered his voice as Nicole resigned herself to listening to him. "He has to figure out a way to bring this to resolution without the public ever getting any knowledge of this."

"I don't understand," Nicole sighed. "You are the last person I would have expected to be supportive of a cover-up."

Sean chuckled at her naiveté. "Have you forgotten what I do for a living? If the everyday people knew just what went on behind the scenes of their governments on a daily basis, then Hollywood would never have another conspiracy movie to produce." Sean gave a cynical smile to Nicole. He then became serious. "If Bobby can gain enough of an alliance, they can perhaps force Stevens to resign or, at the very least, convince him not to run for reelection. Jefferies will be forced to resign, or Bobby will have him stand trial and become the scapegoat. That might be dealt with publicly. Bobby would be walking a tightrope. There is only so much that can be said before it starts to arouse suspicions. Davis can be dealt with through some trumped up moral charge that will ruin his reputation, and he'll lose his seat. Engle, well, Engle is probably the most vulnerable and the most expendable even though he is extremely rich. He's just an average citizen who invested poorly in the end. It made perfect sense that the blame fell on Sipes. Sipes had the motive. It makes the most sense, and it ties everything up nicely."

Nicole looked at Sean in disgust and disbelief. "I can't believe you justified this cover-up. I can't believe that Bobby would negotiate something like that. What would he gain?"

"Power," Sean stated. "If Bobby tells Mercer and Barker—those are the two powerful senators he associates with, correct?" Nicole nodded her head. "If Bobby tells them about the tape, I think it will be out of his hands. He'll be rewarded with more power in his party by both men for bringing it to their attention." Sean paused a minute. "Hence, his being granted the late run for the presidency. Unless of course, he is as ruthless as you think he is and somehow wrestles their power away without telling them." Sean thought for a moment. If Bobby was going to wrestle power away from Mercer or Barker, he would have to have something on each of them. The run for the presidency wouldn't necessarily keep Mercer and Barker in line. "There are a number of ways this could play out, Nicole. But I assure you that it will play out behind the scenes and no one but those involved will know anything about it."

"You think your father would do nothing about this if he knew about it?"

"What do you want him to do? You want him to broadcast to the world that Stevens is a murderer?"

"That would be a good start."

Sean laughed. "It won't happen, Nicole. And my father will be informed about it."

"Who will be informing him?" Nicole asked.

"Probably Jack Kensington," Sean informed her. "He is our director, and since one of his counterparts is part of this conspiracy, I need to let him know about this."

"Sean, I came to you in confidence."

"I know that," Sean replied. "But I can't let this stay under the veils of darkness."

Nicole started to show her frustration. "Then why can't you see that I can't do the same thing?!"

Sean looked at Nicole. "Just what do you want Bobby to do?" He asked seeing for the first time that her sole purpose of bringing him the tape was to expose the conspiracy.

"Stevens and the others committed murder and treason. I think the American public should be informed of that. I think Stevens and the others should be tried and, if convicted, given the death penalty."

Sean shook his head. "And I'd like one of those fast, nifty little cars that fire bullets and missiles." His tone turned more serious. "This isn't fairy tale land. That is a tall order for anyone to live up to, let alone a powerful senator."

"He has the means to do it."

"If he wants to end his career in politics and quite possibly be killed in the process," Sean stated matter of factly.

"If he got public support, he would be a hero. He has the opportunity to change the course of American politics. Why is it that I am the only one who sees that?" Nicole shook her head. "I know I have an expectation that he do the right thing—"

"The right thing?" Sean interrupted her. "Do the right thing according to whom? You?"

"The right thing for America, its people, and its government."

"Oh, I see," Sean said teasingly. "And you know, with all your infinite wisdom, what that right thing is?"

"I know what it isn't. It isn't brushing this under the rug."

"Nicole, while I appreciate your..." Sean's voice trailed off as he searched for a word to describe Nicole's passion. "...patriotism, you are asking an awful lot of Bobby. I assure you that Bobby knows exactly what you want him to do and I'm sure he explained to you why he can't do that." He watched as Nicole shifted in her chair. "He does know you are here, doesn't he?"

Nicole shook her head. "He doesn't know where I am." Sean just closed his eyes. This made disclosing the information a bit more tricky.

Sean's mind was working quickly to ascertain the situation. In a way, Nicole could be a whistleblower if she wanted to come forward with the information. Sean wondered if Jenkins would welcome that situation. He was pretty certain that Jenkins would prefer to be in control of how the assassination plot was announced to the public. Right now, he knew the right play was to wait it out. He opened his eyes and said, "Nicole, you realize that you have put yourself in a very dangerous situation."

"I'm here, aren't I? If I can't trust you with my life, whom can I trust?" Nicole said looking into Sean's eyes. He couldn't help but smile at her. "What should we do next?"

"Wait. Let's see how Jenkins handles this situation." Sean looked at his watch. "And I'm late for lunch with my dad. Would you like to join us?" Sean asked, hoping she would. She would be the distraction that would possibly make the lunch less stressful.

"I don't want to intrude," Nicole responded. "Can you drop me off at the hotel or should I get a taxi?"

"You wouldn't be intruding, and at this point, I'm not sure that the hotel is the right place for you and that tape," Sean argued. He stood up and was about to pick up the phone when Charlie walked quickly through his office door.

"Thank goodness! You haven't left yet," Charlie said a bit out of breath.

Sean looked at Nicole and then back to Charlie with a confused look on his face. "Is everything all right, Charlie?"

"No, not at all," Charlie asserted as he moved to his desk. "I'm afraid I've got bad news, and it impacts you both."

Sean and Nicole were waiting for Charlie to drop the news that Jenkins had gotten in touch with Kensington since he had hurriedly rushed in from the director's office. Sean walked to Nicole's side. "What is it, Charlie?"

Charlie sat down and gathered what remaining strength he had. "I'm afraid I'm getting too old for this." He took a breath and looked at a Sean and then at Nicole. "A very serious situation is unfolding that I don't think you are aware of, well, of course, you aren't aware of it."

"Charlie, just say whatever it is," Sean said with a smile on his face. Charlie was a very endearing man and at times worried enough for all the parents in England. He certainly had a flair for drama.

"Yes, well," Charlie said, focusing on the situation and clearing his mind. "It involves Kent."

Nicole looked at Charlie then at Sean. "What?"

"I haven't had time to tell you, Nicole. Five days ago I called you and asked you to call me back. Obviously my message didn't get to you. I called to tell you that Kent escaped."

Nicole looked at Sean, who turned and walked to the back of the room. "What? How?" Nicole was surprised and confused at the same time. Sean and Charlie took turns informing Nicole of the details of the escape like a tag team.

"What's the new development that has you so rattled?" Sean inquired, as he sat down in a chair across from Charlie and next to Nicole.

"Do you remember a French politician named Babineaux?" Charlie started. "He represented a southern region in France and was very vocal about the Basque rebels who have been committing crimes and fleeing to his district to hide."

"I remember the name, and I also remember that there was very little evidence indicating that was actually happening," Sean recalled.

"You are right. There was no direct evidence, but he kept babbling on about it. Well, he was assassinated yesterday." Sean stiffened waiting for the other shoe to drop. "The French authorities have just forwarded their report. It reads that they believe the Serpent committed the assassination. He used the same caliber of gun, and he left his calling card. There was also this." Charlie presented a photograph to Sean. In the photograph, Babineaux's body was covered with a white sheet, but there was blood marking the ground around the head of the victim. In the blood that was not covered, the assassin wrote a name: Nikki.

Sean swallowed as he looked up at Charlie. He had shielded the photograph from Nicole's sight.

"What is it?" Nicole said. Sean hesitated. "Sean, tell me."

Sean looked at Nicole as he turned the photograph for her to see. Nicole did not gasp at the gruesome site. She had seen worse when she worked in the District Attorney's office. What shocked her was seeing her name written in blood. Nicole's eyes moved from the photograph to Sean's eyes. "As if I don't have enough people after me as it is."

Sean looked sympathetically at Nicole. He handed the photograph back to Charlie. "Thank you for telling us about this. I can't leave right now, Charlie." Sean's eyes were darting about reflecting the conflict that was racing through his brain. A part of Sean wanted to leave immediately to dispose of Kent. He knew an order for him to do so could come at any time. However, Nicole was now in danger from two different parties. He desperately did not want to leave Nicole's side.

"I don't understand," Nicole interjected. "Surely you have photographs of the Serpent lying dead in Bobby's beach house. Why can't you show them that and tell them that Kent committed this murder?"

"It isn't so much who the Serpent actually is that is the problem," Charlie explained. "You see, Nicole, it is more about the resources and connections that an assassin of this caliber has cultivated. It takes many, many years to build that. In fact, the Serpent that you met wasn't the original Serpent."

Wait, what?" Nicole asked. "So this might not be Kent?"

"No, it's Kent," Sean verified. "Your name written in blood confirms that."

"So, Kent is the third Serpent?"

"Yes," Sean confirmed. "The man you and I could identify killed the original Serpent some years before he killed Sarah and Kate." Nicole looked at Sean with a confused look. "The original Serpent was getting old and careless. Saverio and I met when I was in training for MI6. He was a Basque freedom fighter who left Spain to help the IRA. I was assigned after making contact with him to infiltrate the IRA and determine if there was any connection between the IRA and the Basque. The IRA employed the original Serpent to assassinate a prominent figure in the British Government. The Serpent didn't succeed for a number of reasons, but what did happen was that Saverio killed the Serpent and took his identity. Saverio grew the Serpent's reputation and network. He obviously recruited Kent."

"So, because you and I know that this is Kent, we are his target," Nicole concluded. Sean nodded his head in confirmation. "I still don't understand why SIS or the CIA couldn't say that this isn't the Serpent."

"It would be like the CIA telling Israel that Hamas doesn't exist," Charlie said.

"But Hamas does exist," Nicole said.

"Precisely," Charlie said.

Nicole paused, thinking about Charlie's answer. "You're telling me that no one would believe it," Nicole replied.

"That's right. The Serpent has a network of people that, after this assassination, would not believe that the assassin who they are aiding was killed," Charlie clarified. "And there is another twisted reason we don't want to announce that we know who this is."

"What's that?" Nicole asked.

"We may need his services," Charlie said.

"WHAT?" Nicole said emphatically.

Sean shook his head. "I don't think we need to go there." He turned to Nicole. "There are times when governments hire assassins."

"So that's how Jefferies could get in touch with the Serpent."

"Yes. And if we know how this network works, and now we know that the Serpent is Kent, we might be able to thwart a future assassination, if it is in the best interest of our governments."

Nicole shook her head in disbelief. "So...I..." Nicole was grappling for the right words. "Does the head of state, president, dictator, whoever, actually make the call to have someone killed or is this something the intelligence agency decides?"

"I don't think we can tell you that," Charlie replied at the same time as Sean.

"It depends," Sean smiled. "I think we need to leave it at that." Sean turned to Charlie. "About my tracking him—"

There was a knock on the door. "Come in," Charlie called. "We're not asking you to do so, Sean."

A very beautiful, blonde young woman walked into Charlie's office. "I'm sorry," she said in her very pleasant British accent. Nicole was watching Sean and noticed his eyes brighten. He smiled as the woman entered the room. "I can come back, Charlie."

"No, no. I need you in this meeting." Charlie said while waving a hand indicating for her to come into the office and close the door.

Nicole was unsure what to make of Sean's reaction to this woman. She was about the same height as Nicole and had a figure for which most women would kill to have. Her hair was thick and fell just below her shoulders. It was all one length and parted in the middle. Her striking baby blue eyes were intense but welcoming. She closed the door behind her and smiled at Sean who was watching her saunter toward the three of them.

Sean looked at Charlie with a big grin on his face. "Perfect." Nicole had no idea what Sean was referring to.

"I thought you might approve," Charlie responded. "Maggie, this is Sean Adkins."

Maggie's face lit up as she heard Charlie speak Sean's name. It was evident that Maggie was captivated with Sean. Her cheeks flushed and her eyes focused at the mention of his name. Maggie was now doing those little things that women do to catch a man's eye. Nicole sat in her chair watching this unfold before her. Maggie flipped her blonde hair behind her shoulders as she extended her other hand to shake Sean's. "It's such a pleasure to meet you. You're like a legend around here." Sean began to blush at her praise and attention.

Nicole rolled her eyes at Sean's reaction and Maggie's forwardness. She wasn't entirely sure, but she believed she saw Maggie stand up straighter at Sean's name, making her perky little breasts even more apparent through her oxford blouse that was unbuttoned lower than appropriate for the workplace. Sean stood to accept Maggie's hand, the union happening right in front of Nicole's face as she stayed seated.

"It is nice to meet you," Sean gushed all too eagerly for Nicole's liking. "And you can't believe everything you hear around here." They were still holding hands.

"I would venture to say what is being said is only the tip of the iceberg." Maggie maneuvered her head giving Sean a provocative *come hither* look. With a slight tilt so that her eyes looked alluringly into Sean's, she added. "There's a lot I can learn from you."

When did I walk into a bad James Bond movie? Nicole shifted in her chair.

"From me?" Sean questioned. He looked over at Charlie.

"We'll get to that. Maggie, this is Nicole Charbonneau."

"Hello," Nicole said, smiling up at her and not offering her hand. She could tell by Maggie's reaction that she never noticed Nicole was in the room.

"Oh," Maggie said, stepping back and finally releasing Sean's hand. "I'm sorry. How rude of me to have greeted Sean right in front of your face. I didn't see you there."

"Obviously," Nicole shot back. She did not attempt to shake Maggie's hand. She watched as Maggie realized that Nicole had detected her subtle flirtations with Sean. Maggie's eyes started at Nicole's feet moving upward as Maggie sized up her competition. Their eyes met, and Nicole gave a sardonic smile. Nicole tilted her head as if to mock Maggie and said, "What's this all about Charlie?"

Sean motioned for Maggie to take his seat. Maggie moved to it and sat down. Sean turned, bringing the hand he motioned with to his face to hide the smile that was creeping across his lips caused by Nicole's reaction to Maggie. He walked to the other side of Nicole, retrieving a chair that was against the wall. For a moment he considered sitting on the other side of Maggie, just to see Nicole's reaction, but decided that he didn't need to inflame Nicole any further.

"Well," Charlie started with a heavy exhale. "Kent has always had a weakness for women. So, Sean, Maggie will be tracking the Serpent and will report to you."

Nicole and Sean had the same reaction resulting in them speaking at the same time.

"Me?"

"Sean?"

"Yes," Charlie confirmed.

Nicole looked at Sean. "You've accepted a position here without..." Nicole's voice trailed off. How could she expect Sean to consult her on his plans when she was clearly involved with Jenkins? She looked down at the floor realizing how she was acting and that she had no right to be doing so. Nicole's forearm was resting on the arm of the chair. With her other hand, she tucked her cinnamon-colored hair behind her ear.

Sean put his hand on Nicole's forearm. Nicole looked at him. "Charlie, I'm not sure I'm following you," he said. "I didn't ask for this. I didn't ask for a desk job. I'm not sure I'm coming back. That's the whole reason why I've been struggling with whether or not I'd be going after Kent."

"I know," Charlie said. "Maggie will be in the field, and you'll have all the information on the networks and on Kent. She'll just need to check in with you and get your input on things."

"That's another way of saying that I can't leave," Sean replied.

"It's just until you determine what it is you want to do."

"I know what I want to do," Sean replied.

"You do?" Charlie questioned.

"Yes. Nicole is in a bit of trouble in a couple of ways. I would prefer to handle this a bit differently. Maggie can go into the field, but she can report to you," Sean said.

"Well, there might be a small problem with that," Charlie began. "We aren't in the personal bodyguard business, Sean. MI6 has not revoked your license to kill, and you are still considered an employee of SIS. As an employee, you'll do as you're ordered to do."

"Don't play hardball with me, Charlie."

"I'm just telling you, Sean, if that is what you want, you're going to have to resign."

"Wait," Nicole interrupted. Nicole looked at Maggie, realizing she would have to rephrase what she was about to say. "Some circumstances are occurring in my situation that I think warrant an MI6 agent's protection."

"We have plenty of agents," Charlie retorted, cutting her off.

Sean stood up, turning his back on Charlie, and walked to the back of the room. When he turned around, he said, "What does this entail?"

"It's a desk job," Charlie informed Sean. "Maggie will do all the tracking, field work, killing…"

Nicole couldn't contain her reaction. "You just said that it doesn't matter if you kill the Serpent. Someone else will take his place."

"I'm not talking about just killing the Serpent," Charlie quipped.

"I have to be here every day," Sean stated, ignoring Nicole's comment.

"Or we would have to know how to get in touch with you."

Sean realized that his freedom to move around on his own was being taken away from him. "With the desk job, my license to kill isn't necessary."

"That's right; it would be revoked," Charlie confirmed.

Sean looked at Nicole and released some breath that sounded like a defeated chuckle. "Who put you up to this? Was it from this side of the pond? Was it my father or Jenkins? Perhaps it was another of our friends in the US government. Was it Jefferies?" Nicole spun around in her chair to look at Sean, surprised by his questions.

"It's time for you to make a decision, Sean," Charlie responded.

Sean stood in the back of Charlie's office while his mind ran through all the possibilities. If he stayed with SIS, he would be tied to a desk while Maggie tracked down Kent. It was almost as if SIS wanted him dead. With a desk job, Kent would know where he was at any given time. He couldn't protect Nicole from Kent, or anyone else for that matter. It came down to what was more important to him. Sean reached into his shoulder holster and produced his gun. He spun it around so that he was holding it by the barrel. He walked up to Charlie's desk and placed the gun on it. He then reached into his pocket and produced his badge. He surrendered his credentials. "Nicole." She stood up. "I'm sorry, Charlie. I resign."

He took Nicole by the arm, and they walked to the door. Maggie looked at Charlie and then at Sean. "Wait!" she exclaimed. "I can't do this without you."

"Talk with Elliot. He knows as much as I do," Sean shot back. He opened the door, allowing Nicole to walk through first. "Nicole is in danger, and I put her there laying a trap for the Serpent the first time. I'll be damned if I am going to leave her side in a foreign country with no protection. You can tell Jefferies or whoever told you to do this—tell them I said to go fuck themselves." Sean walked through the door, slamming it behind him. He took Nicole by the arm as they stormed out of the building, not speaking a word until they got into Sean's car, which was parked outside the building on the street.

"Thank you," Nicole said, finally breaking the silence. "Sean, if there is any doubt in your mind; I don't want you to throw everything away for this. If there is any part of you that wants to track Kent down—"

"I won't have to track Kent down," Sean interrupted. "He's going to track us down. It's just a matter of time."

{III}

Jenkins entered the Senate and walked to the floor. Most of the senators were milling around as a vote was proceeding. It wasn't a major vote, but a vote on an amendment to a major bill having to do with veterans' benefits.

Votes in the Senate were a time when all the senators were actually in the chamber at once. Conversations ranging from light, humorous chats to serious arm-twisting were occurring throughout the chamber. As Jenkins walked to the floor to cast his vote, he was greeted by senators from both sides of the aisle. He reached the table, glanced over the bill quickly, and then looked up to catch the eye of the gentleman recording roll call votes.

"Senator Jenkins of North Carolina," the man said into the microphone before him.

Jenkins gave the thumbs up sign and said, "Aye."

"Senator Jenkins: aye," the man confirmed and marked the paper before him.

Jenkins turned and acknowledged a number of senators as he made his way to the stairs that led out of the chamber. He was leaving shortly on a campaign trip and wanted to get more work done. Across the way,

Barker could see that Jenkins was starting to leave and excused himself from his conversation.

Jenkins reached the top of the stairs and was opening the door when he heard Barker call to him. Jenkins continued through the door, not wanting to talk to Barker in the chamber. Barker had been asserting a lot of pressure on Jenkins to run his campaign Barker's way. Even though Jenkins had won Iowa and New Hampshire and was now considered the front-runner, he continued to frustrate his campaign manager and Barker with what they considered to be Jenkins's rebellious attitude. Jenkins stopped outside the door.

"Bobby," Barker said as he walked through the door. "I was just wondering where Nikki is these days."

"She's fine," Jenkins assured him. "She's been rather busy and with my schedule, it's been difficult to make our schedules sync."

"Busy doing what?" Barker asked. "Louise said that she phoned her the other day and hasn't received a call back."

"Yes, well, she isn't in Washington right now," Jenkins responded. He was not willing to say anything more. "I'll tell her to call Louise the next time I talk with her." Jenkins started to walk away in the direction of his office. "I need to run. I've got so much to do before I leave for Alabama and then up to New England. Good to see you, though." Jenkins turned and quickly walked away from Barker.

"Just what are you hiding?" Barker mumbled to himself as he watched Jenkins scurry away. After several seconds and a few taps to his lips with his reading glasses in his hand, Barker turned and headed to his office.

Jenkins opened the door to his office and walked in quickly, closing it behind him. He looked at Chris and then over to Thompson. "Kevin…" He walked into his office with Thompson right behind him.

"Where is she?" Jenkins asked as Thompson closed the door to his inner office.

"As far as we know she is still in Paris," Thompson replied. "Nobody has spotted her coming or going from her room. She paid cash for the room, and her last day there is tomorrow."

"She hasn't returned my phone calls," Jenkins complained. "I am beginning to think that she isn't in her room. Can't one of your friends go in and check on her?"

"That might be a little tricky," Thompson said with a smile on his face. "You didn't want her to know that you were having her followed."

"At this point, I don't care if she knows," Jenkins snapped as he sat down. "I need to know that she is okay. Have them check on her."

"Yes, sir," Thompson complied. "Is there anything else?"

"What time do we leave?" Jenkins asked.

"We leave for the airport at around two."

"There's nothing else. I have a lot of work to get through before then. As soon as you know something in regards to Nikki, let me know."

"I will, sir." Thompson turned and left the inner office. When he returned to his desk, he called the number of his friend who was tracking Nicole. He ordered him to enter the room to check on her. The friend was then told to call him afterward. Thompson was hoping that he would hear from his friend before they left for the airport. Otherwise it was going to be a long flight.

{IV}

After Sean's white-knuckled driving; Nicole was happy to finally reach his flat. Sean entered with Nicole and immediately went to his living room. He removed a painting that was hanging over a faux fireplace, revealing a safe. After unlocking the safe, he removed a gun—the exact same type of gun he had surrendered to Charlie—and ammunition, placing both on the hearth. Nicole was intrigued to witness several stacks of money in the safe. Sean removed one of the stacks, setting it next to the gun. He removed the proper amount of ammunition and placed the rest back in the safe. He closed and locked it, and returned the painting to its proper place. He loaded the gun and put it in his shoulder holster. He looked up to see Nicole watching him. "We'll be here a while. You might want to make yourself comfortable."

Nicole moved to the couch and sat down. She flipped on the television, turning the sound down.

Sean moved to a desk that was situated under a window toward the back of the room. He sat down and dialed a number. "Is he in?" Sean waited for the secretary's answer. "I'll wait."

"I guess this is why they call you secret agents," Nicole joked.

Sean looked up at her. "Hello, Jack. I suppose by now you know what happened." Sean listened to the voice on the other end of the phone. "You know what I'm asking." He waited again, listening to the man on the other end speak. "I appreciate that. How long will it be?" There was another pause. "Thank you. I'll be here." Just before hanging up, the man on the other end of the phone asked a question. "She's here with me, why? I see. Thank you. I'll see you then." Sean hung up the phone. He looked at Nicole. "Turn that bloody thing to channel thirteen."

Nicole did as she was instructed and was surprised to see Jenkins, at an airport talking to the press. She turned the sound up.

A reporter was asking a rather long question. "...We've been camped outside her apartment, Senator, and there has been no activity. She's not there, and she has not been by your side for the last six or so days. Where's Nikki? Is everything all right between you?"

"You are quite the detective," Jenkins said. "Really, gentlemen, Nikki likes her privacy, but if you must know, she is in Paris." Jenkins smiled. "I told her it was a bit premature, but she wanted a very special outfit for the inauguration ball."

"Don't you think that's bad luck?" another reporter shouted.

"I don't believe in bad luck," Jenkins returned with a smile. "I really must go now."

"Where is she in Paris?" a third reporter shouted.

"Where ever women buy expensive dresses," Jenkins shot back as he made his way through the crowd.

Sean looked at Nicole. "I thought you said you weren't followed."

"I didn't think I was, but I'm not good at this sort of thing," Nicole replied, stunned by the news. "But Sean, that's why I bought the ticket to Paris. I checked into a hotel and paid cash for a week's stay. I left the hotel and took the train ferry here. I don't remember seeing any familiar faces, people that I had seen on the plane or at the hotel, so I don't think

I've been followed to London. Jenkins has connections all over the world. Maybe he contacted someone in France?"

Sean stood up and walked to his window. He cautiously drew the drape from the wall, standing at the side so he could not be seen. He looked up the street and in each building that he could see from that side of the window. He didn't see anything out of the ordinary. He switched to the other side of the window, repeating his actions. "I don't see anything suspicious, so maybe they think you are still there. In any case, your supposed whereabouts have just been given to Kent. We'll need to be a bit more careful."

"Kent! Sean, do you think Kent will go after Kevin? He did shoot Kent and knows what Kent looks like." Nicole asked.

"Possibly, I've never really thought about it," Sean confessed.

"Don't you think we should tell him?"

"I can have Charlie get word to him."

"After today, I'm not sure I trust Charlie." Nicole frowned. "I'm not sure I trust Bobby, either."

"That's true. I'll ask Jack to do it." Sean ignored the comment about Jenkins. If Nicole disappeared while in his company, he would have been looking for her as well.

"Jack? As in Jack Kensington, the man that was in Charlie's office?" Nicole asked, bringing Sean out of his thoughts.

"Yes."

"Do I have time to change before Jack arrives?" They had retrieved her suitcase from the hotel after having lunch with Sean's father.

"Yes," Sean confirmed. "Jack should be here in about thirty minutes or so. We'll go out for dinner after that."

Nicole left the room to go upstairs. She decided to dress up a bit, deciding on a nice pantsuit for their dinner out. The look on Sean's face when he had seen Maggie was still fresh in Nicole's mind. She asked herself if she was that jealous back in Charlie's office. Maggie was a beautiful woman. Was Jenkins behind it, trying to tempt Sean with another woman? She shook her head to try and clear that ridiculous thought. She looked in the mirror as she was putting on the last touches of her makeup. "The man gives up his job for you, and you are standing here wondering if he cares for you," Nicole said under her breath as she applied blush to her cheeks. "You are insane."

As she was putting on her lipstick, the doorbell rang. She heard Sean greet a man by the name of Jack. She finished up, giving her hair a little primping, and started for the stairs to the living room.

"I'm very happy you called me, Sean," Jack said, accepting the drink that Sean had poured him. "You know I don't want to lose you, but I couldn't give the impression that I would lose the cooperation of the US over one agent, either. It was clear that they didn't want you anywhere near this."

"I understand," Sean replied. He looked up to see Nicole at the bottom of the stairs. Sean raised an eyebrow and gave an approving smile when he saw her walk into the room. He quickly turned his attention back to the business at hand. The look on Sean's face was all the confirmation Nicole needed. "Would you like something?" Sean asked as he reached for the gin. He poured the gin over ice for himself.

"No, thank you," Nicole responded. "Good to see you again, Jack."

"Good to see you, Nicole."

Sean moved to the couch, and Nicole sat down next to him. Jack sat on a chair across from them separated by a coffee table. He set his drink down and reached into his suit jacket. He placed a black wallet on the table. "Your credentials complete with your ID badge," Jack said as he picked up the drink again.

"Thank you," Sean said as he reached for and examined the contents in the wallet. He placed it back on the table and took another drink.

"This is our secret, Sean. You can't just waltz into SIS any time you want." Jack reminded him. "Charlie thinks that you have quit, so no contact there, either."

"I understand. I'm a black op and no contact with SIS." Sean confirmed.

"What does that mean?" Nicole inquired. "It sounds pretty ominous."

Jack looked at Nicole. "It means that only four of us know that Sean is still working for SIS."

"Well, not entirely true," Sean said. "I don't plan on telling Geoff anything, so he will still think I'm an agent. So, my Dad makes the fourth and Geoff makes the fifth."

"Fair enough. I guess I should have said that Sean is reporting directly to me and I've permitted him to operate without specific orders."

"I see." Nicole was not entirely sure she understood the situation at all.

"There are only a few I would trust to do this. Sean is one of them. Maggie is going after Kent. We all know what his weaknesses are." Jack was saying this to Sean more than Nicole to make the point that he wouldn't give this kind of carte blanche to just any agent in his employment.

"Kent never could resist blondes," Sean said.

Jack finished his drink and stood up. "You have everything you need?"

"Yes. If not, I know where to get it," Sean said standing up. He extended his hand. "Thank you, again."

Jack shook his hand. "I think of you as the son I never had, Sean. Keep this pretty lady safe as well as yourself." He winked at a standing Nicole and took a step toward her. "I'm sure I'll be seeing you again." He shook her hand and started walking to the door. Sean followed behind Jack, bidding him a good evening, then came back into the living room and sat down on the couch.

"I'm confused. Are you going after Kent?" Nicole asked.

"No," Sean replied. "That is a different operation." Sean picked up the wallet from the table that Jack had given him. "This is just my license to kill if Kent gets too close to either one of us. We need to determine our next steps though. Do you want to expose the contents of that tape?"

"Yes," Nicole confirmed without hesitation. "If this conspiracy doesn't see the light of day, it will change the path of our government forever." Nicole thought back to the Kennedy assassination. "Remember when JFK was assassinated?"

"Yes," Sean replied, unsure where she was going with that question.

"It took the Warren Commission a year to report their findings. The summary was published, and the findings weren't very credible in some people's minds. The single-bullet theory was not a strong theory, which led some to believe there was a conspiracy."

"That doesn't mean there was a conspiracy." Sean never looked into the assassination, but he knew from experience that less knowledgeable people needed something to ramble on about at dinner parties.

"That is exactly my point. The controversy of whether or not there was a conspiracy in Kennedy's assassination has begun a rift in the trust of our government. Andrews, a mild-mannered, middle-of-the-road president, who probably couldn't hurt a fly, was brutally murdered—and for what reason? What story will Bobby's investigation put out? If he provides a cover-up theory, which I am sure he will be pressured to do, will that cause further distrust? We allow a traitor and murderer to remain as president. If Bobby won't do something to expose this, then I believe I have to do so. To put it simply, it's just the right thing to do."

"You realize that you become a target yourself when you do this. You realize that you will be exposing information that the chairman of the Intelligence Committee has in his possession. You'll never be able to travel to the United States again, and Bobby might have to consider you an enemy of the state."

"Yes, I know I will probably need to seek asylum. As for Bobby's actions, I can only hope he uses the opportunity to bring this out in the open and call for the conspirators to be arrested and tried."

"Let's go get something to eat and talk about this further. There has to be a way that we can do this with Bobby's help. We just need to think about the process a bit more."

Nicole was happy to hear Sean's comments. "Your loyalty to your friends is quite commendable."

Sean helped Nicole with her coat. "Friendship is a luxury in my line of work. True friends have your back regardless of the consequences.

Bobby has been a true friend to both of us. If we can save him or aid him, I rather like that option."

{V}

Jenkins arrived at the airport with Thompson at his side. Having just finished answering questions at an impromptu press conference outside the terminal, he was surprised to see Barker with Carson waiting inside. He motioned for Thompson to stay back as he walked up to greet the men. "This is a surprise, Larry. Are you traveling to Alabama with us?"

"Yes, we have business to discuss," Barker informed him.

"I see. Shall we board the plane?" Jenkins asked. He didn't like the tone in Barker's voice and knew he wasn't going to like the upcoming conversation. He motioned for Barker and Carson to board the plane before him. Thompson walked up to Jenkins as the men passed through the gate to the private plane. Jenkins was eyeing them with suspicion.

"What do you think this is about?" Thompson asked.

"I don't know, but it can't be good," Jenkins replied. He and Thompson walked through the gate. Once they were on board, the flight attendant closed the door, secured it, and shut the door to the cockpit. Jenkins took his seat across from Barker and Carson. Thompson sat in the row behind them so that he could eavesdrop more easily.

The plane's engines whirred as usual when the pilot started them. It was almost as if it was Barker's cue to start talking. "Bobby, Jim and I have some concerns."

"Obviously," Jenkins stated sardonically. "Otherwise you wouldn't be here."

Barker was cunning and could be underhanded when he needed to be. Jenkins had been waiting for this conversation to happen ever since he started writing his own campaign speeches and didn't share them with Carson. If Jenkins had his way, he would fire Carson, who was finding it harder to control his candidate. Jenkins was aware of Carson's frustration; he just didn't care to put an end to it.

As the plane took off, Barker decided it was time to get down to business. "Bobby," Barker started out. The tone in Barker's voice exhibited the mentor tone that Jenkins had heard so many times before. It was meant to ease the tension between them. Barker watched as Jenkins drew in a deep breath showing his impatience and sat up in his chair. Jenkins was clearly marking his displeasure with the tone. Barker ignored it and continued. "You have the best campaign manager in the business. You need to listen to him. You are the front-runner now, and we need to make sure we don't screw this up."

"Yes, I am the front-runner, Larry. It is good you noticed that. Did you also notice that I became the front-runner when I started writing my own speeches? That is what this is all about." Jenkins looked at Carson. "You're upset, Jim, because I won't let you put words in my mouth?"

"Writing your own speeches and not letting me see them is one of the issues, yes," Carson confirmed.

"We have to make sure the message is consistent," Barker added.

"Consistent? Point out to me where I have been inconsistent? I'm not saying anything different than I have said in the past or on the Senate floor. I'm not in favor of weakening the Glass-Steagall Act, and these interpretations by the financial agencies are reckless and just may be encouraging illegal activity. I am not and never will be in favor of drilling in the ANWR, and I will continue to push for tougher CAFE standards. I will also encourage the growth of green energies like solar and wind. I will continue to push for oversight of our intelligence community. These stances are no different than before I began my campaign."

"Bobby, you have some very powerful backers who have paid a lot of money to your campaign. The PACs and contributors won't be happy with some of these stances."

"Then give them their money back," Jenkins quipped.

Barker was becoming angry. "We can't do that. If you don't change your ways, they will simply back your opponents who will gladly give them what they want." Barker looked at Carson. "Will you excuse us for a moment, Jim?"

Carson made a face but knew what Barker was going to say next was only to be heard by Jenkins. He stood up and started to the back of the plane. He motioned for Thompson to get up as well. Thompson just waved, making it clear he wasn't going to move from his spot. Carson grumbled as he walked away.

Barker scooted forward on his seat and pointed an accusing finger at Jenkins. "Now you look here. I didn't pull strings and call in favors for you to put forth your own personal agenda." Jenkins didn't like where this conversation was going, and he tilted his head, the only indication that he was listening. He restrained from showing any other signs of dissent. Barker felt the need to take his anger one step further. "I can wreck your campaign with one press release, and I can take all the support you have to Sanford."

"I'm curious, Larry, just how would you do that?" Jenkins asked, hiding his own anger at being threatened with what he considered to be a betrayal by his mentor.

"Let's just say that I know how you got your medal in Vietnam." Jenkins looked at Barker with confusion. "The civilians your men shot on the raid when you lost your leg."

Jenkins closed his eyes. Barker had him. If the secret that had been covered up for all these years got out, Jenkins would not only lose his status as a front-runner but could possibly lose his Senate seat, thereby ending his public service career. Jenkins thought for a moment. His mind took him back to the jungle on that hot, muggy night. He loosened his tie. He didn't remember giving the command to kill the civilians in the village. He only knew what John Spencer had told him when he woke up in the hospital without his lower leg. He remembered hearing that the boy who shot him had been killed, and he justified the boy's death. The boy could have announced their arrival to the village, and his entire unit could all have been killed. Jenkins lived with the knowledge every day that things were done under his command. There wasn't a day that went by where he didn't ask for mercy and forgiveness. It was war. But people who never served or hadn't spent a day in a war zone didn't understand the cruel realities of hand-to-hand combat. Defeated in the current moment, Jenkins exhaled the breath he noticed he was holding. "What do you want?" He looked at Barker with disgust.

Thompson listened intently to the conversation. He began to wonder just what had happened on the night that Jenkins lost his leg. He pulled out a notebook from his jacket's breast pocket. He wrote down a few notes to remind him to check on it. He didn't like that Barker was attempting to blackmail his boss. If he could, he would do something to help him.

"You know what I want. I want for you to play ball and give your donors what they want." Barker stood up and tapped Jenkins's knee three times, signifying that he understood Jenkins would now assume the persona Barker dictated to him. Barker started to walk past him. "I knew you would see it my way."

Jenkins didn't answer. He refused to look at Barker, although he could feel Barker's gloating smile. As Barker walked to the back of the plane to join Carson, Jenkins stared at the empty chair across from him. At this moment, he didn't see a way out of being a puppet for big money. He didn't want that; he had always hoped that his service would be different. He began to wonder at what point he sold his soul to the devil and whether or not he could cancel the contract. He felt like he had been hit by a truck. His enthusiasm for this campaign had left him. Now he was going to be a talking head for Carson and his cronies. He felt sick. At this moment, he had lost everything he cared about: first Nicole and now this.

"Here's the speech for tomorrow," Carson said, sliding into the chair across from Jenkins, who didn't see him sit down. "We have a few people who want to meet with you afterward. If we do this right, they will be willing to support you and donate to the campaign." Carson was still holding the speech. "Senator?"

Jenkins blinked his eyes but did not acknowledge him. Carson set the speech on the seat next to him. "Make sure you look this over. We'll be in Birmingham in about thirty minutes." Carson looked at Jenkins. Nothing he said was causing any reaction in him. He began to wonder just what Barker had said to Jenkins. Carson decided to change the subject. "Not that I miss her, but have you heard from Nikki?"

Jenkins didn't respond.

Chapter Seven

Mid-March 1980

Sean and Nicole discussed several options available to her over a few days. It was clear with each option that seeking asylum in the United Kingdom would be the first step. Sean wouldn't have it any other way, and he felt this would help ensure her safety. After finally reaching agreement on their plan, Sean called his father to arrange a dinner date so that he and Nicole could share some information with him. Since Nicole wanted to expose the confession tape, they needed to secure a contact in the media. Sean evaded the press, so he had no connections to any reporters. Peter did have those connections and could engage the right person.

Peter suggested that Sean and Nicole arrive at his home at seven and his staff would prepare the dinner. Nicole was upstairs getting dressed, as Sean waited downstairs flipping through television channels when he happened onto a campaign speech given by Jenkins. Something had changed in his demeanor, and Jenkins didn't seem as enthusiastic as he had been. Sean wondered if it was because of Nicole's absence. The thunderstorm produced a bolt of lightning pulling Sean from his thoughts. The rain was pouring down, and Sean frowned realizing he and Nicole would be heading out into it shortly.

Nicole finished dressing for dinner; she walked down the stairs. Sean turned off the television and stood up to meet her in the foyer. Nicole was wearing the dress that she had worn on the campaign trail. It was one of her favorite dresses, and the violet color set her eyes dancing. She also had to admit to herself that she was wearing it because the last time she had done so, Sean couldn't keep his eyes off her. As she descended the steps, Sean looked up to see her in the dress he had imagined slipping off her many times since that day in North Carolina. He smiled his approval with a devilish grin that confirmed his desire for Nicole. They arrived at Peter's house promptly at seven as directed. Sean was a bit nervous about the evening. He wasn't entirely sure why.

"Come in," Peter said as he opened the door. "I've always wanted to get a canopy for the front stoop. I'm sorry you were standing in the rain." Nicole and Sean did have an umbrella, and both were donning coats. Sean deposited the wet umbrella in the appropriate bin by the door. Peter urged Nicole to take her wet coat off and hand it to him. Sean did the same. Peter hung them in the foyer closet and then led them to the living room.

"Would you like something to drink?" Peter asked while motioning for them to sit on the couch. "Dinner will be ready shortly."

Sean walked over to the bar. Peter was pouring himself gin on the rocks. "I'll get ours, Dad," Sean said taking the bottle of gin from his father.

"I see we are all gin drinkers here."

"Evidently the chip doesn't fall too far from the tree," Nicole responded. "Gin on the rocks is one of Sean's favorites."

"I always told the bartender just to give the vermouth the ole look, but not any in my martini. Then I determined, just order the gin on the rocks. It's quicker to say, you see."

Nicole smiled when Peter winked at her. She saw so many similarities between father and son: The most obvious being Sean's mannerisms and facial features. Their emerald-green eyes were beautiful and captivating, not to mention they were almost the exact same shade of green. While Peter's hair was graying at the temples and he had a smattering of gray throughout, Sean's dark black hair was still present in Peter's hair. It was a rare but interesting combination of eye and hair color, which caused Nicole to wonder what Sean's mother looked like. She glanced around the room to find a photograph. The only one she could locate was a black-and-white wedding photo sitting on the mantle above the fireplace. While it was very apparent that Peter was from a family of some importance, Sean's mother seemed a bit ill at ease in the photograph. Peter looked dashing while his wife looked dazed and uncomfortable.

Sean never talked about his family. It dawned on Nicole that neither one of them spent much time talking about their pasts. Was she projecting her unease at being in Peter's home onto the disposition of Peter's wife in the photograph? She stood up and walked to the mantle to take a closer look. As beautifully dressed as the woman was, she didn't have a smile on her face. It was meant to be the happiest day of her life, and she looked stoic at best, sad at worst. It was the most interesting conundrum. Nicole smiled as she thought that the look on Sean's mother's face reminded her of a look she had received from Sean a time or two.

Peter walked to a chair and sat down. He noticed Nicole looking at the photograph. "There's a story behind that photograph—besides the obvious that it is our wedding day." Nicole returned to the couch where Sean was waiting with her drink. "I'm not sure if you know this, but Sean's mother was Irish, hence the spelling of Sean's name. Her brothers were quite a rowdy bunch, and her upbringing was a hardship."

"Dad is politely saying that a poor family raised mum in Northern Ireland," Sean interrupted.

"Yes, well," Peter started again, "my family was prominent in London, always have been really, and when the two families met—"

"Met? You mean clashed," Sean corrected, taking a drink of his gin.

Peter smiled and gave a little laugh. "That is true. There wasn't a time when one of her brothers wasn't trying to pick a fight with my family. I mean literally a physical fight, not a verbal one. On the day the picture was taken, the photographer posed us, and all seemed to be going well, when all of a sudden her older brother dropped his drawers." Nicole covered her mouth dropped in astonishment, which quickly turned to a smile. "It seems my younger brother had commented the unruliness of Brighid's family. It wasn't so much that her parents weren't polite; it was directed more at her siblings. My parents and Brighid's parents got along very well, actually. So when her older brother caught wind of this comment, he essentially mooned my brother right there in front of everyone. To this day, I have no idea what the comment was. That explains the disapproving look on Brighid's face and the grin on mine!" Peter took a drink. "I rather liked traveling to Northern Ireland during our courting. It was the one place I could go and throw aside the shackles of my life and destiny. She always brought out the rebel in me—or, maybe it was her brothers who brought out that side of me."

"Despite the look on her face, she was a gorgeous bride," Nicole complimented Peter.

"Yes, she was," Peter agreed. "And a wonderful mother." Peter lifted his glass, as did Sean and Nicole. "To Brighid." They all took a drink. Peter swallowed and then added, "Sean was her favorite," he winked.

"I was not, Dad," Sean protested. "She loved us all equally if that is even possible."

Peter turned his attention and statements to Nicole. "Sean was most like her family. He was quite rebellious and didn't want anything to do with the upper crust, stodgy—I believe that was the word you used—family members. I can't say I blame him. He was a handful when he was a child. Yes, the MacBride genes are deeply instilled in my son." Peter took another sip. "And I'm sure they are one of the reasons for his current profession."

Nicole noticed the disapproving tone in Peter's last sentence. She looked at Sean, who rolled his eyes and took a drink to keep from saying anything. "Well, sir, if it is any consolation, I am very grateful Sean chose that occupation. I probably wouldn't be here if it weren't for him."

Sean smiled, and Peter nodded his head in acknowledgment more than agreement. "I've heard from Jack that there has been a bit of a development. No need to talk about it in depth, but it seems that the Serpent, or his reputation, isn't dead."

"Yes," Sean replied. "And I'm sure that Jack told you about my new assignment."

"It doesn't sound any less dangerous, but I am glad that you are not going back undercover to track Kent," Peter said. "I hope you feel whatever debt you had to pay has been settled."

"It has," Sean confirmed. Both men were referring to obtaining revenge for the deaths of Sarah and Kate. "But Dad, you also have to realize, my work was also for Mum." With a confused look on her face, Nicole looked at Sean.

Peter could tell by Nicole's reaction that Sean had not shared what had happened to his mother. "Brighid was killed in a train station bombing long attributed to the IRA, but they have never claimed responsibility. It was in the early days of the uprising, so very little was known at that time. Our MI5 division was terribly corrupt and just getting their feet on the ground." A servant came into the room and announced that dinner was ready to be served. "Shortly after that, Sean entered the training to be an agent." Peter stood and walked to the bar. "Does anyone's drink need to be freshened?"

"I'm fine, thank you," Nicole replied.

"I'll have a bit more," Sean said walking over to his father. When their drinks were poured, they walked to the dining room, which was exquisitely decorated with vintage furnishings. It was, Nicole would come to discover, the last room that Brighid had decorated. Brighid was very proud of the room, and many dinner parties were given here even after her death. To Peter, it became her shrine—his memory of her and her impeccable taste that developed over the years of being in society. "This room was always off limits to me and my brother growing up," Sean added, with a devilish grin which told Nicole he broke that rule on many occasions.

Dinner conversation was a combination of Peter telling tales about his life and, consequently, Sean's life. Nicole drew her own conclusions about Sean's childhood, determining it wasn't much different than any other child's aside from the position of importance Peter and his family held in the London elite. While they were not part of the royal family, Peter's father was also in politics. It was fated that Peter was to follow in his father's footsteps. Peter said that he truly fell in love with Brighid, whom he met during the war. However, Brighid was not who the family intended him to marry. When Peter left for his service, he was not officially engaged to a very refined and high society debutante, but it was clear that if Peter did return, he would marry this lovely lady. Peter was shot in the leg and taken to a military medical unit where, Brighid, who was serving as a nurse, tended to his wound. They spoke fondly of home and of family. Peter developed an infection, and Brighid never left his side. While in the throes of the high fever, Peter said that he focused on this angelic voice reading Yeats to him. "I've said it before, and I believe it to this day: She pulled me through. Right before the fever, the idea of returning to that muddy, wet, disgusting foxhole weighed rather heavily on me." Peter paused for a moment. "It was inevitable, my returning to the battlefield. On my way back to the front, just before the truck pulled away, she handed me her rosary." Peter's eyes went to the rosary, which had been framed and placed on the buffet table next to a picture of Brighid in her nurse's uniform. "I told her I wasn't Catholic, and that I would return it to her. She was a clever girl. The crucifix opens and inside she had managed to write her parents address down and fold the paper so that it fit inside. I didn't realize that until after I had returned home."

"This is the good part," Sean said beaming.

Peter laughed. "Yes, Sean says this is the one and only outright act of defiance I have managed to accomplish in my whole life." He looked at Nicole. "I hope I'm not boring you."

"Not at all," Nicole proclaimed, smiling at Sean who seemed to be in utter agony. He was sitting across the table from her. Their eyes met, and she knew exactly what he was thinking. His gaze confirmed her suspicion of his agony.

"I returned home to my mother planning my wedding to the lovely woman I had been dating prior to my service. All of this was a complete surprise and evidently set into action when my mother read the letter from me, in which I had written about Brighid. Of course, every letter after that one mentioned Brighid in one way or another. I was smitten and—," he paused. "No, Brighid had stolen my heart. There I was, in the middle of the horrendous acts of war, head over heels in love with her." Nicole smiled. "You can imagine my dismay at the train station, where I was met by Mother and Anne, the former girlfriend. My mother was politely applying pressure, shall we say, that I bop into the jewelry store and buy Anne a ring." Nicole's smile became larger as Peter spun his tale. She anxiously waited for the moment of defiance. "I pulled my mother aside and told her that I was tired, had no money, and no intention of buying any kind of ring at the moment. The money part she had taken care of, she explained, and the selection of the ring had been taken care of as well. My mother was determined that I was not going to marry an Irish woman, you see."

Peter paused a moment to take a drink and few bites of his dinner. "We all returned home, and I was devastated." Nicole asserted to herself that the British were excellent storytellers. "I sat in my room and fondled the only thing that I had to remind me and make me feel as if she were real—her rosary." Nicole looked at the rosary again. "As I was examining the rosary closer, I noticed that there was a clasp on the crucifix. I opened it and out fell this piece of paper. Now, mind you, at dinner, I was told by my parents the date of the wedding, which was only three days away. Imagine my surprise, and then my mother told me that she and Anne had written to tell me. I had never received the letters. It hadn't appeared strange to my mother at all that I never mentioned a word about the wedding. I only talked about wanting to find Brighid after the war. In fact, I had even stopped writing Anne. Of course, my mother explained that away by telling Anne that my letters must have gotten lost, and that all I spoke about in my letters to my parents was marrying her."

Nicole gave the most charming and seductive laugh—a sound Sean had never heard from her before but took great enjoyment in hearing. He looked at her, his eyes almost glowing at the sound. The devious quality in the laugh followed by a pleasant sound made Sean's desire for her leap. "Oh, how deliciously evil this whole story is," Nicole said with a coy tone in her voice. She was thoroughly enjoying the story. Anxiously, Nicole asked, "What happened next?"

"As I said, I was sitting on my bed, and I opened the crucifix and out fell this meticulously folded piece of paper. I picked it up and very carefully unfolded it. On the paper were written, 'Please find me' on one side and the other side had her street address." Peter paused to finish the last bite of his dinner and take a sip of water. "When I say street address, there was only room for the number and name of street. I was somewhat heartbroken because for the life of me I could not remember what part of Northern Ireland she was from—the town she was from. I figured it was all a lost cause. I did lose hope as I wracked my brain trying to remember the town. The next day after breakfast, my father took me aside and told me how his marriage had been arranged and how he never, for a second, doubted his mother's selection for him. I was absolutely abhorred at this. Then, my father mentioned that it was my duty to go through with this. I was utterly dashed. Depressed, I returned to my room and threw myself on my bed. They forced my younger brother to acquire the ring and take it to Anne on my behalf. They made up some story about how I was locked in my room, writing my vows or something. I barely ate, I was so depressed."

Nicole looked at Sean. Yes, they were more alike than Sean ever wanted to admit. Peter stood, noticing that all of them had finished their meals. They retreated to the living room where tea and coffee were served. After-dinner drinks were offered, but Sean and Nicole declined.

Peter sat down in a chair, his Courvoisier cognac in his snifter, and resumed the story. "The night before the wedding, my younger brother entered my bedroom and sat on the edge of my bed. He asked several questions, and when I told him about Brighid, he encouraged me to find her. He helped me pack, and in the still of the night, I left for Northern Ireland, without a word to my parents or Anne."

"Of course I knew that you weren't going to marry Anne," Nicole began. "But sneaking off the night before the wedding?"

"Yes, that is why Sean thinks it is my only defiant act." Peter smiled, taking a sip. "I searched for a month until I finally found the address. It was a wonderful reunion. I was walking down the road, and she saw me from her bedroom window. By the time I had reached her block, she was running toward me, and we embraced. I knew she was the one for me."

Nicole's thoughts took her back to her reunion with Sean in North Carolina. Sean was sitting next to her on the couch, and she wanted so badly to take his hand at that moment. She resisted and turned her attention back to Peter's story. "How did you manage to get your parents to agree for you to marry Brighid?"

"It wasn't easy. Neither of our parents was thrilled with our choice. Many months after our reuniting, I bought Brighid a ring and asked her to marry me. When I finally told my father that I was willing to throw it all away for her, he decided that it was for the best to start working on Mum to accept Brighid. My mother and Brighid never really got along, but they tolerated each other. When Geoff was born, it got much easier, and then when Sean was born, I'd say that was when they had decided to accept Brighid. Brighid's parents accepted me far sooner." Peter took another sip. "That's enough of that. I hope we'll have more opportunities to share family history in the future. Sean, you said there was something of importance you wanted to discuss."

"Yes," Sean started. "It is Nicole who needs to discuss this with you."

"Thank you for sharing that story with me. I did enjoy it," she said. Peter bowed his head in acknowledgment and lifted his snifter to his lips. "I don't really know where to start, so I'll get right to it. I am in possession of some evidence that pertains to the assassination of President Andrews. The evidence is a confession tape made by Norman Sipes, who owned an oil company and was preparing to drill illegally in the ANWR. The tape asserts that he and now President Stevens, along with three others, conspired to kill Andrews because he had switched his position on drilling in the ANWR."

Peter couldn't believe his ears. "I'm sorry. Did I hear you say that President Stevens was involved in the assassination of President Andrews?"

"Yes," Nicole confirmed.

"It gets worse, Dad," Sean added.

"The other three men involved are Michael Jefferies—"

"The director of the FBI?!" Peter exclaimed.

Nicole continued, "Representative Davis and Joseph Engle, a wealthy businessman."

"My word! How on Earth did you come to have this extraordinary tape?" Peter was in shock.

"Norman Sipes was a client of my former and now deceased employer, Tony Shafer. Sipes made the payment to the assassin, and he was killed. Sipes had made this tape and left instructions for his butler to deliver the tape to Tony if or when he was killed. Tony mailed it to me from Key West, days before his yacht was found scuttled on an obscure barrier island in the Caribbean. His body hasn't been found, but his blood was found on the yacht." Nicole paused as she thought of her friend.

"There was a large amount of drugs found on the yacht. Nicole thinks it was planted, and I can't rule that theory out," Sean added. "A letter that Nicole received from Tony mentioned he was being followed, and since he was good friends with Stevens, we need to assume that Stevens knows about the tape." Sean looked at Nicole.

"Just what are your plans regarding this tape, Nicole?" Peter asked.

"I want to expose the conspiracy," Nicole stated without hesitation.

"Dad, she has left out one important fact. Senator Jenkins also has a copy of this tape but has not made it public yet."

Peter closed his eyes, trying to rein in all the information before him. After a few seconds, he started, "Aren't you involved with Senator Jenkins? Why not just go to him and ask him to come forward with this?"

"Really, Dad, do you think that Bobby would put his life on the line like that?" Sean replied.

"I encouraged him to do so. It wasn't a pleasant discussion," Nicole informed Peter. "Which leads me to my next request: I would like to ask for asylum."

"Asylum?" Peter questioned.

"If I expose this tape, I'm exposing evidence that is in the hands of the Intelligence Committee chairman. They could extradite me and charge me with espionage."

Peter smiled and said, "I take it you and Bobby are no longer an item, as they say?"

Nicole sidestepped the question. "Sean and I differ on this, but I feel Bobby threatened me. I wanted him to make this tape public."

"Yes, well, I can understand you not agreeing on that point." Peter took another drink. "My office can certainly facilitate the asylum request with the Border Agency; however, I'm not so sure you should make this public."

"Good luck with that one," Sean said with a chuckle. "I've been trying to convince her for days."

"I just need to know a name of someone you trust in the media here," Nicole stated. "Norman Sipes was no friend of mine, but he says on the tape that he wasn't about to let the others escape without some kind of retribution. I agree with him. Sipes is dead. I will not allow Stevens to win reelection as a payoff for this crime. He has committed murder and treason; he does not deserve to be president. The others deserve the same fate as Stevens. They need to be charged with their crimes and stand trial, just like anyone else would." Nicole paused for a second. "It's obvious that they planned for Sipes to be killed by the Serpent, and they clearly planned to blame Sipes for the assassination. I can't let it end there. I don't expect you to understand this. I just can't." Nicole ended with a shrug of her shoulders, shaking her head.

"Do you plan on just surprising Bobby with your announcement?" Peter asked.

"No, I'm going to call him, and we need to warn Kevin about Kent as well," Nicole explained. "I want to be able to tell Bobby that I am asking for asylum and that the process has started."

"It's started," Peter verified. "I won't allow an extradition to start." Sean smiled, knowing his father was powerful, but not powerful enough to stop an extradition without the proper process being followed. "I see your smile, Sean. I'll be talking to the prime minister tomorrow."

"No, Dad," Sean protested.

"How else can I be sure that the extradition request from the United States gets squashed? The minute that the content on this tape is viewed, Stevens will be calling for her head." Peter stood up and refilled his glass. "Isn't there some way we can back channel this thing and force Stevens to step down?"

"What would you do if someone came to you with evidence that the prime minister committed a felony, and it is completely viable to keep his name clean and blame it on some other bloke?" Sean asked. "Now, add in that the United States has the information and wants you to do something about it."

Peter snickered. "I suppose I'd tell them to f-off." Peter sat down, smiled, and took a drink. "You are putting your life in danger, Nicole. Beyond that, your life may never be the same. I doubt you will ever be allowed to return to the United States."

"I think that depends on what Bobby does," Nicole countered. "If Bobby does confirm the tape and uses the opportunity to charge the other four men, then I might be able to return sometime in the future." Nicole looked at Peter and Sean, both of whom had skeptical looks on their faces. "If not, I'm all right with living in England." She looked at Sean.

Peter watched the exchange between them. "Does Bobby know you have feelings for my son?"

Sean was about to answer when Nicole interrupted him. "He knows I care for Sean. He has always known that. And just to be clear, Lord Adkins, I'm no longer in a relationship with Bobby. When he threatened me, that relationship stopped." Nicole paused. "I won't be manhandled by anyone in a position of power just for that person's political gain. Bobby's feelings may have been sincere at one point, but I can't be with someone who doesn't see what the right path is on this issue. He isn't the man I thought he was."

Peter stared at Nicole, who did not squirm under his scrutiny. "Do I get to see this tape?"

"You may see it whenever you like," Nicole responded.

"Tomorrow morning in my office," Peter stated. "Be there around ten, and I will have the others assembled then as well."

"The others?" Sean questioned.

"Yes, someone from the agency to start her asylum, and I think the prime minister may want to join us as well. Perhaps we should call Bobby at that time, too."

Sean looked at his father. "I suppose there is no talking you out of this."

"There is as much of a chance of that as talking Nicole out of exposing this tape," Peter retorted. "Are you sure you don't want something to drink?"

{II}

Sean and Nicole drove back to Sean's flat in silence. Nicole was concentrating on what she might say to Jenkins when she called him.

She was annoyed that he had had her followed, but she should have realized he had connections around the world. She knew his reaction to what she was planning to do would seal their fate. Jenkins could hate her for the rest of his life. While Nicole knew she didn't love him as much as he loved her, she did care for him. She knew she was about to hurt him, but all this could have been avoided if he had exposed the tape when he received it.

The car stopped, and the lack of motion drew Nicole's attention as Sean turned off the engine. Sean and Nicole exited the car and walked to the flat. "Are you okay?" Sean asked as they got to the door. "You are awfully quiet."

"I'm fine," Nicole replied. It had stopped raining, but it was rather cold. Sean opened the door and allowed Nicole to step inside first. "I enjoyed hearing your father talk about how he met your mother," Nicole said. The foyer was dark, so she didn't move very far inside, not being too familiar with the layout of Sean's flat.

Sean closed the door and in a soft voice replied, "He misses her so much." To Nicole's right was the light switch. Sean reached around her to turn it on, fully expecting Nicole to step back. She didn't move. Their bodies came close together, although they did not touch. Sean could smell her perfume and feel her warm breath caressing him as he leaned closer to the light switch. He paused. Should he take her in his arms? His body ached from the want of her. He slipped his right arm around her waist and pulled her closer to him. There was no resistance. His left arm was intercepted by Nicole who guided it to her waist. Their faces, their lips were so close. Sean hesitated.

Nicole brushed her lips gently against his, and then pulled them back ever so slightly. It was a quick brush, teasing him to take her. Her body tingled from head to toe, something she had never felt before. It was mysterious and exciting. There was a brief pause, and then Sean pulled her even closer, bending her back slightly as she melted in his arms. Their lips met as Sean tried to bring Nicole's physical body as close to him as he could. It was a brief kiss. Then Sean kissed her again, deeply this time. Nicole parted her lips. The tingling intensified with a warm energy that she had never experienced before. It was only a kiss, but it felt as if they were already one on another level. It felt as if their souls were dancing and intermingling as if there was no physical body between them. The kiss ended, but the tingling that radiated out from her chest and throughout her body continued. She kissed Sean's neck and removed his coat. He did the same to her, their bodies staying as close as possible throughout the process. They fell into another kiss.

Sean pulled his head back from Nicole. Their eyes had adjusted to the darkness of the foyer. "Are you sure?" Sean asked.

Nicole didn't answer with words. She caressed Sean's cheek, moving her hand to teasingly play with his hair. Then, she kissed him passionately on the lips, her mouth parted again, and her tongue traced Sean's lips. She hugged him tightly. When the kiss ended, she kissed his neck, nibbled his ear and in a breathy whisper cooed. "I'm sure. Are you?"

"Since the day I first met you in that trashy nightclub," Sean whispered. Sean heard that seductive laugh that made his desire leap. He ran his hand up Nicole's naked back and then down her arm. He took her hand and led her up the stairs to his bedroom. He closed the door behind them as he recalled his dream of removing the violet dress from Nicole's body. That dream was finally coming true.

Chapter Eight

End of March 1980

Jenkins was sitting in the green room with Thompson and Barker, feeling utterly defeated. Barker was in full command of his campaign, and he felt like a puppet. Barker was already making plans to set himself up as Jenkins's vice president. Jenkins was wondering if there was any way out. He was waiting to make a campaign speech at a rally in Kansas City. With the Kansas primary falling on April Fool's Day, only a few days away, Jenkins felt like his whole campaign was a sham.

The phone rang. Thompson, who was standing by it, picked it up. "Jenkins for president," he said. He paused as he listened to the voice on the other end. "Just a second. Sir, it's Chris. He says he has a call for you that you need to take."

"Now? No," Barker snapped with displeasure. "Bobby needs to go onstage in a few minutes."

"Chris says you would want to hear from this person," Thompson prodded. Jenkins looked at Thompson and raised an eyebrow. "It's Nikki."

Jenkins jumped out of his chair with the most energy anyone had seen from him in weeks. He grabbed the phone. "Put her on, Chris." Jenkins waited until he heard Nicole's voice. "Hello, Nikki. How is Paris? It's so good to hear your voice."

"I'm not in Paris, Bobby," Nicole replied. "I'm in London."

"London, what are you doing in London?" Jenkins asked. He could think of only one reason why she would be in London. "Is Sean with you?"

"Hello, Bobby," Sean interjected. He was on the extension. "Is there a way for Thompson to be on the call?"

"No," Jenkins snapped. The rising anger was apparent in his voice. "What's going on, Nikki?"

"There are a couple of things going on that you need to know about. First, the reason we wanted to talk to Thompson—"

Sean interrupted her. "We'll talk to Thompson after this, Nicole. I'm sure Bobby will be good enough to pass the phone to him when you are done."

"Yes, of course," Nicole said. "Bobby, I'm going on the BBC's morning show in a couple of days to show the confession tape."

"What?!" Jenkins exploded. "Nikki, you can't do that! You'll ruin this for me. You'll ruin *me*! Please, I beg of you, don't do this. Let me handle this." Jenkins's pleading caught Barker's attention. "I need to go onstage now. Give me some time to handle this in the right way. Can't you do that?"

"No, Bobby. I've asked for asylum. This needs to come out before the American public votes for their next president. I'm sorry. I have to do this."

"Jesus Christ, Nikki! You are so damn stubborn! You know there is nothing I won't do to stop you!" Jenkins yelled into the phone. Everyone in the room was stunned.

"I know," Nicole said. She looked at Sean with tears in her eyes. Her voice cracked. "I guess we have nothing more to say. Can you put Thompson on the phone for Sean, please?"

"Why, so you can do some kind of counterplot or something?" Jenkins was still angry, and the hatred could be heard rumbling from deep within him.

"No, Kent escaped..." Nicole couldn't stand hearing the hatred in Jenkins's voice any longer. "I'm sorry. Kevin needs to know..." She hung up the phone.

Sean took over the conversation. "This shouldn't be that big of a surprise to you, Bobby. You know she'll always do the right thing."

"Fuck you," Jenkins said bitterly.

Sean shook his head. "I'd like to tell Thompson about Kent. His life could be in danger."

"I'm supposed to believe you give a shit about anyone's life?" Jenkins handed the phone to Thompson. "He wants to talk to you."

Thompson looked confused as he took the phone from Jenkins. "Yeah?"

"Kevin, Kent has escaped from prison and is assuming the identity of the Serpent. He made it clear he was going to come after us. We haven't gathered any intelligence yet that confirms that your life is in danger but thought you might want to know."

"OK, thanks," Thompson replied. "I'll get back in touch after I do some checking over on this side of the pond." Thompson hung up the phone and watched Jenkins storm from the room with a confounded Barker trailing him.

{II}

Andrew Fitzsimmons, who had met with Nicole several times over the past few days, was the best in British broadcasting and lead interviewer on the *Today Programme*. Nicole was escorted to the stage from the green room where she met up with Sean. Sean had accompanied the tape to the production room where a copy had been made. He handed the original tape back to Nicole, who secured it in her purse. She walked to the stage where the sound technician fitted a microphone to her dress. Andrew walked from another stage to where Nicole was seated behind a counter that separated Andrew from her. He smiled as he approached and extended his hand. "Good to see you again, Nicole."

She shook his hand. She felt the dryness in her throat as she started to answer. "Morning," was all that managed to come out of her mouth.

"Can we get some water for Ms. Charbonneau?" Andrew called out. An intern scurried away to retrieve the water. "Try to relax. I know that is easier said than done but just pretend that we are in my office, talking like we have done over the past few days."

"Thirty seconds," the stage manager called out. The intern placed the glass of water next to Nicole. She took a drink and placed it to her right. "Five seconds, four, three…" the stage manager's voice trailed off, counting the last two seconds quietly.

"Welcome back. You have seen the promos over the past few days, and we've been chattering on about this interview all morning," Andrew started. The camera pulled out to show them both. Nicole sat up straight and tried to look professional. "A few days ago, I met a rather extraordinary woman who showed me an even more extraordinary taped confession. I'd like to welcome Ms. Nicole Charbonneau to the show.

Of course, some of us know her because of her relationship with presidential candidate, Senator Robert Jenkins. Good morning, Nicole."

"Good morning," Nicole responded. She swallowed, trying to keep her throat from drying.

Andrew could see that Nicole was nervous and thought a little chitchat would loosen her up. "How is Senator Jenkins doing?"

Nicole looked at Andrew slightly confused. "I haven't seen the senator for a couple of weeks now, but I suppose he is doing well."

"Yes, of course. Let's jump to the reason you are here. You obtained a rather interesting recording, a taped confession. Can you tell us before we run the tape, how you obtained it?"

"The tape was sent to me by my colleague, Tony Shafer. It was mailed to me at my residence in Washington, DC," Nicole stated. "Included with the tape was a notarized affidavit from Mr. Shafer, which explained how he acquired the tape."

"Can you share what that letter said?" Andrew asked.

"The letter said that Norman Sipes, CEO of Sipes Oil Company, and who was killed a few days following President Andrews's assassination..." Nicole paused for a second. "It was Mr. Sipes's butler who delivered the tape to Mr. Shafer. The butler was instructed to do so by Mr. Sipes in the event of his death."

"Mr. Sipes was murdered?" Andrew asked.

"Yes, he was killed at his residence. A bomb exploded when he started his car," Nicole explained.

"I think this is a good time to show the tape to our audience. Without the tape, it might be a bit confusing to our audience to ask any further questions." Nicole nodded in agreement. This was it. The whole world would see this tape now. Andrew turned to the camera. "Take a look at this and then we'll have more questions for Ms. Charbonneau." The stage manager indicated the tape was rolling.

Nicole glanced at the monitor. Norman Sipes was toasting Tony and urging him to get his yellow notepad. She looked at Sean, who gave an encouraging smile. She then turned her attention to Andrew.

"You're doing fine," Andrew said. "Just answer the questions like you did the other day in rehearsal." Nicole gave a nervous smile and acknowledged Andrew's comment. She took another sip of water. She wondered how long it would take before the media descended on Jenkins. The tape ended, and the stage manager pointed to Andrew. "This is shocking, to say the least. It's a taped confession and states very clearly who ordered the assassination of President Andrews."

"Yes, that's correct."

"What is being done about this—to your knowledge?" Andrew asked.

"To my knowledge, nothing is being done about this. Mr. Shafer made a copy of the tape, which he gave to Senator Jenkins the day following the murder of Mr. Sipes. I am not privy to what Senator Jenkins or his investigation is doing with this tape."

"Senator Jenkins has a copy of this tape?"

"Yes."

"Nicole, you were in a relationship with the senator. Did you not bring this to his attention?"

"Yes, but to my knowledge, nothing has been done with it. I truly believe that no one else knew about this tape except Tony and Senator Jenkins. I don't know what the senator's intentions were in regards to this tape."

"Does Senator Jenkins know you are here?"

"I informed him a few days ago, that I was going to air the tape," Nicole replied. "He wasn't too happy with me."

Andrew gave a little laugh. "I should say not. Nicole, you are risking your life bringing this tape out in the open. Why are you doing this? What do you hope to gain?"

Nicole didn't flinch even though more butterflies launched in her stomach. She felt queasy but held her head high. "Mr. Shafer and I want one thing to happen: The murderers of President Andrews to be charged and tried for their crimes. It is believed that my friend and former colleague, Tony Shafer, is now dead. As you just heard, this tape provides damning evidence that President Stevens, Representative Davis, FBI Director Michael Jefferies, and wealthy businessman Joseph Engle are involved. There are those who want to sweep this tape and other evidence under the rug, giving our government a get-out-of-jail-free card. No government official, no officeholder—even if it is the president of the United States—should be above the law." Nicole took a quick breath. "I left the United States a few weeks ago because I couldn't be part of this cover-up. It became clear to me over the past few months that Senator Larry Barker was tying Senator Jenkins's hands. I'm not sure of all the details, but I know that Senator Jenkins wants to do the right thing and announce the findings of his investigation. I want the people of the United States to know what happened and who plotted the assassination. I want them to have this information before the next election. I want those who committed this heinous act to be brought to justice. With the tape now in public domain, the US government is forced to deal with this tragedy. I'm not naïve. I know there are many cover-ups or conspiracies created by governments for the good of the sovereign nation, but this is one conspiracy that can't be pushed aside."

"This is just unbelievable! A vice president at the time, a representative and the FBI director all plotted this assassination." Andrew looked at Nicole incredulously. "What are you going to do next? You can't go back to the United States."

"I've asked the British government for asylum. I love my country, but I can't keep this a secret any longer. Tony Shafer would not want this to be brushed aside, and he was good friends with three of the conspirators."

"Did he know about the plot prior to its execution?"

Nicole smiled. "Interesting choice of words—no he did not. Tony and I had a rather strange conversation the last time I saw him alive. He made it clear he was not involved in the plot and, since finding out about it, had ended his friendships. This tape cost Mr. Shafer his life."

"Don't you want to be able to return to the United States if these men are tried and found guilty?"

"I'm sure that the US government would like to extradite me and that is why I sought asylum. I would love to return to the United States someday. After today, my life will certainly change." Nicole paused, looked down, and then back at Andrew. "I just want justice."

"Thank you." Andrew reached over to shake Nicole's hand.

She accepted his hand and said, "Thank you for the opportunity to start the wheels of justice turning hopefully."

"I think there are many who, in the long run, owe a debt to you." Andrew turned to the camera, which zoomed in on him. "We'll be back after this short break."

The stage manager signaled they were off the air. Nicole remained silent and removed her microphone. After thanking Nicole again, Andrew was off to another staged area for the next segment of the show. He managed to catch Nicole's eye, and he placed his hand over his heart. He then gave the thumbs up and smiled. Nicole returned his smile.

She laid the microphone on the counter as the director and others informed the crew that the switchboard was lighting up with callers. She grabbed her purse, which contained the original tape, and secured its handles over her shoulder. Nicole walked off the stage and into the arms of Sean.

"Let's get out of here," Sean said as he turned, keeping his arm around her to lead her out of the soundstage.

Sean had arranged for his father's car and chauffeur to wait for them outside the entrance to the studio. There was a roped-off area, keeping the crowds out of the way on their path to the car. An endless number of reporters had gathered outside the studio entrance waiting for Nicole to exit.

Upon exiting the building, the reporters were calling her name, trying to get her to stop. Sean and Nicole were hurrying to the car when Nicole thought she heard a familiar voice call her name. She turned instantly, slipping out of Sean's arms, to look behind her. Sean stopped immediately, turning to gather Nicole back in his arms. They were a few feet from the car's open door, manned by the chauffeur. All of a sudden, the right side of Nicole's neck, where it met her shoulder, had a feeling of searing, intense heat followed by excruciating pain. She reached her hand up as she heard everyone scream. Sean looked at Nicole and saw blood streaming out of Nicole's neck area. Nicole looked at her hand. Her eyes widened as she saw the blood and it dawned on her that she had been shot. She started to feel faint, and her knees started to buckle as Sean grabbed her wrist, pulling her into his arms. Nicole collapsed as Sean swept his other arm under her knees. Carrying her, he moved quickly to the car. Sean noticed the chauffeur was already moving to the driver's seat, and with Nicole still in his arms, he dove into the backseat. He grabbed at the door, shutting it, while he screamed at his father's chauffeur to get them to the nearest hospital.

Sean applied pressure to the wound, which was bleeding profusely. Nicole's eyes were open looking at Sean. He could see the fear in her eyes. "You're going to be okay," he reassured her. Nicole didn't blink. She continued to stare at Sean and tried to speak. "No, don't speak. Just keep looking at me. You're going to be okay. Do you hear me?" Sean's voice had a commanding tone to it. "You keep looking at me!"

Nicole could tell she was losing consciousness. Sean's hands were covered in her blood, and the cuffs of his white shirt were quickly becoming red. She felt cold, and she knew that she would not be awake for much longer. A tear rolled down her cheek as the thought of leaving Sean became a reality to her. She tried to speak again and Sean, whose own eyes were tearing up, leaned in close to her. Nicole whispered, "I...love...you..." A tear ran down her cheek.

"If you love me, then fight to stay here, Nicole," Sean said to her as he applied more pressure on the wound. "Do you hear me? Don't you leave me!" Sean maneuvered his hands to keep applying more pressure. "Stay with me, Nicole. I love you, and I can't lose you!" Nicole's eyes began to flutter as consciousness began to leave her. "Nicole!" Sean shouted. Her eyes fluttered open again. "Damn it, Nicole; you stay awake!"

It seemed like an eternity, but finally, the car swung wide around a corner, narrowly missing other cars, and into the emergency drive of the nearest hospital. The chauffeur stopped the car and placed it in park while opening the door. He ran into the hospital and shouted that he had a dying woman in his car and demanded immediate assistance. He grabbed a nearby gurney and started to roll it out to the car. Nurses followed along, and when the backseat door opened, rushed toward it. They awkwardly managed to get Nicole on the gurney as Sean kept applying pressure. As they got to the surgery room doors, another nurse removed Sean's hand, replacing them with her own. "We've got it from here."

Another nurse came up to Sean and directed him to a nearby chair. Sean slumped into it, bringing his blood-soaked hands up to his head. It was then that he noticed all the blood. It was on his shirt, hands, pants, and jacket. *How can she survive this?* The thought was debilitating. He sat staring at his hands as the memory of Sarah infiltrated his mind. Was he going to lose another woman he loved? He didn't think he could stand it again.

A nurse walked by and saw him staring at his blood-soaked hands. Grabbing a towel off a nearby cart, she hurried into a water closet. She wet the towel, wringing the excess water out, and ran back over to Sean. "Here, let's take care of that. Are you hurt?" She knelt down before Sean, taking one of his hands and began to clean off the blood. Sean shook his head. "Is she in there? Is it your wife?" the nurse asked, her head pointing to the doors—the same doors Nicole's gurney crashed through only a short time ago.

"Yes," Sean confirmed. Everything seemed so surreal, and he knew he was in shock. He didn't want this attention, and he certainly didn't want to speak to a stranger.

"She's in good hands." The nurse continued to clean Sean's hand when Sean's father and brother entered the hallway.

"Sean," Peter called. Sean stood up, revealing all the blood on his clothes and his other hand. "Oh, dear God, are you hurt?" Peter walked briskly; Geoffrey was right behind him, into his son's arms

"I'm not. It's Nicole," Sean said. "She's been shot."

Peter noticed Sean's body temperature. "You're freezing cold. Are you sure you haven't been shot or injured?" Peter stepped back, looking over Sean's body.

"I'm not, Dad. I'm just in shock. I have no idea who…" Sean looked his father in the eyes. Tears formed again. "I can't lose her. I can't go through this again." Geoffrey put his hand on his brother's shoulder.

"Let's hope you don't have to do so," Peter said. He held his son once more. He released Sean and took him by the arm, walking him back to his chair. "Can you tell me what happened?"

Sean sat down and rested his head against the wall. He was trying to envision the scene. "She had finished the interview, and we were walking to your car." He lifted his head from the wall and looked at his father. "Your car…it's probably a mess."

"I'm not worried about that," Peter replied.

"Nicole turned suddenly back toward the building. I'm not sure why, but when she did, she was out away from me, just barely out of my reach." Sean thought for a few seconds. "The shot had to have come from my left. I didn't hear the gunshot. There were so many people yelling questions and calling her name. Then when she started to bleed, there were screams, and I turned as she started to collapse. I grabbed her and basically threw both of us into the car. Your driver was marvelous and got us here as quick as he could."

"Where was she shot, Sean?" Geoffrey asked.

"Her neck," Sean answered. "I was applying pressure here." Sean pointed to his neck and shoulder area. "Shouldn't there be some news by now? It seems like I've been here for a long time."

"Well, maybe it is good that there is no news yet," Geoffrey said optimistically.

Sean acknowledged his statement with a quick nod. He looked at the doors and wished there was some kind of window he could peer through.

"I hate to ask this, Sean, but do you have any idea who might have done this? Did you see anyone or anything?" Peter asked.

"I didn't see anyone. As for who might have done it—Barker, Stevens, Jefferies, Jenkins…" He stood up. He then paused, furrowing his brow as he looked at the doors. "Kent."

"Kent?" Peter asked.

"The shot was to her neck. It was meant to paralyze her just as it did Andrews. But she turned, and everything went too fast. I wasn't holding her so he couldn't get the second shot off."

"You don't know that for sure," Peter said. "Isn't it a bit early for Kent to have gotten everything together?"

"I don't know," Sean uttered helplessly.

"Do you think that Jefferies or Jenkins could have had someone mobilized in these few days?" Peter asked.

Sean looked at his father. "You're joking, right? Of course, they could have—especially if he had help over here." Sean paused.

"But why shoot her afterward? It would have been better for her to be killed before the tape was exposed," Geoffrey added.

Sean was about to agree when a nurse who worked the check-in process reticently walked up to the men. She was holding a clipboard and pen. "Excuse me, sir," She was speaking to Sean. "You were with the redheaded lady who had the gunshot wound?"

"Yes."

"I know this isn't the best time, but if you could fill this out..." She extended the clipboard and pen. "We need her information for our records."

Geoffrey intercepted the items. "Thank you. We'll do the best we can."

The nurse smiled, "Lord Adkins, they wanted me to tell you that there is a room with a little more privacy if you would like to follow me."

"Yes, yes," Peter replied. "That would be wonderful."

They followed the nurse out of the hallway and back to the emergency waiting room. It was full of reporters and others who had seen the incident and wanted to provide support in some way. Just as Sean started to round the corner, his blood-soaked clothes drew the attention of the cameras. Light flashes were exploding, and Sean tried to shield his face. They entered the private room and shut the door behind them.

Geoffrey was looking at the clipboard. All he had written was Nicole's first name. "Two n's in Charbonneau?"

"Yes," Sean confirmed.

"I'm afraid that's all I know about her," Geoffrey stated. Sean walked over to look over Geoffrey's shoulder.

Sean sighed, "I can drive to her house in DC, but I have no idea what the street number is. I don't know her insurance carrier or any of that."

"They'll just have to wait," Peter said, taking the clipboard from Geoffrey and setting it on the table.

"Dad, if she survives, we'll need some protection," Sean stated.

"Yes, well, I'm sure the police will be glad to lend a hand," Peter agreed. Just as Peter finished speaking, a surgeon with blood on his green surgery garb opened the door and walked into the room.

Sean felt his knees begin to crumble. He collapsed into the chair next to Geoffrey. Geoffrey placed his hand on Sean's forearm that was resting on the arm of the chair. Sean swallowed hard trying to control his wildly swinging emotions. The doctor walked to the end of the table and sat down.

"Gentlemen," he started and then noticed Peter. "Oh, terribly sorry, sir." He was about to stand when Peter waved it off, telling him to continue. "The bullet went through her. It grazed her collarbone, which changed the trajectory, only nicking the artery." He looked at Sean. "She lost a lot of blood because there were two wounds." The surgeon pointed to his shoulder area. "The bullet exited out the back of the lower part of her neck—where the neck and shoulder meet. Once we got the artery repaired, we managed to start pumping blood into her rather quickly. She's very weak but stable." Sean felt the air leave his lungs. He closed eyes and said a quiet thank you. "We're moving her to ICU."

"Can I see her?" Sean asked.

"Not right this moment. We need to get her situated and make sure she stays stable. I would give them about thirty minutes. You should be able to visit her in ICU."

"I'd like to request that security be posted outside of entrances into ICU, and only those with the proper credentials be admitted. You see, she is a person of some importance and has asked for asylum here in the UK," Peter asserted. The surgeon informed Peter that could be worked out with the hospital's head of security, who was out in the emergency waiting room dealing with the press. Peter nodded and handed him the clipboard. "I'm afraid we weren't much help on that piece of paper there."

"We'll worry about that later. Her name helps. I'm sure hearing all your voices will help her as well." The surgeon stood up.

"Thank you," Sean said.

The surgeon walked up to him. "The pressure you applied gave her a fighting chance. Prepare yourself. When you walk into ICU, she will have tubes running everywhere. It will be quite a shock."

Sean acknowledged his comment with a quick nod. "Thank you again."

The surgeon left the room. Sean took a deep breath and let out a sigh of relief. Geoffrey and Peter both hugged him. "I'll run by your place and get you some clean clothes," Geoffrey said.

"No," Sean countered. "No one goes near my flat until we figure out who did this. I assume the police are working on the crime scene. That bullet has to be somewhere."

"It may be a while before we know anything and you need some clothes," Geoffrey insisted.

"Just buy me some," He opened his wallet and pulled out some cash. "Here."

"We'll settle up later," Geoffrey said, denying the offer. "Anything in particular you want?" Sean said that there wasn't and provided Geoffrey with his sizes. "Maybe the nurses will let you shower in one of the rooms."

"That's the least of my worries right now," Sean said. "I need to get up to ICU."

"And I'm going to line up her protection," Peter added.

They all left the room, Peter finding the head of security and Geoffrey leaving the hospital to secure some clothes. Sean found his way to ICU. He entered the locked-down unit only after identifying himself and the patient he wanted to see. They were still getting Nicole situated in her room, resulting in Sean having to wait outside on a row of three chairs just inside the doors. Finally, a nurse greeted him.

She led him down the bustling hallway. Before reaching the room, she stopped to prepare Sean. "Nicole is unconscious. She has a number of tubes running everywhere, and she is currently on a respirator. This may shock you. I want to make sure you are prepared for this."

Sean smiled and nodded his head. She started to walk a little farther, stopped by the open doorway, and motioned that he should enter. Sean wasn't aware that he was holding his breath, but he was. He exhaled and took a few more steps.

"She can hear you, and we encourage you to touch her—hold her hand and, above all, talk to her." The nurse noticed the blood on his clothes. "There's a shower down the hall, and we can get you some scrubs until you can get a change of clothes."

Sean looked at the nurse and then at Nicole. He was blinking his eyes repeatedly, although no tears were forming. It was as if he was in some dream that he desperately wanted to wake up from to find Nicole perfectly healthy and in his arms. And then it hit him. He had failed her. He failed to keep her safe. He promised her that he would keep her safe. *Look at her!* Sean looked down at the floor and then back at Nicole. His lower jaw moved side to side in agony that he couldn't describe. He bit his lower lip so that the scream of anguish deep within him would not escape. Sean heard a voice—the nurse's voice—encouraging him to hold her hand. He slowly moved to her bedside. He couldn't talk yet; the scream was too close to the surface. The agony, his agony, was like a freshly torn open wound. *Damn them! Damn Jenkins! Damn Jefferies! Damn Kent! Damn whoever did this!*

There was more urging from the nurse. "It's OK. You can talk to her. Just say her name or hold her hand. Let her know you are here."

Sean was at the side of the bed now. Nicole's hand was within his reach. The respirator was clicking away forcing air in and out of her lungs. He looked at the machine. He hated the noise it made. "Will she need to be on that for long?" Sean asked.

"It depends on how quickly she recovers consciousness." The nurse gave Sean an encouraging smile. "We're just helping her breathe and helping with other functions so that she can concentrate on healing."

It was a nice try to explain it that way, but Sean didn't believe for a minute that Nicole was out of danger. He recalled the doctor reporting that Nicole was in stable condition. He wondered if she was in stable condition thanks to the many machines. He reached down and gently touched Nicole's hand. While Nicole's fingers felt cold to his touch, the heart-rate monitor told another story.

"Did you see that?" the nurse asked. She grabbed the endless stream of paper from the machine. "We rarely see this, but I love when it happens." She held the paper for Sean to see. "She knows it is you. Look, her heart jumped when you touched her. Here..." The nurse pointed to the spike on the sheet. "She knows it is you. Remember, she can hear you." With that last urging for Sean to speak, the nurse left the room.

Sean pulled a chair over so that he could sit and hold Nicole's hand. He slid one hand under hers and wrapped his fingers around the palm of her hand. He watched the heart monitor as it reacted to his touch. He gently laid his other hand on top of hers, fully engulfing her hand in his. Another spike on the monitor appeared. Dare he talk to her? What should he say? He paused, looking at her face. He noticed her cinnamon-red hair was pulled to her left side, but the length was still intact. "I'm so sorry, Nicole," Sean whispered quietly and calmly. "I failed you. I failed to keep you safe." He lowered his head to her hand and kissed it. He laid his head next to her hand, his breath caressing her fingers. He fought back the tears. He told himself that she was going to make it back to him. She had to make it back to him. In a low, barely audible voice, he said, "Don't leave me, Nicole."

{III}

Jenkins sat in his hotel room in Kansas City and watched the interview that was being replayed during the morning shows across the United States. He listened intently to what was being said. He watched the confession tape that had been his secret until a few weeks ago when Nicole announced to him that she had seen it.

There was a loud banging on the door, and he knew it was Barker. He stood up and walked to the door. He opened it as the impatient senior senator forced his way through it. "What in the hell were you thinking?!" Barker screamed.

"Good morning, Larry." The calm voice of Mercer froze Barker in his tracks. He turned slowly to see him sitting at a small table on the other side of the room.

"Daniel, when did you get here?" Barker asked calmly as he walked toward Mercer.

"I received a call from Bobby a few days ago. I told him then that I would meet him here." Mercer did not stand nor did he shake Barker's hand. "Sit down." Barker was about to protest when Mercer more forcefully stated, "Sit down."

Barker sat in the chair closest to him. Jenkins walked to the bed and sat on the corner of it. Mercer looked at Jenkins then at Barker. "Bobby told me that you have been holding some information about his service over him, using this information to force him to run your campaign."

"I don't think that is the story we should be talking about here. Didn't you see the news?" Barker demanded.

"Yes, Bobby and I were just watching that," Mercer returned. "Larry, we go back a long way, and I've never doubted for a minute that if you could get close to the presidency, you wouldn't hesitate to take advantage of the opportunity. Of course, that unfortunate misstep during your first term would, if discovered, keep you from reaching that office." Mercer looked at Barker who was scornfully glaring at him. "And just so that we can keep everything on equal ground, I took the privilege of informing Bobby here of our little secret."

Barker looked over at Jenkins who was not smiling. Jenkins detested the dirty side of politics, but he never let those feelings known. "I remember sitting at your dinner table a few weeks back, and your lovely wife made a comment to me that I didn't understand at the time," Jenkins started. "She said to me that she hoped that I would never hurt Nikki so much that she would lose the love she has for me. I had to wonder just what you did to Louise that caused her to lose that love for you." Jenkins smiled. "I have to give Louise an incredible amount of acknowledgment to forgive you for that affair that you had, but I don't know how you repay a woman who raised another woman's son for you. It explains everything: how she looks at you and how you treat each other as business partners. And just where did your lover disappear to? We don't need to say what happened to her out loud, but I do know. I have to say; I am getting tired of your holier-than-thou attitude."

Barker looked at Mercer, who was the only man who knew Barker's secret. Mercer said nothing but returned the stare without blinking. After a few moments, Barker began to speak calmly. "I'm not sure what you gentlemen are up to, but in case you didn't notice, that little filly of yours just blew this whole campaign to hell."

"No, she didn't," Mercer countered. "Bobby and I will take care of that. And we'll take care of Bobby's Vietnam problem, too." Mercer picked up a Styrofoam cup and took a drink of coffee. "You, however, are done with this campaign. Pack your bags and get the hell out of here."

"I was the backbone of this campaign. Without me, Bobby wouldn't be the front-runner, and you know it! I got him his backing, and as soon as I get back to Washington, that just might dry up."

Mercer shrugged his shoulders and tilted his head. "Only if you want your secret spread all over the newspapers and television. I would hate to see Louise hurt again." Mercer gave a sly grin. "If I were you, I wouldn't give her the opportunity to speak to that issue. You just don't know what she might have to say. Of course, your son has only ever known one mother." Barker looked at Mercer. His question appeared on his face. "You're out, Larry," Mercer said, confirming the unanswered question. "I'd have no problem exposing not only what happened all those years ago to anyone who needs to know, but also how you manipulated our very powerful friend here." He nodded to Jenkins. "Am I clear?"

"Fuck you both," Barker said as he stood and walked to the door. "I'm not done yet. I'm just done with you two."

"I'd be careful if I were you," Mercer said. "My staff is looking over your affairs as we speak. I wouldn't be surprised if they found some suspicious money deals..." his voice trailed off as Barker walked out of the room, slamming the door behind him.

"Are there any?" Jenkins asked. "Suspicious money deals?"

Mercer laughed. "There always are." He took another drink of coffee. "Now, we need to deal with this tape and its ramifications, but I don't want us to make an official announcement until after President Stevens plays his cards."

"I have a campaign rally to attend in about two hours," Jenkins informed him.

"No, you don't. We need to head back to Washington. You have an Investigation Committee hearing to organize and evidence to assemble. The subpoenas will be served in a few hours. My plane is waiting at the airport, ready to go." Mercer finished his coffee and threw the cup in the garbage can.

Jenkins stood up to turn off the television when he heard, "This just came in…oh, dear." The news anchor read over the report silently. "I'm sorry. I'm so very sorry to report that Ms. Nicole Charbonneau has been shot. She was rushed to the hospital, and we have no further information at this time." Jenkins stiffened as he heard the words. He turned off the television. Slowly he turned to face Mercer, who had been putting on his overcoat when the announcement came. After exchanging a look with each other, Mercer finished putting on his coat.

"Let's get back to Washington where we can get more information." Mercer started for the door.

Jenkins grabbed his coat and suitcase, falling in behind Mercer. Thompson was walking down the hall joining up with Jenkins and Mercer. Thompson was surprised to see Mercer but was much more worried about Nicole.

"Have you heard?" Thompson asked.

"Yes," Jenkins replied with no evident emotion. "We're heading back to Washington. I need you to cancel the rally and make my apologies. Call Chris; he can help you. I'll see you in Washington tonight." Thompson stopped and watched Jenkins go out the door to the limousine that was waiting. To say that Thompson was dumbfounded at the lack of emotion in Jenkins would be an understatement.

{IV}

Mercer and Jenkins arrived back in Washington, DC within a few hours. A limousine was waiting for them at the airport, the chauffeur standing by the open door as both men exited Mercer's chartered plane. After the two men were inside, he shut the car door and then drove them as quickly as he could to Capitol Hill.

As Jenkins entered his outer office, Chris was in the inner office, turning the television on. Jenkins and Mercer walked into the inner office.

"President Stevens is about to make a statement," Chris announced to the two men. He moved out of the way, and the three of them stood around the television waiting for the president's remarks.

"I hope he has enough sense just to resign," Mercer said. "Then it is just a matter of trying him in federal court."

Stevens was in a dark suit and looked very presidential. There was no smile on his face as there typically was when he addressed the nation. He looked very serious sitting behind his desk in the Oval Office. The fact he was broadcasting from there did not bode well for Mercer's hope. When he was given the signal, he began his speech.

"My fellow Americans, it is with a heavy heart that I must address this nation regarding a longtime associate's allegations that I was involved with the assassination of President Andrews. I believe I owe you the truth." Jenkins gave a little chuckle. He grabbed a chair and turned it around, encouraging Mercer and Chris to do the same. "Norman Sipes was a contributor to many of my campaigns from when I was a representative, senator, and vice president. However, Norman Sipes had some problems and an expectation that, in my capacity as vice president and president, I would help him in exchange for his financial support. Anyone who has attended the many White House dinners with Mr. Sipes knows that he also had a drinking problem. What most don't know is that Norman Sipes also had a money problem. Days before the assassination, Mr. Sipes came to me and asked for money. I denied that request. I had no idea that he was going to use that money to hire an assassin. Had I known, I would have had him arrested." Jenkins noted that Stevens was a bad actor. The index finger stabbing at the desk to emphasize his comments was almost hysterical.

"If you watch the so-called confession tape, you will see that Mr. Sipes was drinking and he addressed a man named Tony. His lawyer, Tony Shafer, and I were also very good friends. Tony represented me on a number of occasions, and I often sought his opinion. His advice was always sound, and we enjoyed a great friendship until I was reluctantly forced to fill the shoes of President Andrews. Mr. Shafer wanted to be my attorney general, but I explained to him that I was not making any Cabinet changes as I saw this as the fulfilling the goals of the Andrews administration. Tony and I grew apart because of that decision. He increasingly became angered that I would not appoint him to a Cabinet position. It would only make sense that Sipes would address this tape to a spurned, angry, and bitter man."

"You have no shame," Jenkins said to the television screen as he shook his head.

"But perhaps the hardest blow in these accusations came with Nicole Charbonneau's traitorous act. What I have to tell you now is not easy, and I must apologize to my wife for the hurt that I am about to cause her. I must confess here that the rumors about Ms. Charbonneau and me are true. I ended our relationship just before her chasing after Senator Jenkins, knowing that the popular senator was about to announce his campaign against me for the presidency. She wasn't happy about me breaking off the…"

"The man is delusional!" Jenkins exclaimed.

"…affair and she swore she would find some way to sabotage me. This is that way. I'm not proud of my actions, and I publicly apologize to

Katherine, who has stood by me even in the hardest of circumstances. Over the next couple of days, you will hear some accusations and calls for impeachment. I love my country, and I respect the power that accompanies this office. While some of my decisions on relationships may be called into question, I need to tell you now that I did not plot to kill President Andrews, and these accusations are the result of three people who have tried or are trying to blackmail me. I thank you for your time, and, rest assured that I will not allow this smear campaign to continue."

Chris walked over to the television and turned the sound down. Jenkins and Mercer sat with shocked looks on their faces.

"Tell me that the president didn't just blame this whole situation on two dead people and one in a hospital in London," Mercer said. He looked at Jenkins. "Tell me that you have evidence that shows without a doubt that Stevens knew about the plot."

Jenkins sat for a moment. He chose his words carefully. "I have evidence that Sipes was constructing an oil rig illegally in the ANWR before the speech where Andrews announced he would veto the bill. I have two witnesses who saw money being exchanged between Davis and Sipes." Jenkins left out that the two witnesses were in London, one in the hospital. "And now that we have subpoenaed Jefferies, I'm sure I can arrange a deal: the country club of prisons for Jefferies's confirmation that Stevens was involved. I can also subpoena the financial records of all involved now and follow the money."

"We have some of that already," Chris alerted the two men. "Thompson has been working on the money trail. I'm not sure if he was even looking at Stevens, though."

"He wasn't. He was looking at Jefferies," Jenkins corrected.

"The subpoenas for the arrests of Jefferies, Engle, and Davis have been served this morning. They are in custody. I'll have my aide call you with their locations. We need to question them and start pulling the evidence together," Mercer said, standing. "Right now, we need to address the press with our next steps. Bobby, I want you to lead the press conference. If a man who committed treason can look presidential, then we need our front-runner to show his strong leadership skills."

"Thank you for your help," Jenkins said gratefully.

"I am glad to be of service," Mercer replied. "Now, make me proud." Mercer shook Jenkins's hand. "Keep me informed, but you are leading this. I'll make sure Barker stays away from the spotlight."

Jenkins smiled. "Thank you again. Chris, inform the press that I will be making a statement shortly. One feed out of this office, behind my desk, so that it reminds the public that there are three branches of power in this democracy." Mercer smiled as he excused himself to leave for his office.

"Yes, sir," Chris said. He called out to two other office workers giving the command to move some furniture and straighten up the office. Chris went to make the appropriate phone calls.

{V}

An hour and a half later, Jenkins walked into his office to find the desk arranged with two photos behind it. One of the photos was of the White House, and the other was of Jenkins in his dress uniform. "No," he said as he walked into the office. "I don't want the photo of me in uniform. Take it down immediately." Chris moved without question and removed it. Jenkins walked into the outer office and grabbed the American flag and stand. He moved that to the left of his desk where his military photo had hung a few seconds before. "What happened to the painting of the eagle that used to hang…" his voice trailed off as he turned to search for it. Chris appeared through the door with it in his hands. "Yes, please. These two symbols are a much better message. Thank you."

"We need you to sit behind the desk, just like you would when you give your address," one of the cameramen said. Jenkins moved to his desk and sat down. The lights were adjusted to minimize shadows.

Jenkins was dressed in his navy blue suit, a favorite of Nicole's, with a white-with-blue pin-striped oxford shirt. He opted for a dark burgundy tie, knowing it would not clash with the colors in his office nor the desk chair.

There were two cameras and three light stands glaring at Jenkins as he sat calmly looking over his speech. His desk was clean except for his nameplate and a few typical desk items. Jenkins laid the speech down in front of him. "This shouldn't take too long," he said to the cameramen.

"Are you going to accept any questions?" one of them asked.

Jenkins looked around. "From whom?"

"The anchorman who will be interrupting the soap operas for your comments could ask questions. We can hook you up with an earpiece." The cameraman replied.

"No, no questions," Jenkins responded. "God forbid that I interrupt *Peyton Place*."

"I thought this place looked familiar." The cameraman joked inferring that Capitol Hill reminded him of a soap opera. "Get ready, Senator, they are coming to you in five, four, three…" He mouthed, "Two, one," and pointed to Jenkins.

"Good afternoon. As you heard earlier today from President Stevens, we have a very dynamic and unprecedented situation occurring. You may recall shortly after the assassination of President Andrews; I formed an Investigation Committee. Over the past few months, we have meticulously compiled evidence. Part of the evidence is, in fact, the confession tape of Mr. Norman Sipes that Ms. Charbonneau released to the press via the BBC earlier today. Please note the confession tape is only one piece of evidence that we have uncovered in this sophisticated plot."

Jenkins took a breath. "The unfortunate and premature airing of the confession tape prompts me to announce that we are forming a formal committee. The Select Investigative Committee on the Assassination of President Andrews will begin holding public sessions in a few days. Rest assured that warrants have been issued for Mr. Jefferies, Mr. Engle, and Representative Davis. As you may have seen on the news reports, they are now in custody. President Stevens will be impeached and will be subpoenaed to appear before the select committee. Senator Daniel Mercer and the Speaker of the House, Randy Davidson, will be working with this committee to begin impeachment proceedings. Since this is the first time a president could be involved in such a heinous act, our committee will be investigating the proper procedure to prosecute President Stevens if these allegations prove to be true."

"It is a dark day for the United States of America. I want to personally reassure everyone that we, the Congress, will act upon these charges with a full and proper investigation fully accessible to each citizen. I ask for your patience as we gather evidence and begin the committee process. Thank you."

"And we're out," the cameraman announced. Jenkins didn't say a word. He stood up, removed the microphone from his lapel, and walked out of his office.

Chapter Nine

April 1980

Nicole had been unconscious for just over two days now. Sean remained by her side the whole time. The nurses were kind enough to allow him to shower in different rooms close by, and Geoffrey had brought some new clothes, discarding the blood-stained ones.

Peter had arranged for security around the hospital and the ICU. He had called the nurse's station earlier in the day to let Sean know he was dropping by to see him. Sean walked out of the room to sit with Peter when he arrived. Sean was glad not to hear the repetitive noises of the machines that were helping Nicole grow stronger—or, at least, that was what the nurses kept telling him. He wanted to believe them.

Peter and Sean were going over some evidence recovered from the scene when Sean's attention was caught by rapid movement from the nurse's station, where three nurses had stood up and were running to Nicole's room. When Sean saw this, he quickly stood up and ran to the room as well, with Peter following a few steps behind. When Sean reached the room, he was amazed at the chaos.

"Nicole, relax, we have a tube down your throat to help you breathe," the nurse was saying, holding Nicole down with her hands. Nicole was awake and fighting the machine, trying to breathe on her own. It sounded as if she was choking as she fought the air being forced down her throat. The second nurse was trying to hold Nicole's head to keep her from moving it side to side. The third nurse was trying to hold the tube and keep Nicole still. All the machines were sounding alarms, causing quite a raucous. Nicole's eyes were wide open, and she was trying to cough. "Nicole, you have to settle down so that we can work on you."

Sean calmly but quickly walked over to the bedside and took her hand. "Nicole, I'm here." Sean bent over so that she could see his face, bringing her hand to his heart. "Nicole, look at me," Sean commanded. Her eyes focused on Sean. He smiled when he saw that she could see him. "Relax, sweetheart. You're going to be okay." He placed his free hand on her forehead and stroked her hair back. "It's good to see those brown eyes again."

The nurses began to work on Nicole while Sean kept her distracted. They worked around Sean as much as they could, and when the tube that was helping her to breathe was removed, the nurses were astonished that Sean didn't make any attempt to shield himself from the discomfort that Nicole was feeling. Nicole coughed a few times, and the head nurse announced that she was going to retrieve some ice to relieve some of the pain in her throat. The other two nurses turned off the alarms and reset the machines. The room finally became quiet.

When all the nurses had left the room, Nicole tried to speak. It was very painful, and her face grimaced from it. Sean urged her not to speak, but Nicole was insistent. Sean bent down so that his ear was close to her lips. "Who?"

Sean stood up. "We don't know," he replied. "I'm sorry."

Nicole closed her eyes and shook her head. She knew that he was expressing his sorrow for not protecting her. A tear ran from the side of her eye as she squeezed his hand. The nurse returned with a cup of ice shavings. She raised the head of Nicole's bed to a more upright position. "Maybe this handsome man of yours will be sweet enough to help you with this," the nurse said with a smile. "He hasn't left your side since you've been here. I'd say he's a keeper. What do you say?"

Nicole smiled and nodded her head. She looked at Sean who returned her smile.

"Well that's good because I can't handle any fights among the nurses over him," she winked at Nicole who was still smiling. "Just hit this button if you need anything, Nicole," she said, pointing to the remote on the bed, and left the room.

"A lot has happened," Sean started, impatient to tell her everything that had transpired. Peter walked into the room. "Bobby has called for a formal public committee to investigate the assassination. He's naturally suspended his campaign. The committee will start meeting in the next day or two. He's gathering evidence." Nicole smiled. "Next time you want something, can we do it a different way?"

Nicole tried to laugh. She made a motion that indicated to Sean she wanted to say something to him. He leaned closer to her lips. "I didn't want to be the one."

"I know," Sean said. He took the cup of ice and a spoon, digging a small amount for Nicole to eat. He fed her the ice. "Dad here tells me that the Republicans are calling for your head. They want you brought up on espionage charges."

Nicole started to object. Sean interrupted her, placing more ice in her open mouth. "We'll talk all about that when you are in full voice." Peter laughed at Sean's comment and actions. "Until then, you need to rest."

"Until the Yanks figure out what they are going to do, I refuse to put you in any more danger," Peter said to Nicole. "Besides, I've been bugging everyone, including the prime minister, and you have been granted asylum. We just haven't announced it yet. I doubt we will." Nicole mouthed her thank-you. "You are quite welcome, my dear."

It warmed Peter's heart to see his son in love again. He stood watching Sean taking care of Nicole and recalled this softer, loving side of him with his first wife and child. It was a side that Peter had not seen in over ten years.

"And then, there is Stevens." Nicole's shoulders dropped, which caused some pain, and she winced. She closed her eyes, gathered herself, and looked into Sean's eyes. "He claims that you were trying to get back at him for…" Nicole's jaw tightened and her facial expression showed her anger. "…breaking off the affair that he claims you were having with him. Stevens claimed Tony was exacting his revenge because Stevens wouldn't make him attorney general."

Nicole shook her head, her mouth open, as she hoped the words that were flowing through her brain would somehow come out of her throbbing throat. In a squeaky voice, she managed, "Are you fucking kidding me?" Sean laughed at the sound. Then, she remembered Peter was in the room. She looked over, embarrassed by her choice of words. "I'm sorry."

Peter smiled. "I think I'll leave you two alone to talk." Peter realized Sean was teasing her in his way with the information. He walked over to Nicole, took her hand, and gave it a quick kiss. "I will see you soon, my dear." Nicole smiled. "And don't give it another thought." He winked. "Sean, I'll talk to you later."

Sean acknowledged him with a nod. "Be careful, Dad. You have security right?"

"Oh, yes. They are waiting outside." Peter turned and walked out of the room.

Nicole swallowed and tried to talk again. "Did…he…announce…this affair?"

"Yes, on national television," Sean informed her, digging more ice from the cup and putting it in her mouth so that she couldn't speak. "Really, Nicole, if you were having an affair with the president, I wish you would have at least told me. It puts me in a rather difficult spot…" Nicole coughed as she choked back her response. Sean laughed and shook his head. "You know I'm joking," he told her with a devilish grin on his face. She smiled back at him. "It is so good to see your beautiful eyes again." He spooned more ice into her mouth.

Nicole pulled him closer. "You look awful. Have you slept?"

Sean pulled away. "Oh, thank you. You're quite a sight too, you know."

Nicole's face turned solemn to reflect her concern. She shook her head, trying to convey that she didn't say it to hurt him. She was concerned that he was not sleeping. She needed him to take care of himself. Sean could see that his attempt at humor missed its mark. He pulled a chair over, placing it next to the bed so he could sit down and still look at her.

"I slept here. I wasn't about to leave your side," Sean told her, taking the hand that Nicole extended to him when he spoke. Nicole's eyelids were getting heavy, and she was tiring. He could tell she was fighting it. "You need rest, Nicole. Go to sleep."

She shook her head. "I'm afraid. I might not…I don't want to…"

"I'll be here when you wake up. I'm not going anywhere," Sean reassured her. He scooted his chair up closer so that he could hold her hand, laying it on the bed. "I won't let go." Nicole fought sleep for a few more minutes, blinking her eyes continually. Sean squeezed her hand a couple of times to let her know he was still there. Her eyelids finally won, and she was asleep. Sean kept his promise; he didn't let go of her hand.

{II}

It had been three very long days for Jenkins and his staff. Thompson was working around the clock following up on leads, looking through financial records, trying to pull together a timeline of events. Chris was making copies of the evidence that Jenkins would use to tie the suspects back to Sipes's confession tape. He and Thompson had an appointment in the morning to visit Jefferies in prison. Thompson was pulling together some details on the evidence they would use to convince Jefferies to squeal. The phones had been ringing off the hook all day.

"Senator," Chris called. "There's a gentleman on the line. He insists on talking to you."

Jenkins was annoyed. "Who is it?"

"He won't say, sir."

Jenkins became even more annoyed. He picked up the phone on his desk. "Yes, what is it?" Jenkins said, his usual charm lacking.

"Senator," the voice sounded familiar, and Jenkins stopped reading the paper that was in his hand. "Do I have your full attention?"

"Who is this?" Jenkins asked, suspiciously. "You sound familiar, but I can't place your..." Jenkins' voice trailed off. Thompson and Chris walked into the inner office when they heard Jenkins ask who it was.

"It might be due to the fact that you think I'm dead. It's Tony Shafer."

"What? Where are you?" Jenkins asked, astonished. He stood up.

"I'm sure you have a thousand questions. I want to testify that I gave you the tape and that Stevens ordered a SEAL team to murder me."

"Where are you? We need to get you protection. I can send Thompson immediately." Jenkins was anxious. "Dear God, how did you survive?"

"We'll get to that. Have this Thompson fellow go to the Old Ebbitt Grill. You all must be starving. I'll pick up dinner." Tony hung up the phone.

"Who was it?" Thompson asked.

"Tony Shafer," Jenkins replied, still stunned. "He's alive. You need to get to Old Ebbitt Grill and bring him back here. We need to arrange for some security for him as well. I think proving Stevens was involved in this just got a whole lot easier." Jenkins sat back down. As Thompson left the room, Jenkins turned his attention to Chris. "Put in a call to the hospital where Nikki and Sean are. She should know that Tony is alive." Chris left Jenkins's office. He buzzed the senator when Sean was on the phone.

Jenkins smiled as he picked up the receiver. "Sean, tell Nikki that Tony Shafer is alive!" Jenkins listened for a moment. "I can't wait to hear what he has to say."

Chris stood and closed the door to the Jenkins's office.

To my wonderful readers,

Yes, it's a cliffhanger, and, yes, I know I hated it when Robert Ludlum did this in the Jason Bourne series of books, which prompted me to write *Blind Influence*.

I recently finished book one in the century trilogy by Ken Follett. I am well aware of what it takes to get through a nine hundred page book. Now, I'm not saying that this could have turned into a nine hundred page book, but it would have been close. The good news is that I have a head start on book three and that I'll be pulling that together as soon as this book is appropriately launched. As usual, I would greatly appreciate reviews over on Amazon, and you yelling from the treetops to all your friends how much you have enjoyed the *Blind Series* to date. When I started this series, I intended for it to be one book and done. So many of my readers wrote to tell me that you couldn't wait to find out what happened next. Now, I have book three in the works, and more books planned that will center on these three characters: Jenkins, Sean, and Nicole.

I hope that you will take a few minutes and connect with me. Here's how:
Email: lfisler@lindafisler.com (Freebies available if you sign up for my newsletter at www.LindaFisler.com)
Blind Series page: https://www.facebook.com/BlindInfluence/
Linda Fisler page: https://www.facebook.com/Linda-Fisler-Artist-Art-Chat-Host-Author-55121546229/
Twitter: https://twitter.com/lfisler or @lfisler

Many thanks to my editor, Sonja Sweeney, who was a gem to work with, and I appreciated her thoroughness and suggestions. I look forward to working with her on book three.

I'll be out and about promoting this series. I hope to see you at one of the upcoming events. If you are a member of a book club, please contact me if you would like me to speak to your club. With all the technology available to us today, I'm sure we would be able to work something out!

Thank you for reading! It is always difficult to make judgments on what should be deleted and what should stay in a book. I choose to tell you more about Nicole, Sean, and Jenkins with this book. Discovery is an exciting path.

Cheers,

Linda Riesenberg Fisler

About the Author:

When award-winning author and fine art artist, Linda Riesenberg Fisler, isn't working on her next book, she is painting in her studio or riding her Trek bicycle along the many bike trails of Ohio. The former P&G manager explores art through her worldwide Internet podcast, *"Art Chats with Linda Fisler."* Linda has been creative since childhood, writing stories, scripts, and TV shows to entertain friends.

Blind Influence, her debut fiction novel placed in three competitions: Paris (France) Book Festival, Hollywood Book Festival, and the Great Midwest Book Festival. She is currently working on the third book in the ***Blind Series, Blind Alliance,*** as well as working on two other fictions books. Riesenberg Fisler is also working on converting ***Blind Influence*** into a script as the possibilities continue to grow.

You can message Linda at lfisler@lindafisler.com and read deleted scenes from all her books at the Blind Series website: http://blindseries.lindafisler.com/

Linda is looking for super fans and patrons. Become a patron of Linda's writing (for as little as a $1) and receive complimentary gifts on her Patreon page: https://www.patreon.com/LindaRiesenbergFisler/memberships

Author readings, sneak peeks, and secret meetings for patrons are available when you unlock the secret posts by becoming a patron of Linda's work.

www.ingramcontent.com/pod-product-compliance
Lightning Source LLC
Chambersburg PA
CBHW030029180626
46810CB00001B/282